# Praise for Melissa Algood

### For The Enhanced Being Series

"An intriguing and easy to lose yourself in book. The last 80 pages made it hard to Mom."
  - Jennifer, reader

### For The Greater Good Series

"I loved reading [Gone]...found myself racing ahead during the action to read what happened [next]...Also, Katey is one crazy biotch"
  -E. Paige Burks, author '*Heart of The Guardian*'

"I loved reading about Sam and Matt, and where their adventures took them. Seeing more of their individual pasts and how those lives intersect is a reader's dream. Sam's amazing, a real super heroine without replying on the trope of a super powered heroine. She's brave and courageous and vulnerable, all at once. Matt has his secrets, too, but he's more than just a pretty face or nice body; he's a good guy. I find myself cheering along Sam and Matt as I delve more into their exploits"
  - Omar, reader

"One can easily find himself sucked into the story so that the book becomes difficult to put down."
  -Jim Cole, award winning author of '*Never Cry Again*'

"Wild ride, strong scenery and not one straight plot point, they all twist!."
  -anonymous reader

"colorful and vivid ."
  -anonymous reader

## For 'Everything That Counts'

"Blake is that part of all of us that makes us genuine...Read, enjoy, and relate."
  -David Welling, award-winning author

"I like the characters...particularly funny and sharp..."
  -Kimberly Morris, author, editor, & speaker

"Dialogue is snappy, sharp..."
  -Sharon Halprin, author

## For Short Fiction

"Featured author, Melissa Algood, was featured for a reason - she clearly has talent."
  -Mallory Hinson, reader

"Fans will delight in the Algood's '*The Silencer*'...Yet the fresh and heartbreakingly vivid centerpiece of the anthology, '*Caroline Hearts Toby*,' describes a murder of the spirit. Nestled in with entertaining crime writing, Algood's story about young love and violence captures the precariousness of adolescence perfectly.."
  -Patricia Flathery Pagan, founder of Spider Road Press

# The Girl In The Fog
## Book 1 of Enhanced Being Series

### Melissa Algood

Copyright © 2022 by Melissa Algood

The characters and events portrayed in this book are fictitious. Any similarity to real person, living, dead, zombies, or underpaid teachers, is purely coincidental and not intended by the author. All rights reserved. NO part of this publication may be reproduced, distributed, or transmitted in any form or by any means, including photocopying, recording, or other electronic or mechanical methods, without the prior written permission of the publisher except in the case of brief quotations embodied in critical articles and review and certain other noncommercial uses permitted by copyright law. For permission requests contact the publisher at the email address below.

melalgoodauthor@gmail.com
https://melalgoodauthor.com
Printed in the United States
Cover Artist Heidi Dorey
Edited by E. Paige Burks

ISBN 978-1-0879-7713-3

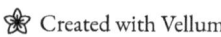 Created with Vellum

*This one is for Baltimore*

"And while I was talking, the idea of actually losing Peeta hit me again and I realized how much I don't want him to die.

And it's not about the sponsors.

And it's not about what will happen when we get home.

And it's not just that I don't want to be alone.

It's him. I do not want to lose the boy with the bread."

**— Suzanne Collins, The Hunger Games**

# 2 YEARS/3 MONTHS/15 DAYS

I don't know how long they'd been chasing me this time, their Flashing Red Auras tailing me long after I'd left Johns Hopkins property. They always found me when I tried to reach out to Widmore, a man I hadn't spoken to in six years. Not since he warned me and Reed that our lives would be short without him, that the Lab would get us, and if we wanted to come back it would be too late.

Leave it to a five-hundred-year-old telepath to predict the most ominous future perfectly.

All I knew was that I couldn't leave Baltimore before I found Widmore. I tried everything I could think of to be in the same room as him again. To be protected by him instead of spending the past two years, three months, and fifteen days running. When I found Widmore I could find a way to control my powers and be a normal twenty-five-year-old who goes out for drinks with friends, has a job and goes for a run for exercise, not to escape from The Lab.

Sweat trickled down my neck, soaking my long sleeve t-shirt and breaching my hoodie. With each ragged breath, steam formed out of my mouth like I was a dragon as my high-top sneakers pounded on the pavement, weaving up and down the streets. I headed south, past the

Baltimore Museum of Art toward Charles Village, a neighborhood that looked suburban even though it was in middle of a metropolis.

The streets were lined with two story brick houses, nearly all of which looked the same – from sedans, a lone kid's bike left in the front yard, to matching hanging plants and doormats. That's when I slowed down; easier to blend in if I wasn't running. I gulped in air as I tuned into the minds around me, checking to see if anybody took notice of a stranger running for their life. I sensed the Red Flashing lights around me, found their pattern, and broke through an opening which led to N. Howard Street and the infamous Ottobar. No better place to blend in than with a bunch of drunk twenty-somethings.

Outside of the club were a few smokers, long since banned from the inside, a couple making out, and a few stragglers like me that came up to the plain two-story block of white, painted concrete. I pulled the twenty out of the back pocket of my jeans. The buzz-cut bouncer gave me back a five since it was ladies night. A woman with cornrows stamped my hand before I walked inside into a world of color and noise.

Cold War Kids played on the stage in the back of the club, or at least that's who I think it was, considering the name of the band was flittering between everyone's thoughts. Don't have much time to check out the music when you're on the run from The Lab that's held you a prisoner for half a decade. But I liked the beat, and the crowd clapped along with it and the guitar melody that seemed to sparkle like fireworks. It was so much easier being in a room full of people when they were all enchanted by the same thing as me.

The dark bar was on the right side of the space, lit with cool purple track lights. People danced in front of the small stage, drank, and laughed, awash in the same tone of purple hue that you saw in the sunset on the harbor. Right before the stars took over the landscape. At least that's what everyone else saw.

For me there were Electric Yellows, Sickly Greens, Florescent Magentas, and even a Cloud of Darkness near the speakers, which I made sure to stay away from. All the musicians were shinning brighter than the sun, absorbing all the energy from the crowd.

People shoved into me as I made my way to the bar, none of them expecting a band of such prestige on a Thursday. I pulled off my beanie and shoved it in the pocket of my leather jacket. I couldn't remember the last time I washed my hair, and I wasn't sure if the crowd was drunk enough to let me fade into the background. I scanned through their thoughts, like people scroll through pictures on social media, and I'd only made it on the radar of one that was Swirling Red.

Apparently, he likes blondes with big tits, *but with an ass like that I'll buy her a drink*, he thought as his eyes skirted me. Instead of waiting for him to join me, I threw a hundred-dollar bill on the bar to get the bartenders attention, which it did. He picked it up and put it in the fishbowl next to the tap, he wouldn't realize until after last call that it was only a single. But then again none of them would remember me either, so who cared if I was a thief.

"What can I get ya?" His blue-black mohawk sparkled along with the thick Purple Haze around him, obviously he was high.

"Double shot of whiskey."

"What kind?"

I shrugged. "Whatever's closest."

He smiled, nodded, and poured me the drink.

Everyone between the ages of twenty-one and thirty-five who resided in the tri-state area must have been there, considering how busy the bar was. Everyone was smushed together, making it hard to filter through all the thoughts that bombarded me. I was wearing a hoodie under my leather jacket and not a skintight leather dress, so I still remained off everyone's radar, save the Swirling Red prick whose eyes locked on mine.

I tilted my head back, letting the whiskey slide down my throat. Cold War Kids finished with *First* then started the vibrating intro to *You Already Know*. The crowd cheered, which distracted the creep as I moved away from the bar and toward the center of the club.

The Red Flickering lights that had been chasing me since I don't know when were still blocks away, which gave me time to close my eyes and turn down the volume around me. Shut out the hundreds of club goers thinking about screwing, or if they could get that guy to buy them a drink, or a girl in the corner who contemplated how every breath she took was pure agony ever since her boyfriend left her.

I brought the memory of Reed to the forefront of my mind, the

Bluest Blue Aura there ever was. His ebony-skinned hands on my nearly translucent ones, his voice steady, *'put everyone on mute, until you need them, Litha.'* The warmth of his breath still on my neck.

He used to sparkle right before he kissed me. Although he hated it when I told him that he looked as if he'd been coated in glitter, that he was the skinniest person I'd ever met, and that I didn't know anyone that that put that much Old Bay on their food. After all, I was from Maryland and he was Dominican, and even I didn't like it that much. When I did sneak into his brain to see if he still thought I was beautiful after what The Lab had done to me, shaved my long blonde tresses to adhere electrodes to my head and sliced into my skin that before only bore the marks I'd marred it with, I found out that he preferred my short, cropped hair, and he thought my scars made me strong. Even if The Lab made me look like a pre-pubescent boy that had been through an autopsy.

But Reed didn't care about any of that, and he was my world, until the morning I woke up and he wasn't Blue anymore. Much less glittering. That was the morning I left Wakefield Laboratories. Two years, three months, and fifteen days ago; and they'd been chasing me ever since. The Lab had killed my boyfriend, and now I was the one acting like a criminal.

With steady breathing, I managed to turn all the sound off, and push the memory of Reed's lifeless body to the back of my mind. The band took a break to tune their guitars, but in reality, the drummer had to make a phone call back home. The DJ put on Justin Bieber, which he thought was a joke, as did most of the club goers who laughed, but it was hard for me to mute it because I liked the song. I didn't have time to be embarrassed for liking a pop star though, because I heard the whispering coming from behind me.

A dozen Deep Purples, armed with stun guns, helmets, and full riot gear surrounded the club. Half a dozen Red Flashing assholes weren't enough apparently, to come after a twenty-five-year-old girl that hadn't eaten a real meal in months. They needed the Baltimore PD.

Deep Purple BPD closed in now that Flashing Red from The Lab had tracked me, probably because I was stupid enough to use my powers to get a drink.

I was so tired, and all I really want to do is go out there and let them take me. Cut me up or take me over the world to use me as a lie detector. It didn't matter anymore because they'd never leave me alone. And my only savior was out of reach; had been this entire fucking time. Reed was the strong one, and here I was in the middle of a club in Baltimore about to get captured and put under a microscope because I couldn't think of any place else to run. They moved in, along each side of the building, but they'd left the alley open. Well technically, they did leave one guy by the dumpster, but under his Deep Purple Aura was Glowing Yellow.

He feared me.

I pulled up my hood, turned the guy's bathroom off mute, since it was the closest to the dumpster, and heard a single male voice, *Wait, did I pay the internet this month? Or my lights? Guess I'll find out when I get home.*

I moved through the crowd, pushed open the door to find a guy at the sink. His brown hair curled on his forehead but was tightly faded on the sides, his eyes, which scanned me, were gray-green, and he had a stubbled jaw that was sharp enough to use as a knife. He had a black leather jacket on too, jeans ripped at the knees, boots, a beer in his hand which I didn't find the most hygienic, but none of that was what stopped me in my tracks.

His Aura was Blue. Bright Mother Fucking Sparkling Blue, like pictures I'd seen of the Pacific Ocean, a color that I'd only seen once before. Only Reed had been Blue, until now.

Not-Reed raised an eyebrow on his long rectangle face at me. "You okay?"

"You're Blue," I stuttered the words and took off my hood.

He looked down at his clothes, then back at me, and his mouth turned up in a half smile. "I want whatever you're on."

*She's pretty,* Not-Reed thought, *pretty weird.*

I put Not-Reed on mute, and I didn't have to close my eyes to see the Flickering Red of rage as they moved like a wave to the back of the club.

To the bathrooms.

To me.

I jumped on the sink, Not-Reed squawked, "Hey, what the fuck?"

I covered my fist with my beanie, punched the square window that led out to the alley, and immediately jumped back down. With two steps I was standing in front of Not-Reed; he was taller than his namesake, over six feet, while I barely met his chest. Sure, he was clueless, maybe so stupid he didn't know if he'd paid his bills, but it was the Blue, Azure really, that floated around him that kept me in his presence. His Aura was hypnotic, something I'd assumed everyone could see until I found out just how different I was.

It was the Blue that made me trust Not-Reed.

"Tell them I jumped out the window and ran right." The whispering echoed louder and louder in my head, drowning out nearly everything, including the band that had started back up.

Not-Reed's face formed a point. "What? Who?"

The Flickering Red was a foot away from the bathroom door.

I grabbed onto Not-Reed's t-shirt and half whispered, half screamed, "Please, they want to hurt me."

He nodded. "Okay, I'll tell them." The Blue around him gained a swirl of white, like a custard treat, wrapping around him. I kept him on mute, because I needed all my strength once they came inside. But I also desperately wanted to know what he was thinking.

I pushed open a stall, shut it, locked it, and sat on the tank, my sneakers on the seat. Trying not to think about how many germs I must be covered in, and thankful that I couldn't get Non-Enhanced diseases, I closed my eyes and shut out the world.

The world went white, and silent.

Peoples' brains appeared to me like a movie theater, mine containing the most advanced projector of all. And I was able to access everyone's personal theater from the bright white corridor in my head. This hallway that was void of air and sound had openings to a litany of minds. Doors appeared in front of me, an endless line of them going to my left and right, but only a few at a time had light leaking out from the sides. Most lay dormant, not worth the energy to keep active when you're on the run. And whenever I thought I'd opened all of them, another would appear. I made my way to the oldest door. The one that always appeared directly in front of me whenever I closed my eyes and went to the hallway. This particular door was made of driftwood, like you'd expect to be the gateway to an old lighthouse. Not in an endless white hallway; the very core of me.

I walked to the slanted frame across the blinding white floor. I wouldn't be able to tell what was up and down in the corridor that was filled with doors, if it weren't for their presence. My hand gripped the knob, which was cold to the touch, turned it, and walked inside to a swirling mass of fog. The atmosphere was so dense it took a minute to get acclimated so I could see.

I don't know how else to explain it—the fog. No matter how hard I tried, even with Reed. But I would let my mind go beyond blank.

Past Zen.

Deep into another plane of existence.

That also existed in this universe.

I was both there and not there.

My fog worked like a one-way mirror, I saw you, but you didn't see me. Untouchable, and safe. The only bitch was it took up a lot of energy, but it was better than being a lab rat again.

So, while the men looked to everyone else, including Not-Reed, like off duty cops with their cheap suits, haircuts, and mustaches, to me they were Flashing Red like a siren. But just like every other Non-Enhanced, they depended too much on their senses. What they could physically understand, when I just knew how to get into the fog, and what I could do once I was there.

Flickering Red: "Did a girl come in here? About five feet, short blonde hair, blue eyes, wearing all black?"

Not-Reed: "Man, that girl was crazy." And even deep in the fog, I kept him on mute, so I'd have enough energy to get out of this club and to safety. It had been so long since I'd had something to eat, too depressed to break into any more homes and steal their food. The pain in my stomach was beginning to compete with the hammering in my head.

Hoping that I was right about the Blue, I held my breath until Not-Reed continued, "She busted open that window and ran to the right."

The whispering started again, giving directions, to the next team of Flickering Red, which in turn relayed it to Deep Purple. But they'd leave one. They always left one. And I'd pry open his mind like it was a can of tuna, but for my recipe I'd implant an image, not mayo and relish.

Flickering Red moved from the position that the team left him in, by the sinks next to Not-Reed, and stood in front of the first stall. The one I was in surrounded by my fog. He kicked in the first stall, and computed the image I'd created in his head. He found it empty, and not with the prize he wanted. He kicked open the other stall, which looked exactly the same down to the stains on the bowl. And it was, in every single way, because in the fog it was easier to duplicate something then create it new.

Flickering Red clicked on his walkie talkie. "The bathroom's clear, going to follow you East to continue the search."

Not-Reed: "Told you she ran away."

Flickering Red: "Thanks for your help sir, and if you do find the fugitive then please call the Baltimore Police immediately."

Not-Reed, nodded, then reached out to shake Flickering Red's hand. When they touched it yanked me out of the fog; the Flickering Red's hatred was more powerful than Not-Reed's earnestness. His Aura turned the edge of Not-Reed's Azure Aura to a Sickly Green. I bit my bottom lip so as not to cry out as the electricity caused by something so evil interacting with something so good tried to melt my brain. Thankfully Flickering Red moved back toward the door, and Not-Reed turned back to his True Blue.

Once the whispers were at the end of the block, I stepped off the toilet, dropped both feet back onto the ground, opened the stall, and turned on the water faucet.

"You, okay?" Not-Reed asked.

The water was cool, and I splashed it on my face, taking in deep breaths until I looked up at the mirror. I'd lost weight since the last time I'd looked in a mirror, whenever that was. My skin was even paler now, lips cracked, probably because I'd left behind my last tube of lip-gloss three safe houses ago. And there was blood under my nails, which I scrubbed as I felt Not-Reed step closer. Very close. The closest I'd let a person get to me in a while.

His Blue glided against my Swirling Gray Smoke. I didn't have an Aura like everyone else, just a hint of the fog that was deep inside my brain exuded around me. As if my very being were a zephyr, whereas everyone else was a consistently fluctuating variance of vibrating color.

I faced Not-Reed. "Thank you."

He nodded. "No problem."

"Can you take me somewhere? Just for a few hours." I leaned against the sink. "I'm so tired."

He chuckled. "Don't you want to at least know my name before I take you home?"

"It's not like we're going to hook up so it doesn't matter what your name is."

That wiped the smile off his face. "Wasn't, like, expecting that, but I'm Carl."

"Nice to meet you Carl, now can we leave? I'm about to pass out."

"Why would I bring home some girl that's being chased by the cops to my house?"

"Because you just lied for me, so you're already involved, and I'm not going to hurt you."

He raised an eyebrow at me. "Aren't you supposed to be afraid of me?"

"No." I shook my head.

"Why, because I'm Blue? What's that even mean?"

I shook my head again, but this time it started to pound so I pressed my hand against it. "I'll explain everything to you, if you could just please help me out one more time."

"I have to at least know your name."

I took in Carl, not sure if I was damning him because I could read minds but couldn't predict the future like Widmore, but he was already on their radar. And if anything happened, I'd just go into the fog and erase all this from his memory. Then I'd be the only one to remember that we'd even met.

"Talitha," I sighed realizing it was the first time in two years, three months, and fifteen days since I'd heard my own name, "call me Talitha."

# JONAS
## 10/9/2020 9:42 PM

"You're telling me that you lost her again?" I sat at my desk tapping my pointed fingernails on the stone. They'd been freshly shaped by Sabine so a slight *tink* sounded throughout the room. My Enhanced soldiers and the glamoured Baltimore Police Officers formed a semi-circle around their commander, who held my full attention.

The commander's thoughts whirled in his mind, trying to pull apart the cacophony of possible outcomes and find the exact words to keep him alive. Unfortunately for him there were no words that would find his way toward the goal of leaving this room with a pulse.

"It seemed that she used her powers, making herself invisible," his bottom lip quivered for a beat, "she slipped right past us."

"She's not invisible, that would be ridiculous." I tented my fingers in front of me, elbows on the freshly polished obsidian desk. "Enhanced Being Eight Fifteen, or Talitha, is able to transport herself into another plane of existence. She calls it her fog."

The Non-Enhanced officer raised an eyebrow at me. "And that doesn't sound ridiculous?"

"You know what the difference is between Non-Enhanced humans and those that I've had injected with the serum?" I looked at the Baltimore Police Commander I'd glamoured to do my bidding. It amazed me that humans found them as a foe, when in fact he was nothing but sinew, blood, and bones. Something easy to destroy, like the wings of a butterfly being met with a hammer.

The officer's breathing started to quicken. "You have superpowers?"

I straightened my silk, lavender-colored tie and buttoned my jacket as I stood up from my high-back leather chair, its legs rubbing against the concrete floor of my office in the sub-basement of Wakefield Laboratories. I would have preferred a residence in New York over New Jersey, but it was more important to keep fewer miles between Eight Fifteen and myself. Although it did mean I had to work with some of the most incompetent humans in this dimension. "And that in and of itself is a fine example of my point. You only see in black and white."

He looked at my skin, the same color as my onyx suit, and internally I knew he was comparing it to his own flaxen epidermis. Not just because I could read his thoughts, but because humans were more predictable than a sunrise.

"Eight Fifteen can see a person's Aura, what some refer to as a soul." I stepped from behind my desk, closer to the officer, who stood at attention in the middle of the room. Glamoured Baltimore Police Officers and my Enhanced underlings made a half circle behind the commanding officer as I stood in front of him, making sure my shoulders squared with his. He might have riot gear on, and more than one gun, but he was the one who's knees were shaking as the tip of my sharpened fingernail scratched his cheek, leaving a line of red.

"She can also alter one's memory. She told her mentor, Gustav Widmore, it's as if she were editing a movie reel. That each one of us has a movie theater in our head and that's where our life story is kept in canisters of tin, and only she can access it. Once she understands the importance of the work we're doing, I'm going to send her into the CDC and retrieve some data for me."

"Can't you do it? I mean, aren't you The Originator?"

I smiled as he stuttered, slobbering on himself. "That is true, and I am more powerful than Eight Fifteen, but she can erase the memories of anyone in the CDC she interacts with, something I'm unable to do. And while I am superpowered, I have no intention of starting a war with the Non-Enhanced until I'm completely ready, with no doubt of the extinction of your kind. So, I need her to make sure that all of it is forgotten, and Talitha could have done that for you."

"Why would she need to erase my memory?"

"So that you wouldn't remember the horrific pain you're about to endure." I snapped my fingers and a drop of blood ricocheted from the tip of my nail off into space.

The muscles in the officer's cheeks flinched, his bottom lip curled, his fists clenched. Sweat dripped down his eyebrow, which was frozen in a sarcastic arch. His knees quaked, and a sliver of saliva made a trail down his chin. All the thoughts in the dark room that rambled on in the Baltimore Police Department's heads rallied around the human, a literal spotlight above us, leaving the rest of them in shadow. Only the most intelligent ones quelled their thoughts quickly in the hopes that I hadn't heard their pleas for my imminent demise.

*Motherfucking pedophile* was the most common phrase used.

I made a turn around the officer as his cells continued to feel as if he were being electrocuted while being set aflame. A waltz of pain. "If you had caught Eight Fifteen, then I could get her to make you think you were eating ice cream right now with your daughter. Strawberry is Mary's favorite, isn't it?"

His pupils tripled in size as he murmured through gritted teeth, "Leave Mary alone."

"She's two, is that right?"

"Eighteen months," he whimpered.

The officer's throat constricted to the size of a needle, and I was the tractor trailer plunging through it. "The serum might do her well, and then she could join us."

"No," the officer gasped. I'd caused a pain that was beyond the bones I shattered inside of him. "Please. Not Mary."

"My beloved always said she wanted children." The image of my betrothed's almond shaped eyes, framed by her long dark curly hair, and cocoa skin flashed in my mind. A smile crossed my face as I remembered the first time I was in a room with the creature that The Lab called One Hundred and Eight. She was the success of the formulation, and thus her namesake. I'd never wanted to possess someone so badly, to grant her every wish, including when she told me that her dream was to be a *Mum* one day.

I cast my eyes amongst the rest of the room, fully aware of the thoughts that they tried to stifle in their minds. Although I was many centuries older than my beloved, their name calling of *motherfucking pedophile* wasn't apt. One Hundred and Eight had been given the name Lola by her peers, and her luscious lips had only graced my anatomy a handful of times, thus their name calling was a lie. Besides, Widmore had loved an Enhanced woman too, and he was hundreds of years older than her. What difference did it make that they'd met when she was an adult, and I had loved Lola from the moment our eyes met?

"I did Lola a disservice when I let Wakefield sterilize her, but it was protocol. Even if I am in charge, if we start bending the rules then we'll surely break under them. The best I could do was let her live in the East End with her family until it is time for Lola to be my wife. By then, I've been assured that we'll have the third generation of the serum, and we'll take it together. Making us the most powerful Enhanced beings on Earth."

I put my hand on the side of the soldier's face. Even if he tried to get away, he couldn't. Our connection was stronger than if I'd stuck us together with superglue. "Tomorrow is Lola's eighteenth birthday, and I'll be flying to London so we can be together, for the first time." For a moment my mind reeled at the thought of touching her bare breasts, my teeth digging into her skin, to thrust inside of her causing her to make sounds she didn't know possible. Every inch of her would finally be mine, in this life, and the next. As my imagination lit up with the endless possibilities of ecstasy when I'd finally bed my beloved, the officer's skin grew so hot to my touch that it began to melt. Tissue dripped onto the floor as I hissed into what was left of the soldier's ear, "And what a joy you have given me, because now I can tell her that I have found us a child."

By the time my monologue was done the officer had turned in a puddle at my feet. It smelled putrid, smoked, and had a texture of strawberry jelly. The larger bones, including his skull, remained intact amid the goo. My eyes scanned the room; they'd all seen enough executions that their faces showed no disgust.

"Any more questions?"

"No," they said in unison.

"Who do I want in Wakefield custody by the end of the week?"

"Enhanced Being Eight Fifteen AKA Talitha," they answered.

I returned to behind my desk. "If she gets to Widmore before you bring her to me, then each of you will end up a puddle on my floor, understand?"

"Yes, sir," they recited.

I nodded at the mess in the center of the room, "Get that cleaned up, and bring in his daughter, Mary."

"Would you like to meet her before we inject her, sir?" Sabine, my most loyal Enhanced solider moved forward, crushing the officer's femur with her boot.

I shook my head. "Had enough with humans today."

Sabine nodded and just as quickly, her long, blue-black hair shortened to a buzz cut. Her bronzed skin turned alabaster, and in turn her dark eyes lightened. She grew a few inches, thickened in muscle mass, and before she left the room, she had completely altered her physical body until she matched the officer that she stood on. Including his pristine uniform, before he turned into a pile of mush on my floor.

"Shouldn't be hard to kidnap an infant," Sabine said as she pulled open the door, although her voice sounded just like the officer that had turned into a pudding. "Then we'll take you to the airport to have your evening with One Hundred and Eight."

Her mouth twitched at the end, giving herself away, demonstrating her weakness, exposing herself to me. Daring me to tear open her throat for wishing to kill my beloved so that I would love her instead. Lola would be my beginning and end – no other being would capture my heart.

I leaned back in my chair. "What would I do without you, Sabine?"

She smiled at me. "Thankfully we'll never have to find out because we're about to get Eight Fifteen."

# TALITHA
## 10/9/2020 9:55 PM

Even expired canned spaghetti in a chipped, sage-toned China bowl is delicious when it's been a month since you had something warm to eat because you're too depressed to even steal something. Being a thief proved lucrative when you could read your mark's mind, but when your only interaction with a human is to con them, it gets lonely – and after a while it made theft feel wrong.

Although I did have fun at first when I'd find out who was on vacation and stayed at their home. I'd sleep in their California King beds, eat all their organic food in their pantry, wear their designer clothes. Steal and promptly crash their cars since I'd never learned how to drive. For a while, I kept the guns and knives, not sure what I'd do with them, so finally I threw them down a gutter. After I was out a few weeks I couldn't stay in the same place more than a night without the Flashing Reds finding me.

But I couldn't leave Baltimore because Widmore was the only soul on Earth that could teach me to control my powers. The last person I really spoke to, much less ate in front of was Reed. Any other person I interacted with had their memory promptly erased. I'd become so invisible that I'd go days without looking in a reflective surface. But I didn't need one to know that I was blushing as Carl's gray-green eyes held onto me from across the small, round table with junk mail and takeout menus taking up half of it.

We didn't exchange a word as we walked to his two-story red brick row house, which had been built over a century ago for the mill workers on Roland Avenue in the Hampden area. It wasn't until then that I realized how lonesome I'd been, and that's why I'd asked Carl to take me home. Not to sleep with him like I know was on his mind, but because it had been ages since I'd been in the same room as anyone else.

I didn't question why a twenty-seven-year-old bartender had a house to himself, when this neighborhood was so costly that he'd need at least a roommate. Nor did I question why the second floor was empty and the bottom floor was nearly bare, with no form of entertainment save a record player and a television that only played VHS tapes. The furniture didn't match, nor had it been manufactured within the same decade.

It was the perfectly square or rectangle faded parts of the yellow rose wallpaper that lined the living room which drew my attention. The tips of my fingers touched a nail near the top third of the square, dead center, and led me to believe that several pieces of art had been removed. I didn't ask about that either.

I just asked him for as much food as he'd allow me to eat as I handed him a real hundred-dollar bill, one of the last dozen that I'd stolen from a woman's purse months ago. After eating an entire box of cereal, Carl's leftover Kung Pao Chicken, and two cans of spaghetti I didn't have to take him off mute to know that he wanted to talk.

"So," he tilted his chin toward me, "you murder someone?"

I swallowed as my escape from The Lab came washing back, full of rage at the death of Reed. "Not technically."

"What's that mean?"

I looked over the empty food containers at him. "I was a prisoner at this Lab, and I made the soldiers think they were shooting me, but they were shooting each other."

"Wait." His eyes narrowed, and his mouth turned up in half a smile. "What?"

"You've heard of Wakefield Laboratories, right?"

Carl nodded, although it would have been more shocking if he hadn't, after all they had as much prestige as they did mysterious buildings full of employees that were forced to sign NDAs. Publicly traded, several Presidents bailed them out each time the economy gasped for breath, and while I'd never met the founder, Jonas, I'd long wondered what color his Aura would be. He was one of us, possibly the first, and even coined the term 'Enhanced'; he tested on us to make sure only the strongest survived. He'd killed everyone I loved in the effort. I was curious what the Aura of the most vile living creature would look like, since he was coated in the blood of Reed, Micah, and so many others like us. No matter Jonas' and Wakefield's reasoning for making so many of us, just to torture us, they were the bad guys. Although I had killed all the enchanted soldiers that were in The Lab that day using my powers, so maybe I was a bad guy too.

I cleared my throat. "You know, about thirty years ago, they were testing this drug to see if they could make, like, a superior fighter for when World War Three starts?"

He chuckled. "That's just an urban legend, and besides everyone was an adult, neither of us were even born yet."

I shrugged. "Guess the scientists wondered what it would do to pregnant women, like my mom."

He tilted his head to the side, a grin on his face. "So you're telling me that you have superpowers?"

"No, I'm telling you that I look like any other girl, but I'm not." I took a gulp of the Gatorade, but my thirst was overpowering, and I couldn't put it back down so I finished off the liter.

"Then *what* are you?"

"I've been asking myself that for twenty-five years." I set the empty bottle back on the glorified card table Carl used to eat at next to the salt and pepper shakers in the shape of the Eiffel Tower and Louvre, respectively. "Some people call me Talitha, and those fuckers at The Lab have me filed under Enhanced Being Eight Fifteen. But I still feel human, even if my DNA is different from yours."

He leaned back and smirked at me. "Can you shoot lightning out of your eyes? Or are you strong enough to pick up a car? Or jump out of a plane without a parachute?"

"I heal faster than you, and I don't get sick like you, but no I can't do anything like that. I can tell if you're a good person or a bad one, though."

"How?"

"I read Auras."

He narrowed his eyes and tilted his head as if I'd started speaking in another language.

"Around everyone is a color, well a bunch of them usually, but one of them is dominant. That's kinda like a person's soul. But it will get Hazy if you're drunk, or Super Bright if she's pregnant, or will Shake if they're scared. And it will flash Bright Red if you happen to be someone that wants to experiment on me."

"And I'm Blue, right? That's what you said when you ran into the bathroom."

I nodded, gazing at the Crystal-Clear tone of Azure.

"So, I'm good then, right?" His eyes widened like a kid that finally figured out fractions. "That's why you asked me to bring you to my house?"

I nodded.

"And how many colors do you see around people?"

"How many colors can the mind perceive?" I wiped my mouth with the sleeve of my gray Henley shirt. Didn't realize how dirty it was until the light above us captured the stains.

He crossed his arms over his chest. He didn't believe me, but they never did. "How many are Blue?"

My eyes met with the table, because I might have to say Reed's name out loud, and I hadn't done that since I screamed it until I lost my voice. "Ask me something else." I pushed the bowl away.

"Why are you telling me all this? I mean, couldn't I turn you in for a reward or something?"

"Probably, but you won't."

"Why, because I'm Blue?"

"That and I'm going to have to erase your memories of me once I leave tomorrow morning."

"You're going to what?"

I waved my hand at him. "It will take like two seconds, and you won't even feel it."

"How do you know?"

"Because I've done it a million times." I leaned forward. "It doesn't matter if you know everything about me. I can give you all the details in the world, and that's easy as pie to delete without a skip in your stride, but to remove a real *relationship*, it's difficult, but really only for me."

"Why?"

"Matter has to go somewhere, so if I take it from you..." I tapped my head. "I can't exactly buy more storage."

He narrowed his eyebrows. "What happens when it's full?"

I shrugged. "System overload."

"What happens?"

"Lights flicker, a few things shake, bad headache." I didn't add that I was essentially in a coma for a week after erasing my mother's memory. But she of all people needed to forget my existence.

Carl leaned forward and bent his elbows, his flannel sleeves rolled up, exposing his left arm, which had what appeared to be a tattooed sleeve of gears – as if he were made of metal and just as not-human as me. A brown curl fell into his eyes, stubble covered his face, and his lips turned into a smirk. "What else can you do?"

I reached out to him, palm up, the sleeve of my shirt up far enough that the barcode on my wrist peaked through the black leather studded cuff. "It would be easier to show you."

Without trepidation he placed his palm on top of mine.

"Don't let go." I gripped onto him. "okay?"

"Okay."

I threw him half a smile. "And you might want to close your eyes."

He closed them without hesitation, and I pulled him through the bright white backstage, directing him through the corridor. I stopped at an ornately decorated red velvet door. The fabric was quilted and had gold grommets, creating a star pattern in the padding. My free hand turned the knob, also in the shape of a star, and went inside the cortex of my memory bringing Carl with me. He smiled when he heard *Hang Me Out To Dry* playing on the speakers, which I made sure was loud enough to drown out my biopic so he didn't hear any of my internal monologue.

I pulled him up the red-velvet upholstered staircase, went back to the projector that played the movie of my life, recording each and every moment, including this one. I hit pause, then rewind, and started to pull the spool, searching for a specific set of frames. So well-worn was the filmstrip that I could have found the cells in a pitch-dark room, the 35mm film gliding between my fingers until I found the exact memory I craved to revisit.

"Where are we?"

"Arizona, thirty minutes northwest of the Mexican border."

"Holy shit." Carl ran up next to me his Doc Marten boots soundless against the sand. "Won't the cops see us?"

"No, because this is a memory."

"Who's?"

"Mine."

"Why didn't you use one of mine?"

I sighed. "You wouldn't want to be in everyone's head all the time if you didn't have to either." The breeze from the mountains came down and blew the sand in our faces, but it didn't sting our eyes, get in our teeth, or fill our lungs.

"The sand isn't real?" Carl's voice wavered.

"Yes, it is, it's just that we're not in 2020 anymore."

"Then, *when* are we?"

"7:45 PM on November 10, 2014."

"Damn you remember the time?"

I looked up at Carl, the never-ending sky above him, each planet and star exactly as it was that night, and it would remain that way for as long as I could recall the memory. It hadn't occurred to me until Reed died, but I could relive this night forever. And I tried that for a while, but my 'power' wasn't near as exceptional as his. When Reed stopped breathing, I couldn't restart his heart, like he'd restarted mine twice. All I could do was go back to November 10, 2014, the last night we were free. I didn't answer Carl, just kept walking toward the caves a hundred yards south.

"Wait." Carl tugged on my arm. "I don't understand, what happened to our bodies."

I raised my eyebrow. "Um, you're in your body."

"But where are we in 2020?"

"This isn't time jumping." I stopped. "This is all in your head and everything else is kinda on pause."

He rubbed his face with his hands and groaned "I don't know what kind of drugs you gave me, but I want to go back to where I'm supposed to be."

"I didn't waste all the energy getting out here just to have you drag me back." Ahead a fire crackled in front of the opening of the cave. I faced Carl. "You wanted answers? I can't explain everything like you want me to, just like you can't explain why you're left-handed, or that you prefer scrambled eggs, or that you're not entirely sure if you paid your internet or light bill this month."

He took a step back, gray-green eyes taking me in. "How did you know that?"

I laughed. "You think I can take you into my own memory, but I can't read your mind?" Then I turned, not waiting for a response, heading toward the literal light. "We're almost there," I called out behind me.

"Aren't you scared those people are going to hear us?"

The words had barely left Carl's lips when we were close enough for him to see who the two people sitting by the fire in front of the cave opening were. Reed's skin was as dark as the desert sky, and I know it sounds weird, but I totally loved it when we held hands. Our fingers knitted together. My skin so fair next to his so dark, like the keys on a piano, and together we made a symphony. And I'd be able to remember exactly what our interlocked hands looked like forever, because it was me that was on the other side of the campfire. The me that was six years younger. Before I'd been locked in The Lab. She was gazing at a Reed who was very much alive and had toasted marshmallow stuck to his upper lip. Young me licked it off.

I didn't have to get close enough to hear what Reed was saying to me, the fire casting a warm glow on his face, his perfectly straight, bright white teeth on full display as he smiled down at me. The very definition of charming. Long ago, I'd memorized every word he'd said and repeated mine back as if we were in a play and the 2020 version of me was the understudy.

Reed tucked a lock of my long blonde hair behind my ear, on

instinct I did the same. Although, now my hair was barely longer than Carl's. Shorn halfway down my ears, not covering the four ruby-red studs on my right lobe and barbell through the top cartilage. The tears came right on cue as Reed took 2014 me's chin in his hand, kissed my nose, and whispered in my ear. I could still feel his breath on my neck, his promise ringing in my ears like a church bell. The old me had a smile on her face, and took Reed's hand back, pleading, "Tell me again."

"I'll tell you a hundred times." Reed's Dominican accent added a melody to his words. He kissed me, his tongue teasing mine. I tried to remember what he tasted like, but it got mixed with the tears streaming down my face and so all I could taste was salt.

Reed stroked the side of 2014 me's face as he recited the words, I couldn't just remember them, but feel the beat of his voice. The phrases he stressed and the ones he let float up into the air above the old me, thought to be completely lost, yet six years later they reverberated inside of me. Our connection was deeper than a tattoo, or any scar. And now it was my curse, the ability to relive any moment of my past, but not the ability to change it. A part of me would always be here, in this night, as Reed recited *Un Amor* by Pablo Neruda, haunted by what I couldn't change.

"He's Blue, too, right?" Carl asked.

I wiped my face, then turned to Carl. His lips turned down along with his gaze as I said. "Yeah."

It seemed as if all the angles in Carl's face softened along with his voice, "But he's not with you now?"

I shook my head, biting my bottom lip.

Carl looked back at Reed as he finished reciting the last stanza to a younger me. "They killed him, and you've been running ever since."

I didn't answer, because it wasn't a question. Younger me pulled Reed to her, wrapped her arms around his neck, and whispered into his ear. Reed responded with a kiss, and not just any kiss, but one you only see in the movies or hear about in songs. The kind of kiss that you feel in your entire body, and even six years later my lips tingled. Reed took younger me by the hand and took her into the cave. Recalling how the evening ended, I nodded back the way we came, and Carl followed me. I might share a make-out session with my dead boyfriend with a stranger, but I'd never share the rest of the memory with anyone else.

But if I could have stayed... To feel Reed's hands run along every inch of me, over the scars that I'd given myself, or that others had left behind when they tried to figure out what made me work. The way his lips glided against my skin, how I reacted when he made his way between my thighs. He was smoother than chocolate. To feel his weight on top of me, and the ecstasy to have him inside me. My Swirling Smoke started to light up at the mere memory of being with Reed. What I wouldn't give to have him touch me again. Even if it was just to tuck my hair behind my ear as he told me, 'I love you, Litha,' and I could tell him, 'I love you too Reed, forever and ever.'

My throat watered, and my knees weakened as Carl and I walked back the mile and a half to where I'd brought us. I took Carl's hand in mine and looked up at him. "Close your eyes."

He did, and it appeared that a tear escaped past his dark lashes, but that might have been a trick of the light as we moved out of my film reel and back to 2020. When he opened them, we were both back in our chairs. He instantly reached for his phone to verify the time, only to show it to me noting that not a moment had passed, "but we were gone for at least half an hour."

I took the phone from him and turned it face down on the table. "We didn't go anywhere in time, all I needed to do was touch your hand and I could bring you into my memory, right before my fog."

"Your fog?"

I rubbed my face with the palms of my hands. "It's like a parallel timeline in my head." I let my hands fall to the table. "It's a place I can go, and not be here. It's what I did at the club, so that asshole couldn't find me."

"What happens to here?" He pointed down at the card table in the center of his poorly lit kitchen, surrounded by celery-colored walls with the paint chipping. His entire house was an artist's study on colors that brought about depression. "While we're gone?"

I stood up, rocking my neck back and forth. Sometimes there was static in my head when I went back to the same memory too many times. Or at least that's what started happing the last fifty times I went back to November 10, 2014. "I'm not so important that time stops for me," I said as I looked around the kitchen, "you have some liquor?"

"Yeah." Carl stretched up to the cabinet above the oven, which was littered with a pizza box of which I'd consumed all of the week-old pepperoni and mushroom. He set the bottle of whiskey on the table, and while he searched for glasses I started to drink. Before he could set a glass in front of me, I'd finished a quarter of its contents. Once my throat was scorched enough, I set it on the table with a clunk, sloshing liquor.

"You probably shouldn't drink so much, you're kinda little." His gray-green eyes flittered over me like a butterfly. "And just ate all that food."

"If you don't get that I'm not like you, then no amount of words is going to work." I started toward the couch, which was about ten feet from the table and four chairs made of avocado-green plastic. When I plopped down, millions of particles of dust floated around me. I unlaced my Chucks, kicked them off, pulled my hoodie up, and threw myself horizontally on the couch facing the wall.

"Are you going to sleep?"

"Yeah, dragging random guys through my memory kinda takes it out of me."

He stepped closer to me; his Blue Vibrated like it was afraid to touch the Swirling Smoke around me. It was a common reaction, so I didn't take it personally, but Carl obviously wasn't much for intuition as the tension rose in the room with each step he took toward me.

"You're not going to tell me anymore?"

"No, I just want to *sleep*." I stressed the last word, and my tone neared a growl.

"And you're not worried I'll hurt you or something?"

"Like kill me or something?"

"Yeah?"

I scoffed. "Don't make me any promises."

"You want to die?"

I sat up and looked up at Carl. "There's nothing that you can do that will be worse than what they've already done to me. I have no family because I made them forget about me, and they killed the only person I had left. So yeah, I'd much rather you get a knife and slit my throat then go back to that fucking Lab." I gasped for breath not realizing I'd assaulted him with words, and my voice cracked once I spoke again. "There's no one left that I love."

"Talitha..." His Blue started to lighten, a glow from the center.

"Don't even waste your time with an apology. I won't exist to you tomorrow."

"What if I don't want to forget?" He bent his knees, so our faces were level. "What if I want to help you?"

"Carl, you're a nice guy, but that's all you are." I lay back down and faced the back of the couch.

"I could help you."

"I thought talking to someone again would help, but I was wrong."

Everything was on mute, my entire world was Carl's avocado paisley couch, but I could still feel his shimmering Blue. "He was singing a song to you, right? A love song in Spanish, right?"

"A poem," I sighed.

"What's it called?"

"*Un Amor.*"

The title ate at me. Deep in the center of my soul, the cruel irony that I'd had Reed recite a poem about how terrible it would be to lose me was heavy. How sad he'd be if I died and he couldn't bring me back. That life would have no meaning without me, the pain all too great that he'd have to block me from his mind.

"What's it about?"

"How much he'll miss me when I'm gone." I pulled the hood over my face trying to block out his Shimmering Blue.

# Talitha
10/10/2020 8:38 PM

"You know it's creepy to watch people sleep, right?"

"Well, you are on my couch."

I sat up and rubbed my face with my clammy palms. "How long was I asleep?"

"A while." Carl's gray-green eyes scanned me as he stood halfway between the kitchen and the couch. He nodded at the empty side, then threw me a look.

I tipped my chin and he sat next to me.

Pine wafted off of him and while the hair on the sides of his head were cut short and faded, the curls that hung in his eyes were damp. His black t-shirt said *Stop Reading My Shirt* in block white lettering. I could tell he was nervous because his Blue Aura Wavered on the edges, but I didn't want to break into his head to find out why.

"Thanks for not calling the police or whatever."

"Yeah, no problem." He nodded. "Guess this is when you erase my memory?"

"Yeah, but is there any way I could, take a shower first?"

He blushed and I didn't have to read his mind to know what he was thinking. "I can make you something to eat, and I might have some clothes for you."

I cocked an eyebrow at him. "You're a foot taller than me."

"No, my ex-girlfriend Jenny, she left some stuff behind." His face turned brighter, as did the Blue that Swirled around him. "And you're about her size."

"She hates you so much she didn't come back for her stuff?"

"She might," he shrugged. "But I think that her new boyfriend, Tom, is jealous of me or something. Probably bought her a whole new wardrobe just so she wouldn't talk to me. Which is funny because I guess I should be the one that's pissed off."

"Why?"

"Jenny moved in here with me, did that for about a year, didn't realize she was sleeping with Tom the whole time." Carl shook his head, his eyes on the floor. "Just figured when she said she was working on her dissertation that she really was."

"That doesn't make you stupid, you trusted her, so why wouldn't you believe her?"

His Blue started to Lighten back up. "Yeah, guess you're right. It's been a few months so you might as well see if there's anything in there you want." He pointed to the door at the end of the hall, beyond the staircase to the second floor. "That's my room you can get changed and there's a lock on the door if you're worried or whatever."

I took off my beanie, ran my fingers through my hair and it came out covered in a week's worth of sweat. Then I balled up the beanie and shoved it into my leather jacket before I shrugged it off. "I already told you that you can't hurt me, but I could hurt you." I met his eyes. "And you don't seem afraid of me at all."

He tossed me a chuckle. "Should I be worried you'll trap me in an embarrassing memory?"

The muscles in my mouth started to ache because it had been so long since I'd smiled. "You have a lot of those?"

He shrugged, still grinning. "Doesn't everyone?"

I nodded, but kept my mouth shut.

Carl stood up, and started toward the kitchen. "I'll give you some privacy."

"I've been alone for so long," I sighed unaware that the words has escaped my head.

Carl turned back to me. "You say something?"

"Thanks." I stood up and bit my lip before I continued, "thanks for being so nice."

"Hey, so I was thinking..." His Summer Sky Blue Aura dared to reach out to my Swirling Gray Smoke but stopped short as Carl continued, "There's a party tonight in the neighborhood, and if you're going to just leave anyway, thought you might want to have a few beers first."

Maybe there was something about him, and it wasn't just an accident that he was at the bar, because my Swirling Smoke Aura began to lighten on the edges, threatening to turn the Deep Coal center of me into a diamond.

"Okay," I said, and thought better than to add that I'd never actually been to a party, at least not one with music you can choose, much less beer.

"Cool." He smiled, and I realized that he had a dimple in his right cheek but not his left.

"Feel better?"

I nodded. "You make some great scrambled eggs."

"Kinda the only thing I can make."

"I'd never even made toast until I broke out of The Lab."

"Really?" He rose an eyebrow. "You always order food?"

My eyes slid to the floor as I laced up my high-top Chuck Taylors that were covered in black peace signs in different sizes. "At school we had meals made by humans that had been enchanted by Professor Widmore, and at The Lab they'd push a tray through the door."

Carl didn't say anything, but his Aura Flickered.

I rolled the bottom of my newfound black jeans up because they were three inches too long. "Thanks for letting me have one of your shirts, I don't really like to look like a disco ball."

He chuckled, happy that I'd broken the tension as he put on his own jacket. "Looks better on you anyway."

I looked down at the gray t-shirt, which on me was nearly a dress, and read *Whisky Made Me Do It*. "Do all your shirts have a witty phrase on it?"

He shrugged. "If you can't have fun, then what's the point?"

That's when reality started to choke me, that I was twenty-five and had never had fun in the conventional sense like Carl had. I only knew how to communicate with people because I could read their Aura's and minds. Not that I wanted kids, nor could I have them since I'd been sterilized by Wakefield, but what stories would I tell those hypothetical nonexistent children?

My mother's eyes would sparkle when she'd talk about her first school dance, first job, learning how to drive a car. Hell, I hadn't learned how to ride a bike. And every moment that I wasn't in the hands of Wakefield being torn apart to see what made me work, I was terrified that they were on my trail, too depressed to even break into people's houses to feed myself. The irony was, I didn't even have a chance to become anything, I'd been stuck in a prison for so long. Bars surrounded me nearly my entire life, whether it was at school with Widmore, or at the Lab; I wasn't even aware who The Cold War Kids were until I happened upon a spontaneous performance while I was running for my life, damned to die in pain, all alone.

But not tonight.

Tonight, I would be normal, a dream I never thought I could have.

I slid my jacket on and nodded at Carl. "Let's go."

# Talitha
## 10/10/2020 9:55 PM

My hair was still the slightest bit damp, strands of it stuck to my forehead as I shoved my beanie on when we stepped out into the brisk Baltimore night. We headed west, traveling the two city blocks to the party. Nervous energy began to build up inside of me, causing my Swirling Gray Smoke to darken into a Storm Cloud. I shoved my hands deep into the pockets of my jacket, feeling the silk interior, rubbing it against my thumb and index finger as I breathed in through my nose, and out of my mouth in an attempt to calm down.

Needing to escape my own head I looked up and over at Carl. "So you're from Baltimore?"

"Born in France, but been here since third grade. Still live in the house I grew up in."

"You speak French?"

He smiled, "*Oui*."

I smiled back. "You still sleep in the same room?"

"Nah." He shook his head and his Blue Aura started to darken to Navy in the center. He was remembering something painful. "Don't really go upstairs anymore." The sound of his boots and my sneakers on the sidewalk were the only sounds either of us made until he asked, "What about you?"

"From the burbs, out in Anne Arundel County."

He threw me a smirk as the Navy shifted to Ocean Blue. "So you're rich then."

"Yeah, that's why I pick up random guys in the bathroom and beg them to let me take a shower and eat their leftovers."

"Isn't that how rich people stay rich then, they don't spend any money?"

"So, based on your decor I'd have to guess you're loaded?"

The smile fell from his face. "Jenny took it all when she moved out, never got around to getting anything to replace it."

"She took all your furniture, but left her own stuff?"

"No, she kinda made me sell all my stuff, and use the money to buy what she wanted."

"She sounds like a real bitch."

"Yeah, I wasted a lot of time on her." Then he looked at me. "Glad I'm not anymore."

"Me too."

I found it difficult to pull my eyes from him, but it was probably just the way the streetlights were hitting his profile, or the cars passing by making that *swooshing* sound as their wheels turned on the slick pavement like it was our soundtrack. He added to it when he started to hum, and I peeked in his brain just enough to know it was called *Take Care* by Beach House. It sounded like a sad song, echoing, cold, and distant. Like him. The moon was out, but the stars were mostly blocked by the luminescence of the city. Everything was bright, and maybe that's what was causing the bubbles in my stomach as we got closer to the party. I could sense the group of thirty or so Auras the second we turned the block. While it would have been smart to pay just as close attention to the outlying neighborhoods, I kept my scope on the few blocks that surrounded Carl's house.

But reserving my energy didn't keep me from sounding like a freak when I did break the stretched-out silence between us. "You should just tell people that your decorating scheme is based on nihilism."

He chuckled, but only half-heartedly, his Aura Flickered Tangerine with embarrassment as he held my eyes with his. "What's that?"

"A philosophy that life is meaningless. So, like what would be the point of decorating your house if everything means nothing?" Once the words left my mouth, I instantly regretted their creation. "Sorry if that sounded harsh."

"No I get you, it's just that I'm not as smart as you I guess," his voice softened toward the end, "because I've never even heard that word before."

I probably should have told him that street smarts were just as important as book smarts. Because I might understand the different types of ethical and physiological lifestyle choices because Widmore made sure of it, but I would never survive on my own in the world like Carl. Not without using my powers. Instead, I elbowed him as we turned to the row house with music pumping out of it, and all the colors imaginable pouring out of all six windows of the brick building. "At least you're pretty then, right?"

He laughed, this time for real. "You think I'm pretty?"

I rolled my eyes. "Like a million girls haven't told you that already."

He tilted his head to the side. "You're pretty too, you know."

"Yeah." I stood at the top of the three shallow steps that lead up to the door. "I know."

Carl opened the door to dancing, laughing, drinking, a thousand swirling colors, and even more thoughts. From love, loss, to how many drinks could a Peach Aura have and still drive home. I put everyone on mute once I figured out that it was The xx with their vibrating love song that played on the speakers throughout the house. The vibe of the partygoers was slow like honey, with most Auras being Relaxed Pastels, rather than the Fired Up Chili Pepper at the club last night. Probably because everyone seemed to already know each other, and trusting an outsider like me was a mere blip on the radar.

A *Jaws*-themed pinball machine sparked and chirped as a small crowd stood around and watched a guy with a Nationals cap try to get the metal ball between the black eyes of the Great White. Christmas lights were strung around the staircase, underneath which was a bookshelf filled with records, a leather couch, and a set of high-back emerald green velvet chairs sat atop a ten-foot circular Persian rug in the living room. The fireplace was lit, the keg in the sink in the kitchen made of white tile, and a fridge was stocked with bottles of beer, both local and domestic. Honey mustard pretzels, UTZ potato chips, and Fischer's caramel popcorn filled the bowls on the coffee table, which was an old door cut in thirds and folded just so the glass inlay didn't crack.

It made me wonder if Carl had killed me and now I was in the afterlife, because I was living in a dream I'd never thought I could experience in this lifetime. But even that couldn't be true, as I had died twice already only to be surrounded by endless empty black. Here the most stressing drama was a late response to a text, or a question as to whether politicians really had our bests interests, or how much it sucked to find a parking spot in Baltimore. Everyone's thoughts started to bombard my brain, *it's so fucking cold, should I have brought a jacket? Will Jessa ever call me back? I think I'm going as Luke Perry to Chris' Halloween Party since it's a Riverdale theme.* I double-clicked the mute button, sometimes it went on the fritz when I was around a lot of people.

Carl moved through the crowd with ease. He greeted the other bartenders at the bar in Fells Point that he worked at, The Tin Man; waved at the few couples that lived in the neighborhood; high-fived a few guys from school; nodded at a slender, ginger-haired vixen who eyed me up and down before she reminded Carl 'about that crazy trip to New York back in 2018 .' She was the first person to actually notice me, and her Aura shifted from Baby Pink to Jade Green as she measured the distance between the Carl and me. Although, it obviously wasn't a love story for the ages, since he hadn't bothered to introduce me to anyone. Until he was forced to.

"Anderson!" A fair-haired guy with dark eyes, shredded jeans, high-tops, and a black hoodie with the image of music producer DJ Khaled crossed the room. I recognized the cover art from his single *Popstar*, a video which starred my crush, Justin Bieber. He wrapped his arm around Carl's neck in a chokehold, a beer in his other hand as he laughed. "You left me at that show last night, man, and didn't answer your texts, thought the BPD got you or something."

Carl laughed and pushed him off. "Sorry man, got caught up in something."

Chokehold Guy's eyes darted to me, and he might as well have licked his lips the way his Aura turned from Deep Burgundy to Bright

Red. "I can see that." He smacked Carl in the chest with the back of his hand.

"No, Danny, it's not like that." Carl shook his head, his Aura Flickered, and his face started to flush.

"I'm Annie." I reached out to Danny, shook his hand, and made sure to time stamp this part of the film so I'd be able to quickly find it and erase this conversation from existence.

"Pleasure to meet you, Annie, couldn't have picked a better guy to chill with. Known him since we were kids at summer camp, and he spent the first week crying for his Mom." Danny nodded over at Carl whose face continued to turn bright red.

"Some wingman you are," he muttered.

I shrugged. "I like guys that are in touch with their emotions."

Danny took a sip of his beer. "You guys meet at Ottobar last night?"

I nodded and continued with a well-crafted lie. "There was a creep bothering me. Carl told the jerk to get lost and I was pretty upset so he took me to his place to calm down. We ended up talking all night, sorry that he didn't answer your texts."

"That's our man, Carl, definition of chivalry." Danny nudged him in the arm. "We're going to have to get you a cape, man."

"I'm gonna grab a beer," I said as I looked over at Carl, who was still blushing. "I'll bring you one." Then I moved through the crowd to the kitchen to leave the friends to talk. Didn't want to include myself in too many memories of others if I could help it, not when I could be a voyeur and be able to remember this party for the rest of my life.

I only remembered what freedom felt like because it was my superpower, and I wanted to create as many canisters of film as I could while I was experiencing it so I'd have something to hold onto when I wasn't anymore. A group of girls with varying shades of Tangerine and Lemon gossiped in the corner of the kitchen, most of them glancing at a group of guys in the living room near the record player and their various shades of Sherbet and Raspberry. I popped open the top of the beer and took a drink, the hops filtering down my throat as I saw a Sunshine Yellow girl turn into a Deep Jade Green and make her way to Danny and Carl. Her hair was deep chocolate and pulled up into a high ponytail, her leather pants looked painted on, and her jacket was coated in gold sequins like a disco ball. She drew me in like a spider wrapping her prey in her web.

"Why didn't you meet me this morning?" Jade Green whined to Carl.

He scoffed. "Did you tell your *boyfriend* that you were texting me every ten seconds to meet with you?"

"I would have if, there was anything to tell." Her hand reached out to Carl, her index finger trailing down just shy of hitting his belt buckle on its way. "But you have been ignoring me since I moved out."

"I'm not interested in whatever you have to say, so please just go." Carl took a step back, nearly bumping into me.

"Sorry, Annie," he muttered as he righted himself.

My heart skipped a beat when he said my name, my *real* name never sounded sweeter, but I played it cool and handed him the beer. "No problem, Carl."

He took the beer and half his mouth turned up in a smile. "Thanks."

"You're welcome."

Jade Green Jenny looked me up and down, before zeroing in on Carl. "Are those *my* jeans, and *your* shirt?" Her tone sounded like nails on a chalkboard, so I couldn't tell if it was a question or a screech.

Carl shrugged. "I told you to get your shit the day you told me you'd been fucking Tom for a year."

"So you just give them to the whore you're fucking now?"

"Hey." I couldn't help but interject myself into the conversation, making another time stamp for review later. *I'm going to have to erase a lot of tape tonight,* I realized before I continued, "You don't know me, but I'm not a whore."

"Then *who* are you?" An eyebrow rose on her fair skin, she would have been really pretty if she weren't shrouded in a thick haze of Jade Green.

"We were doing just great without you talking to us." Carl's shoulders hung heavy.

A Neon Yellow guy began to fade into a Sickly Green as he approached Jenny. His eyes were glued to her, I jutted my chin toward the guy in the button-down shirt tucked into his jeans. "I think he's looking for you."

Jenny's head pivoted back, she muttered, "Shit." Her eyes skirted over me before she turned away and became enveloped in the Sickly Green until she turned him Jade Green like her.

Danny laughed. "That was fucking awesome."

Carl looked down at me and smiled. "Yeah she is."

Danny nodded. "Well it's good to see you man, I hear that Gabby's coming." He looked around the room until he connected with a Strawberry Aura who was leaning against the fridge in the kitchen. "Gotta go." He patted Carl on the shoulder without waiting for a response and made his way to the kitchen, his Aura started to Sparkle the closer he got.

The song switched to *Two Weeks* by Grizzly Bear the crowd told me, and although Jenny's Jade Green negativity had walked out the door along with her boyfriend, the hair on the back of my neck stood up. My mouth became dry even though it was full of beer, my pulse quickened. I could feel it coming.

It wasn't Black, because even that was a color, more like the astronomical phenomenon of a black hole that encapsulated an evil so severe that it made me physically ill. My free hand searched for Carl's, laced my fingers with his and held tight.

"Talitha?"

*Someone very bad*, my voice a whisper only he could hear as I spoke directly into his mind, *he's at the door.*

And when it opened the bottomless pit of evil fell over the rest of the party like an eclipse, clouding out all of their Auras. Everyone's except Carl's, although it had turned to a Flicker of Bright Blue rather than its full glowing glory.

"That's just Joe, he's cool."

I knew that Carl, and all the other partygoers saw an ideal specimen of the male form, with his broad shoulders, bright blue eyes, blinding white smile, and a charisma that outshone most any other human, disarming them into believing he was what he appeared to be. Instead, his mind opened up to me like a Venus Flytrap, which curled my toes and created bile in my stomach that reached toward the back of my throat. One of Joe's hands could easily cover my face, and even though he was across the room I could feel his palm pressed against my lips. Iron filling my mouth. His full weight on top of me, my clothes discarded as he pushed himself inside, tearing me in half. Even though I felt it, there was another girl under Joe, but I couldn't read her mind because she was unconscious. He'd drugged her. But the girl woke up with the taste of the liquor he'd given her.

*Who's Tanya?* I telepathically asked Carl as the depth of evil slowly made its way to me. Joe might not realize it, but I seemed to be a beacon that he'd be unable to avoid.

*She's over there,* Carl thought as his eyes locked in on a girl sitting on the bench next to the pinball machine. Her hair was long, auburn, and curly just like the girl in Joe's memory. I also knew her whole body was covered in freckles just like her face, and that Joe hadn't just drugged and raped her once, but I was bombarded with the memory of him violating her at least two dozen times.

As I scoured Tanya's memory, I couldn't find a clear bit of film in the movie of her life that correlated with what I'd seen in Joe's biopic. Bits and pieces, one time she woke up and the condom was still inside of her. When she asked Joe about it, he told her she must have forgotten to pee after they had sex. But he remembers defiling her as she slept; it was a true horror movie, one that he played on a loop even now with a new victim by his side.

*He drugged and raped her a lot,* only Carl could hear me as I gripped onto his hand as if he were the only form of gravity.

"No way," Carl began, "They almost got married."

I shook my head hoping that I could get it out of my head. *He's done it so many times, so many girls,* I insisted to Carl.

Their faces flashed through my mind, at least nine, the youngest was sixteen and used a fake ID to get into the bar where they'd met. She'd been a virgin before he drugged her drink and raped her in the back of his car, and although she never could remember exactly what happened, there were enough flashes of consciousness to make her take a bottle full of pills before she slit her wrists. Joe had laughed at her mother when she came to his door, her daughter's diary in hand. He threatened to call the police on her for trespassing.

Joe's eyes connected with me, his mind ignited with what he wanted to do with me. Starting with shoving Carl's t-shirt in my mouth so I couldn't scream as he bent me over the leather couch I was standing next to. He couldn't help but grin as he pictured gripping onto my throat until I blacked out which nearly made him climax in his jeans at the mere thought.

*Don't let him touch me.* I closed my eyes and started to step backward bringing Carl with me.

*He won't hurt you,* Carl thought as he squeezed my hand.

The Black Hole known as Joe tried to meld with my Swirling Gray Smoke. Lightning crackled around me. My heart skipped a beat as the electricity began to build. My skin was crawling. And when his Never-Ending Darkness finally broached my Gray Smoke all the footage I'd collected from Joe and Tanya spewed out of me. Faster than the bolts of electricity that swirled around me, the memories flooded out into the room, flowing out of me before I could pull down the iron shield between me and the world.

It might as well have been gunfire that I shot out into the party, because one second the guy at the pinball machine was laughing, the next his Aura turned into Bubbling Lava when he came up to Joe's side. Bubbling Lava gripped Joe's shoulder, face as red as a stop sign and snarled, "Did you rape my sister?"

Joe's eyes left me and were directed toward the nearly foaming Bubbling Lava man. "It wasn't like that, we were dating, and she liked to party."

"Then why'd you crush pills in her soda?"

Before Joe could answer, Tanya's Bubbling Lava brother decked him, and as he fell to the floor I let go of Carl's hand and ran.

Ran out of the room.

Out of the building,

Out into the street.

Not stopping until I was three blocks away and had to because the vomit wouldn't stay in my mouth anymore.

# CARL
## 10/10/2020 11:45PM

I ran back toward my house, the image of Joe on top of Tanya, his hand covering nearly all of her face ignited in my brain. I could feel my breath being taken away from two hundred pounds of weight on top of me. My heart raced in my chest just as Tanya's had. I'd known Joe since high school, and had no idea who he really was, but Talitha did. Somehow, she managed to put the memory into my head, and at least Tanya's brother Clint, seeing as he was the one that started to beat the shit out of Joe as I chased after Talitha.

*How many other people did she give the memory to?*

It seemed like an accident, or something she did unintentionally. Her voice was trembling inside my head, as was her grip on my hand before she raced out faster than a cheetah. She didn't check to see if I was following her, when I caught up with her, she was bracing herself against a mailbox, barfing in the gutter.

"Are you okay?" I asked, but I already knew the answer before she wiped her mouth and looked up at me with the biggest bluest eyes I'd ever seen in my life, some of her golden blonde hair sticking out from her beanie, cheeks and nose red from the cold. Or maybe the barfing.

"I'm sorry."

I rested my hand on her shoulder, so narrow and small. The four ruby studs in her right ear glittered, the end of the silver barbell in her cartilage piercing sticking out. She wore no makeup, but was still so beautiful. A perfect mix of Debbie Harry and Tinkerbell, and I wanted nothing more than to take away all of her pain. "You didn't do anything."

"I didn't mean to let the memory out." A tear fell down her face. "It's never happened like that, with the lightning, usually I can control it."

"You've never done that before?"

She shook her head. "This time the lightning, it took over."

"I didn't see any lightning."

"I see a world that you don't, and it seems to get more complicated every day." She covered her face with her hands. "I can still feel him everywhere."

I wrapped my arms around her, hugged her, and she let me. She lassoed my neck with her arms, standing on her tip-toes, and buried her face in my shoulder as she trembled.

*What the hell is happening since I met this girl?* I wondered, but for some reason I didn't want to question too much because it felt really good to hold her. She smelled like leather and my shampoo.

"It's okay, Talitha, I won't let anything like that happen to you."

She stopped shaking and slowly pulled away from me, like taffy. "Carl, you don't even know, that wouldn't even be the worst thing."

I took her face in my hands, and it felt like we were both pieces of a puzzle, and I'd finally figured out where my missing piece was. "I want to keep you safe from guys like that."

"You can't."

"Not if you don't let me."

"I'm not some princess locked in a tower waiting to be rescued."

"I'm not saying you are."

She pulled my hands from her face and held them in hers, my skin rejoiced, but her tone told me that we weren't about to celebrate. "Let me show you something."

"What?"

"August 13, 2003, the last day I was normal." It was as if her words wrapped around me and carried me like ash on the breeze that made up her past.

The sun was pummeling down on us as we walked on the sidewalk that wrapped around suburban homes where all the backyards opened up into a dense wood. But I didn't sweat under all my layers, leather jacket, and Docs. Just like I hadn't felt the sand swirling in the wind when she took me into her memory in the desert. Kids rode their bikes on the empty streets, wind chimes dinged as the air breezed through them, although I didn't feel a gust at all. Talitha hadn't said a word, but held onto my hand as we continued walking. I wasn't sure if she had to in order to keep me with her, but I wanted to believe that she wanted to hold my hand as much as I wanted to hold hers.

We made our way to a two-story pale green house, with a wrap-around screened in porch, tire swing, and two Toyota sedans. A little girl came bounding out of the house, giggling, two yellow braids hanging on each side of her face with pink ribbons at the end that matched the dress that danced around her as she spun in a circle. In a fit full of giggles, she collapsed on the ground under the White Oak in the front yard.

I figured the little girl was Talitha, but I couldn't be sure until another figure exited the house, with the same delicate features and bright blue eyes as the woman next to me, even if her hair was a darker blonde than My Talitha's. The woman had a big smile and started chasing the girl around the tree as they both laughed, until mother caught daughter around the middle, picked her up, and put her in the swing.

"Higher, Mommy!" the little girl pleaded.

"Want me to send you out into space, Annie?"

I felt an icicle hit me in the heart, Annie wasn't a name Talitha made up when she met Danny, but her real name. Which made sense; after all, no one called him Matt Murdock when he was fighting crime in Hell's Kitchen or Daredevil when he went to the grocery store.

"Yes! I want to fly to the moon!" Annie answered as her mother pushed her even higher, but nowhere near the tree limbs much less the moon.

I looked over at Talitha, truly examining her for the first time since we'd entered her memory. Her face was as stiff as stone, her own eyes glued to the scene on the other side of the block.

"You were Annie right, before whatever happened?" I asked tentatively.

She nodded, but still kept watching her younger self and her mother.

"You said this is the day you got your powers or whatever?"

She nodded again.

I looked above us, but there wasn't a cloud in the sky, so she wasn't struck by this lightning she kept talking about. It was doubtful that nuclear waste was going to start leaking from the tree, or that aliens were about to land in front of us, so I couldn't figure out how it happened. "You're not about to get hit by a car that spews radioactive spiders? Because I'd really appreciate a heads up on that."

"No radioactive spiders." She shook her head. "I was born this way."

"Then why are we here?"

"Because although I've never *really* been normal up until now, I could pretend. Tonight, everything changes for me, like the first eight years I'd had goggles on, but in a few hours they're going to be ripped off."

"What happens?"

Her chin jutted out to the man walking down the steps to the mother and daughter. He had yellow-blond hair like Talitha, broad, squarely built like he was a wrestler when he was younger. When he picked up Annie from the tire swing, the muscles in his face tensed like it hurt to pick her up and throw her into the air.

"He was my hero," she murmured. "I never blamed him for putting my mom in that study which made me this way so he could buy this fucking house, but tonight I'm going to find out who he really is."

"You read his mind?"

"Everyone will just think I'm crazy. Including me."

She didn't say anymore, let the sound of mother and daughter laughing take over. And maybe I wasn't the smartest guy, but I'd only begun to connect the dots. "Your Dad, he's like Joe."

"Worse."

She took a deep breath as we both watched the happy family play in the sun-dappled front yard of their modern-styled farmhouse in one of the most expensive counties in the country. "When I read his mind and heard what he thought about me, it was so confusing. I don't know if telling my Mom what I saw brought him to the brink, or if he was always going to do it. But in a week, I'm going to wake up because I feel him before he's even in the room, as if the evil inside of him spilled out and flooded my room. I won't be able to move. Not even cry out because it will hurt so bad." She took in a deep breath before she continued, "I didn't mean to show my Mom what was happening, but she'd tell the doctors that she saw it all, even before she came into my bedroom."

"There were a million tests, and it was decided that I would be sent away, to a school with other kids like me. Given over to Widmore. I was there for a few years until my Dad found another blonde haired little girl." She looked up at me, her blue eyes turned red. "He didn't last long in prison."

I wasn't sure what to say, but I could see the love in Annie's mother's eyes as she looked at her daughter. "Why don't you go back to Anne Arundel County, stay with your Mom?"

Air escaped from between her lips like a deflating balloon. "I erased her memory of me, so she didn't have to live with any guilt of marrying a pedophile and giving birth to his victim."

"I thought you said you couldn't do that if there's a deep connection?"

"No, I said that it's very difficult, but that it really only hurts me." She looked back at her mother, who blew her father a kiss as she backed out of the driveway. "She lives in Portland now, with a husband and twin sons, completely unaware that I exist."

Her story hung heavier than the air around us. "I'm sorry."

She shook her head. "I didn't bring you here to get you to feel bad for me, it's to let you know that you *can't* protect me. Terrible things have happened, and I can't run forever, so I'll be captured again by somebody, and more terrible things will happen. That's why we should just go back and let me erase your memory."

I don't know why I said it, only that I knew it to be true, although I really had no evidence. "I don't think you should."

"Because you're Blue just like my dead boyfriend?"

"Yeah, that has to mean something." I faced her while in the background, Talitha's mother continued to play with Annie in the front yard.

"Like we're soul mates or something?"

"Maybe?"

Although her mouth turned up it still wasn't a smile. "Why would I need a human when I've made it on my own this whole time?"

"You said it yourself, you can't run forever, and maybe it's because I need you."

"So you can take me to more parties and have me confirm that your ex-girlfriend is still fucking that guy she cheated on you with?"

"No." Her words cut into me. "Because you're the first person in my whole life that I just trust." I hoped my words drew her back to me. "And I know that doesn't make sense, but I'd go anywhere with you." I motioned around us. "Obviously."

"I'm not even a person." She mimicked my hand motion. "I'm a science experiment."

I didn't know how to get through to her, that we met for a reason, and just like she didn't know why her powers had changed at the party, I didn't know why I needed to be by her side, but I knew it was what was right. "Can you take me into one of my memories?"

"Why would I do that?"

"So, I can prove to you that I understand losing everything too."

"Don't know why I should."

"Because if you erase my memory before you do, then you'll always wonder where I wanted to take you." I crossed my fingers hoping that she'd go with it.

She bit her bottom lip, her fingers locked with mine stronger than before. "You got half an hour, I'll have to eat by then anyway."

"Okay, how do we do it?"

She faced me and took my other hand in hers. "Just think of it."

"You don't want to know when we're going to?"

"It's not often a telepath gets surprises." Her words were barely above a whisper and they carried us out of August 13, 2008 and to the 18 of November 2016.

# Talitha
## 10/10/2020 11:45PM

"Where are we?"

He smiled down at me. "Thought you were a telepath?"

I rolled my eyes. "That would have spoiled the surprise."

He nodded behind me. "I think this will be a clue."

I turned around and before us was the Eiffel Tower, with a myriad of tourists in hooded rain jackets, most holding umbrellas, although not a single drop of water fell on either of us. The Seine River reflected the landmark. Winter was about to take over, so only the most resilient plants still existed, but it was predominantly stone, concrete, metal.

"It's beautiful," I mused as I tilted my head back to gaze at the structure that reached up into the cloudy sky, the sun peeking through the rain clouds lighting up random spots around us like a spotlight.

"Yeah." Steam formed out of his mouth along with the words.

"That's weird," and when I spoke it happened as well.

"What is?"

I exhaled a lungs worth of air. "We can see our breath."

"Yeah," he shrugged, "it's cold."

"No, *this* is a memory of a day that was cold. That's why we're not wet." I felt the world shrink in on me for a moment as I looked around, desperately trying to find some way to safely test the memory.

He shrugged, and inhaled deeply. "Smells like they just got finished making bread."

The aroma of perfectly risen yeast wafted in my nose as well, igniting my taste buds. I pulled Carl along with me as I followed the sound of chatter as the locals stood in line for the bakery. Without disturbing a single person, I pulled a baguette from the rack that a young boy with a cigarette in his mouth had just put out. He didn't notice us, nor did anyone in line seem to realize that a loaf was missing, so at least we were still invisible. But the bread was warm, and when I tore off a piece steam rose from it. The crunch in my teeth was equal parts delightful and terrifying.

"*Délicieuse baguette*," Carl mused in French as he shoved a piece in his mouth as well. "We should find some cheese and wine, maybe have a picnic?"

I gripped onto Carl's hand. "We shouldn't be able to eat the bread."

His light eyes widened as if he'd only just begun to understand the gravity of the situation. "This isn't normal either?"

I shook my head, wishing that I came with a user's manual, but fully aware that ever since I'd taken Carl into my memory, my powers had shifted drastically. I no longer understood the rules or boundaries, although I didn't have time to worry about that before Carl's eyes locked on a woman in a canary yellow coat as she walked past us.

She pulled her cigarette from mouth leaving the mark of her matte red lipstick. "Carl," her French accent gave the name a rhythm, "will you please get off your phone and at least pretend you're having fun with us?"

My Carl's gray-green eyes widened, and started to shine with tears. I turned around to follow his gaze, seeing the family of three strolling through the shops along the Seine as they headed toward the Eiffel Tower. An eighteen-year-old Carl rolled his eyes and put in his earbuds as he shoved his phone back into the pocket of his skinny jeans and forced his hands into the pockets of his leather jacket. The same motor-cycle-style jacket that a twenty-seven-year-old Carl wore as he stood next to me.

My Carl interlocked his fingers with mine as his bottom lip quivered and we followed a few steps behind his family. Young Carl's hair wasn't shaved on the sides, but bushy, curly, and long. He wore a distressed M83 t-shirt with a bunch of sardonic bohemian goth teens dressed as if they were torn between Prom and a Halloween party from their *Saturdays=Youth* album cover. His Docs followed behind his parents who both had dark hair as well. He'd gotten his light eyes and his nose from his mother, but I couldn't find the angular jaw which was in desperate need of being touched on either of his parents. Carl had the kind of jaw you could chisel an ice sculpture with while both his parents had oval faces, soft next to his harsh lines.

My Carl pulled me along as he tried to catch up with his mother, and once their strides were matched, he murmured, "*Maman?*"

But she didn't turn, not even to look at the Young Carl who was ignoring her. She kept chatting with her husband as My Carl drew so close that I could smell her perfume. Which I shouldn't have been able to do, no matter how close we were. His family kept moving toward the structure, and part of me wondered if they'd feel us if we knocked into them. But in truth, I didn't want to find out.

I tugged on My Carl's hand a bit so he'd slow down. "She can't see you, it's like a movie, I just rewound it."

The family stopped ten feet closer to the Eiffel Tower than us, and his mother gazed down at her watch, then pulled down the hood on her jacket and let her head fall back as she took in the landscape. She reminded me of some actress from a black and white movie with her fair skin and coal-black, perfectly waved hair.

"She looks just like I remember," he murmured.

I wanted to tell him, *no shit because this is your memory,* but I saw a tear break through his dark lashes, so instead I squeezed his hand.

Meanwhile, Young Carl seemed highly unimpressed with the architectural landmark. His Dad elbowed him in the side, they were matched for height, but Young Carl slouched. Although at twenty-seven, I noticed My Carl was easily four inches taller than his six-foot-tall father now.

"Your great-great-grandfather helped build this, Son." His Dad's

French accent sounded like a melody, his tone a clear tenor, as if they were in a musical and about to break into song.

"Yeah," Young Carl shrugged, "so what?"

"This is your past, and it's just as important to remember as it is to design your future."

"Whatever." Young Carl pulled his phone back out and started scrolling.

"Carl," his father's voice wavered from its joyful tone.

His mother put a hand on her husband's arm. "Charles, let's just get on the boat, he'll appreciate this when he's older."

His Dad sighed. "I hope so."

And the family walked off toward the Seine, and to their boat to tour the beauty of the City of Light.

"Did you ever come back with them?" I asked.

My Carl shook his head, looked down at me, tears streaming down his face. "They die in a car wreck a week after we get back to Baltimore."

We'd finished the first baguette, so we stole another, along with some cheese, a few bottles of wine, and an eclair. None of which we should have been able to savor, but as we walked along the Seine, that's exactly what we did. The night had begun to fall, the streetlights glittered on the water reflecting on his face, softening all his sharp angles.

"It was a hit and run, on their way to one of my Dad's Opera performances. They were running late because I was acting like a prick and refused to go." Carl took a swig of wine straight from the bottle as we walked down the cobblestones along the Seine. We'd left his family hours ago as they boarded a boat for a late lunch.

"Whoever it was ran a red light and pushed the town car into a light pole." His Aura darkened to a Navy as he recalled burying his parents before he graduated high school. "Ended up skipping college, not that I was smart enough to go anywhere amazing, could barely get into the University of Maryland." Carl's eyes sunk to the ground. "Since then, I've been working all kinds of shitty jobs, just kind of living because that's what I'm supposed to do. I figured that I'd get a line on what I should be doing." His gray-green eyes held me. "Like if I have a purpose, I'd get a sign at least to know which way to go."

"You believe in signs?" I asked as I tore off a piece of bread and tossed it in my mouth.

"I never thought I'd see my parents again, and you gave me that." He stopped amid tourists and Parisians moving around us as if we weren't there.

I couldn't help but stay in his orbit, he had become the Earth, while I was his Moon. "I gave you nothing you didn't already have; this is your memory after all."

"I wanted to come and see her, at least one more time. And now this day isn't so bad; it's not just the day I was an asshole to my parents on our last trip to the city we were all born in." He brushed a lock of hair behind my ear, the tips of his finger lingering on my earrings for a beat. I felt all the blood in my body rush to the spot. "I got to rewrite this and not look back and feel like shit because I wasn't nice to my parents."

I didn't know what to say, especially since it felt I was floating when Carl touched me. "Thanks for showing me this." I bit my bottom lip.

"Yeah?"

"Yeah, you showed me around Paris, probably won't ever get to go to the real one."

"If only people could see us, then I could impress you even more with my French." He tore off a piece of bread and tossed it into his mouth.

"It's a memory, you can't interact with the people, Carl."

"You said you couldn't eat the food either." He hoisted up the bottle of wine and took a swig. "But it seems like we can."

"It's never happened before."

"Like how you put that memory in everyone's mind at the party?"

I nodded.

"Told you, it's a sign."

"What? That I'm one step closer to world domination like I always dreamed about?"

"Nah." He shook his head and smiled enough so I could see his dimple. "I think it means we were supposed to meet."

I scoffed. "Yeah because every great story begins with two people meeting in the bathroom of a club."

"Is that the weirdest thing that's ever happened to you?"

While he had a point, I wasn't really in the mood to have a philosophical conversation, at least not sober. "I think we need some more wine and a place to sit."

I handed him the half-full bottle of red we'd swiped before we ended up on a bench in a park. It was the longest I'd ever been in memory. I'd lost track of time as we spent the whole night talking about everything and nothing.

Dawn had taken over, and it competed with the lights that kept the city alive. The stars had begun to fade away, yet a few still hung above us in a city I was completely unfamiliar with, and a language I didn't speak. I didn't question how we could go deeper into Paris when this wasn't part of Carl's actual memory. Before, I'd hit an actual wall or skip like a record to where I started if I strayed too far from where my past-self existed in the biopic of my life. The reel only had so many frames, and they could only contain so much; never before had I moved out of the boundary of memory, but remained invisible to everyone that existed that day. Fear attempted to creep in and take complete control of me as I realized that all of this was because of Carl.

For some reason, once we met, I'd become more powerful, and now in his memory I could feel the wine coat my throat, taste the baguette which was so fresh it was like tearing into flesh, and we'd even made a memory of our own in his memory. None of that had been possible before, even with years of The Lab attempting to heighten my powers. There was something about Carl that made me stronger, but I wouldn't think about that now. Right now, I wanted to pretend to be normal as best I could.

I leaned closer to him and his knee touched mine. "I'm sorry, about your parents."

"I didn't bring you here to get you to feel bad for me." His face turned up in a half-smile showing off his single dimple.

"Then why did you?"

"You showed me two memories that I'm just guessing you don't share with anyone else."

I suddenly felt very bare and nodded decidedly, shoving both memories so far back an atomic bomb couldn't bring them back up.

"Guess I was hoping that you'd want to know about me too, because I've liked getting to know you." He sighed. "At least until you told me that you could spend the rest of your life eating only mac and cheese."

"Pizza's better?" I scoffed.

"Yeah, you can get lots of different toppings on a pizza."

"And like there aren't a million different types of mac and cheeses? How can you live in Baltimore and never had it with crab?"

"Oh. Well." His Blue Aura started to Shimmer. "If it's not just the instant stuff then maybe you're right about mac and cheese."

I tried to bite my bottom lip to keep from smiling, but I couldn't help it. I'd shown him my scars, and he'd shown me his. He'd saved my life before he even knew my name. And between the way his hair fell in his eyes and the way he rubbed his chin, covered in scruff, when he was thinking, I wasn't sure if I could stand another minute not touching him. It seemed like forever that I'd gone over the reasons not to get involved with a someone who wasn't Enhanced like me, but I didn't care about that list I'd created in my head when I was with Carl. I pressed my lips to his while he was mid-sentence, describing the song *We Own The Sky*. And for once, my mind fell completely still as my entire soul ignited into a thousand Fourth of July Firework displays.

"Sorry," I whispered as I pulled away. I quickly stood up from the bench while grabbing the wine and threw back my head, letting alcohol coat my throat in the hopes of drowning out the chatter in my head of *'what the fuck did you just do?'* My sneakers crushed the plush grass under them as I started to walk back to the Eiffel Tower so I could eject myself from this embarrassment, but with the softest touch, his hand brushed the back of my neck.

I turned around and looked up at Carl. Sparkles consumed the Blue around the hand that touched me, and it began to take over his entire Aura as the tip of his index finger traced my bottom lip.

I'd never wanted anyone to kiss me back so bad.

His long eyelashes sunk down over his eyes as he bent his head down, the Swirling Gray Smoke around me lightening to Angelic White as he pushed his tongue past my lips. I dropped the bottle on the ground, wine poured out onto the grass, and I nearly stepped in it when

I moved closer to him as he wrapped his arms around me drawing me in. The rain started to trickle down causing thousands of prisms of color as the sunlight cut through each drop as it feel from the sky.

Our faces were inches apart when I whispered, "You're covered in Glitter."

"Cool." He grinned as he bent down to kiss me again.

I took a step back when I remembered who I was and where we were. "We shouldn't."

He took a step forward. "Why not?"

"Seriously I gotta spell it out?"

He leaned down, his mouth at my ear. "Take me off mute."

"Carl." His name got caught in my throat.

He brought me closer, let his hand fall down my side, and rested on my hip. "Talitha."

It had been so long since I wanted anyone to touch me, much less like that. I traveled through his lips deep into the crevasses of his imagination. I fell into the middle of a porno that Carl had played in his head starring me. My body tingled. In his fantasy, Carl lay me down on his bed, slowly peeling off my clothes. His hands traced the curves of my body. His tongue followed along. In his mind my skin was flawless, like fresh ice on a pond. When in reality, it was anything but. I'd only been with one person, and it had been so long ago, *what if I'm not good at it anymore? What if once he sees what The Lab had done to me, he won't want to be with me?*

It was then that the rain started to hit us. Stuck to our bodies as we kissed in a memory of a rainy Parisian morning in Carl's mind.

Finally, his X-Rated imagination caused me to moan, when he put two of his fingers inside of me. My Aura had officially turned the Brightest White, the falling rain drenched us, the cold water clinging to our skin. I made a fist clutching onto his t-shirt, my lips on his again as I stopped the sex tape in his brain as a shiver ran up my spine. "Yes."

"Yes?" He held me tight as I took us back to October 10, 2020, on the sidewalk in Baltimore where he'd caught up with me hours ago.

My lips danced on his, still wet from the Paris rain. "Take me to your place and do that to me, please."

# WIDMORE
## 10/11/2020 12:27 AM

"It's of the utmost importance that you bring Eight Fifteen to me the moment she reaches out to you, Gustav." Jonas' words were as cold as his office, which was miles below the Earth.

"So that's why you've taken your lackeys off me, hoping to lure Talitha?"

Jonas nodded, seated across from me behind his desk made of a solid piece of onyx roughly the size of a pool table. I didn't understand why he had it, since I never saw any paperwork on it like my desk at the University. I couldn't recall a single time he'd put pen to paper in the five hundred some-odd years that I'd known him. All those years ago, when I'd wanted to study the human mind, Jonas offered me a job to help him with research, only to become the first person who successfully took the serum. I thought it was an inoculation, but instead, I was transformed into a telepath.

My job was to be a father figure to our charges, or at the very least get them to forget about their past. While I didn't see them as superheroes, it proved useful to change their names. *Much easier to control when you get them to answer to a completely new name.* Jonas helmed the actual experimentation at Wakefield Laboratories. As long as I kept him updated, he allowed me to keep our subjects at The Manor, who were of course unaware of the arrangement. Every breath they took was part of the experiment, not just when they were in The Lab. Never had an Enhanced being been out of our care for so long like Talitha, and I knew he was desperate to have her back with him.

I too was curious as to her powers, but there was a reason Jonas never called Eight Fifteen Talitha or One Eleven Reed. And it had nothing to do with the fact that I'd given them new names so they could fully shed their Non-Enhanced life, as he would never have called them Annie or Domingo anyway. Jonas was a scientist who spent most of his time in the sub-basement of Wakefield. I'd made a tie that bound me and my charges closer, giving them names as if they were my children; children that I betrayed by following my mentor Jonas' orders. But I *had* to continue on with the research in the hopes that we could replicate the formula for immortality because there was a woman, Enhanced like me, that I would love nothing more than to spend an infinite amount of time with.

"Pity I can't read your mind anymore, Gustav." Jonas' burning red eyes connected with my light gray irises. "But I suspect you'd prefer to have her back in your care?"

"I would find that preferential." My right knee started to throb: *rain is coming*. "Yes."

"And why should I trust you, when she ran away from you before?"

"Give me a chance, let her reach out to me, and I know that I can get her to come back."

Jonas let the minutes pass as he thought; when one was immortal, waiting to contemplate the many outcomes your decisions would make was not a luxury but a ritual. "Alright," he nodded. "You bring her in, interview her, and if her abilities have advanced, then alert us and we'll evaluate her."

"You kept my charges four years last time." I rubbed my wrinkled hand against my polyester slacks to quell my aching knee. "Will it be as long this time?"

His bright white teeth reminded me of a shark and contrasted against his ebony skin. "You are fond of Eight Fifteen, aren't you?"

"We've already lost so many, we only have six left in North America, we really should conserve what we have."

"Well we do have the phase two specimens. In fact, I just returned from spending an evening with my beloved. You remember her, right?"

I did recall the little British girl, Lola, whom Jonas referred to as his beloved or One Hundred and Eight. Cordelia, the Enhanced woman I loved, was nearly four hundred and fifty years younger than me. However, I'd met her when she was a college graduate, not in year two of school like when Jonas met Lola. *Maybe Lola will learn to love Jonas and it's all for the best?* But as my eyes grazed Jonas' neck, I found scratch marks, and even with his advanced healing powers, the knuckles on his right hand were swollen.

I cleared my throat. "Has Lola's strength increased since you last saw her?"

He smiled at me. "She had a bit of fight in her, even punched through a steel wall to try and get away from me, but I found myself winning in the end. Her brother can replicate the power of another Enhanced being, so we'd have two of the strongest soldiers in our army, and once we find Eight Fifteen, imagine what we'll be able to do then. No human would have a chance against us."

"We can't forget the science, Jonas; finding out how far we can take a human with the serum. The latest specimen lived for nearly a week and had been the first one to grow wings after being injected with the third evolution."

"That's exactly what I'm telling you, Gustav. Why stop at giving ourselves wings, when we can control everyone and everything with no fear of retribution?" His coal-black irises, outlined in a rim of crimson, glowed. "Who will say no to us now?"

# Carl
## 10/11/2020 11:27 PM

We were barely inside and we'd already lost the first layer of dripping wet clothing. My heart beat out of my chest, and not just from the run to my house. I couldn't get Talitha naked fast enough as I pressed her back up against my door. My lips were on every wet inch of skin that I could find. I raised my arms as she pulled off my shirt. It stuck to me, making a sucking sound before Talitha tossed it on the floor. My skin burned under her touch, her fingertips tracing the gears tattooed on the left side of my body.

"How far'd you take this man of steel thing?" she mused as her hand moved along my side.

"I'm half machine," I joked, although it was true in two ways. Literally, in the gears which were etched on all my joints, bolts inked on my collarbone and wrists, and screws along the way, holding the pipes that matched the bones under my skin. I'd even had the artist add an anatomically correct heart above my own and put a cage around it. And figuratively, because after my parents died, I didn't care how much pain the nearly two hundred hours in the chair caused. In fact, I think I ended up liking how much it hurt because it was the only emotion I felt for so long. That is, until Talitha ran into that bathroom at Ottobar and asked me to lie for her and I felt something else for the first time in years: Hope.

She brushed her lips against my heart in the cage. "It's hot."

"You have any tattoos?"

I started pulling off her long-sleeved t-shirt and on instinct she raised up her arms. But before it could hit the floor, her head knocked against the door as she breathed, "wait."

I stopped, but didn't have to ask her what was wrong, because now I knew why she always wore long sleeves. The evidence of torture created a pattern of scars that ran down her arms, breaching her torso, reminding me of those cop shows where they stood over the victim in the morgue after their autopsy. Along Talitha's chest, the imprints were the same shape as those sensors they put on you when you're in the hospital to check your heart, but I couldn't imagine how long they'd have to be on in order to mar her ivory canvas.

As my eyes charted the rest of her skin, there were lines of white that spiraled around her hips reaching up past her belt to her black cotton bra. Some deeper and darker than others, from many hands, over many years, attempting to get a piece of flesh. My index finger traced around a few, her breathing quickening as I neared her. She looked up at me, her eyes wide, but she didn't say a word.

"Does it still hurt?"

She shook her head, took off the leather cuff on her wrist, and showed me her only tattoo – a barcode and the number 815 printed underneath. "Look I get it if you don't want to anymore, since I'm a freak."

With a curved index finger, I pulled her chin back toward me. "How can you find evil in a room full of people and not know how I feel about you?"

"The people that are looking for me do stuff like this for fun," she straightened up her back, "and I can't do anything to protect you but make you forget about me."

"I could never forget about you, and I'm not going to let them get you back." I took her face in my hands. "Just tell me what you want."

For a moment she just looked at me, her crystal-clear blue eyes holding me. I couldn't even shake them when she started to unbutton her jeans. Talitha took my hand from the side of her face, brought it down her stomach, and put it down her underwear. We both sighed when I put my fingers inside of her. She was so wet my erection practically busted my zipper.

Her eyes were crushed shut, her breathing quickening until it matched my speed. "I need you now." She took my hand out of her jeans and pushed me back toward my bedroom.

She kicked off her Chucks, and I hopped as I unlaced my Docs while we made our way to the most nihilistically decorated room in the house. All it had was a bed, side table, and a few milk crates full of records—the only possessions I really cared about. Not that it mattered because neither of us bothered to turn on the light. My body was electrified every time she touched it, her lips always finding their way back to mine. She was practically wrapped around me like a vine as I laid her on the bed. I tugged her jeans off and kissed her calves, which had more patchwork scars, like she'd been taken apart and sewn back together.

My tongue made its way between her thighs, when she took a fistful of hair and brought my face up to hers. "Please no more foreplay or my brain will melt." She took me in her hand, about to direct me inside, when I stopped.

"I need a condom." I sat up and rustled through my bednight stand and made a silent prayer that I still had some from when Jenny lived with me.

Talitha sat up halfway on the bed on her elbows. "You don't need one."

I rose an eyebrow at her. "Yeah, I do."

"They sterilized me." Her voice softened nearly as much as her skin, but darkened like the night sky. "Wouldn't want monsters making monsters."

I moved back to her and brushed hair off of her face, her cheeks and lips red. "You're not a monster."

Her eyelashes fluttered, and her voice was a murmur. "Compared to the me that was in your head."

I lay next to her on my side. "You're so beautiful, it's crazy."

She let her head fall on the pillow and faced me, her big blue eyes holding me when I asked, "Are you okay? We don't have to do this."

"I do, it's just," she sighed and her face reddened. "I've only been with one person, and it's been a long time ... what if I'm bad at it?"

I couldn't help but smile. "You don't need to worry about that. I'm the one that has a lot to live up to if I'm the second guy you're with." And for a horrific second, I realized how true that was. *But if I'm bad, she'll erase my memory and I won't even know, right?*

She smirked. "I promise if you suck, I'll wipe your memory."

My heart stopped. "I thought you kept people on mute."

"It's hard when we're both on the same wavelength." She ran her index finger along my jaw and for a while we just looked at each other. "I like you."

"I like you, too."

"It kind of scares me," her blue eyes were my world, "how much I want you."

I felt it too, an equal amount of heaviness and weightlessness when I was in her presence, and somehow that had bubbled over into an overwhelming desire for her. I didn't want to know what it would feel like to not be with her, now that I'd experienced life with her. "I'm never going to hurt you."

"I know," she smiled. "Remember I can read your mind?" She pressed her lips to mine and pulled me on top of her. I rested an elbow on the right side of her head, my left hand still searching the unexplored territory of Talitha.

She looked up at me. "Go slow, okay?"

I nodded, and she parted her legs and directed me inside. As I eased into her, every cell in my body celebrated.

I breathed her name, "Talitha."

"Carl," she moaned back.

I found a rhythm, sinking into her, a fire that started burning inside of me threatening to become a natural disaster. The need for more of her was beyond intoxicating, to go harder and faster until I broke the damn bed. Better than any drug, or drink, was being with Talitha, but what overrode my overpowering need to fuck her, was the desire to please her.

I brought my hand down to her hips, and tilted them up, but kept at the slow rhythm as I reached even deeper into her.

She moaned as she pressed herself closer to me. "Keep doing that."

It was as if her center were a magnet, and I was made of steel. When I moved inside of her, every synapse of my brain went off. She kept one of her hands on the small of my back, pressing into me with the same rhythm as the Logic's *Hit My Line* one of the neighbors was playing. Her legs were wrapped around me, her lips on mine, not even parting to breathe because we even did that together. My hand moved down to her butt, which was easily the best in Baltimore, gripping onto the thick muscle, tilting her hips slighting to the left.

"Yes." She dug her nails into my back.

I kept my hand in place and thrust into her deeper, and harder, and each time she said yes with more urgency than the last. It got to the point where the neighbor turned up the music to drown us out, or maybe everything was just intensified the closer I brought her to the peak.

Her body started to tremor. "Carl, I'm going to..." But I didn't hear the end of the sentence, because I was transported to the Ocean, the water wrapping around me instead of Talitha.

The sun was on the horizon, tones of pink, orange, and yellow as I got atop a surfboard and paddled toward the setting sun. Seagulls were chirping in the air, salt hanging on the breeze. A wave at least forty feet high came barreling toward me, and I felt no fear as the wave crested on top of me. But instead of being crushed toward the bottom, I floated, surrounded by bubbles, which dissipated so that I saw Talitha's face. Her blue eyes matched the water. She pulled me toward her, off the surfboard, lips on mine as she kicked us back up to the surface.

When we reached the surface, we were back in my bed in Baltimore, but her skin tasted salty like the Ocean.

"How?"

"Happens sometimes." Her breath caressed me. "Like the opposite of the party."

"That's how I make you feel?"

She brushed my hair back so it stopped hitting her in the face. "Keep going," she murmured, and I returned to the pace we were at before I was surfing, and I felt myself nearing the wave again.

"*Tu te sens si bien*; you feel so good." I reverted to my first language.

She'd turned me into putty, so close that I couldn't help but fall into her. I buried my face in the pillow next to hers as I emptied everything I had into her. I managed to take in a few deep breaths before I thought, *when can we do that again?*

She giggled.

"What's so funny?" I looked down at her.

"You were thinking what I was thinking." She kissed me.

"That right?" I started to roll off of her, but she held onto me.

"Not yet, if that's okay?"

"Yeah." I pressed my lips against hers, her pale blonde eyelashes fluttering.

She stroked the side of my face. "I didn't think I'd be with anyone ever again."

"I'm glad that wasn't true." I brushed away her yellow hair which was stuck to her forehead with sweat.

"Me too." She wrapped her arms around my neck, her lips on mine, stoking the dying embers.

# Phoenix
10/12/2020 10:28 AM

Sometimes I wonder if Mamá would have still left me, Alejandro Ramos, her only son, and my twin sister, Estrella, with Widmore all those years ago if she knew what would happen. If letting some ancient white man change my name to Phoenix and my sister to Frozenstar like we were action heroes was the best idea. By changing our names, like all my other Enhanced friends, Widmore took the place of both my dead father and my tired mother. It all happened in a few short hours; my dreams of working in the auto shop with my father, having a family of my own, and living peacefully in a small town on the West coast of Mexico had been shattered—all because I could conjure fire.

That day, Papa was robbed on his way to the bank and killed by the thieves. When I heard the news, I was so upset, and unaware that I had superpowers, I accidentally set fire to my second-grade classroom. Thankfully no one died, but everyone was treated for smoke inhalation. That's when the paramedics panicked when they realized I had a temperature twenty degrees above normal, and my twin sister had a temperature twenty degrees below normal and a slow heart rate. Before they had time to rush us to the hospital, Widmore was at my mother's side, with his pasty-white wrinkled skin, but his Spanish was perfectly accented. True, my mother was grieving, but I still wondered if he glamoured her to get her to let us go before we could even say our final goodbyes to our father.

Now we both had new names, learned a new language, and had been a prisoner of either Widmore or The Lab. One held us at The Manor, in which he forbade electronics, reading outside materials, and choosing our own clothes. The other took classmates one by one, trying to see how far they could be pushed until there was no coming back. For years, my sister and I were imprisoned and tested on by Jonas—the traitor to our kind. After they murdered Reed, and Talitha made all those soldiers kill themselves, I set The Lab aflame. I let the fire reach into the sky, turning any human left inside into bits of carbon. By then there were only four of us left, and we did what we'd been trained to do: return to The Manor. Only that was gone too, but Widmore was there, and he took us to a replica of The Manor north of Baltimore, which was alike in every way, including its name. But even though he'd cut the rooms in half, it was always quiet compared to when I was a teenager. So very quiet.

I don't want to sound ungrateful for what Professor Widmore has done for me and my sister, after all The Manor has an enchanted staff that cook and clean for all the Enhanced inhabitants. There are twenty rooms, not including the living room, which has a record player with thousands of music options, six libraries, each housing texts in another language, an indoor pool, tennis court, and movie theater. Since Reed died, he loosened up on some rules, but we couldn't leave. Not if we didn't want to chance getting caught by The Lab again. I'd been a prisoner longer than I'd ever been free, and my only crime was that I'd been injected with the serum when I was still inside my mother's belly.

Long ago, Frozenstar and I agreed that we would never put someone else above the other. Never love anyone that isn't blood. *What was the point of falling in love if you were only going to have to watch them die?* I wasn't sure if she'd technically broken the pact because she *was* in love with Fidget, but she wouldn't admit it to herself, so I didn't feel I had the right to be betrayed. *If anything, Fidget should be pissed at her.*

Only proving how much love sucked, and how right the pact with my sister was, Talitha, the only woman I've ever loved, never saw me as more than a friend. Maybe it was for the best, since I would have broken every promise to Frozenstar for one night with Talitha.

It was so easy to fall into Talitha's blue eyes; they haunted me. Her hair, the color of the sun, had brushed against me a few times, and it had felt softer than silk. She could always be found on the outside of the crowd, claiming that being trapped inside with all the colors and chatter in people's minds was too much. But I knew it was because she was more introverted, spending hours in the meadow behind the school watching the birds in the trees, often climbing up to them. But now, Reed was gone, and I didn't know where Talitha was, much less if she was alive. I assumed she was in Baltimore, but she'd never be able to find the rebuilt Manor unless Widmore brought her here.

I started my day like every other; after waking with the sun and stretching, I ran around the ten acres of property that surrounded The Manor with Shakira playing on my earbuds. Because even if my life was a living hell, I'm still a man, and to hear a woman's voice that wasn't my sister's or Fidget's was just about the only good thing I had left. *Mierda, the only other guy here is a mute, but it's not like Siren would want to talk about cars anyway.*

After, I'd work on the weights on even days like today, or some boxing on odd days. Then I'd shower, shave my face and head, then take a look in the mirror, because even if it was only for myself, I wanted to look good. An addiction to exercise proved more than destressing as I flexed my muscles, *too bad it was the ultimate rarity that anyone else saw them.* I put on an undershirt, oversized t-shirt and extra-wide-leg jeans, which were all the same exact shade of gray. I lay my silver chain with a crucifix around my neck, kissing Jesus's feet before I let it fall between my t-shirts. I polished my crisp white sneakers before slipping them on, snapped on my watch over the barcode on my wrist and the number 451. For breakfast, I'd eat an egg white omelet, chorizo, and a ton of hot sauce, with a glass of fresh-squeezed orange juice, all prepared by the humans Widmore glamoured. Then I'd go to the living room and place my daily call. I'd always been a creature of habit, finding solace that every morning had been the same for the past two years, three months, and eighteen days. But I'd give my own life to have Talitha back.

I didn't wait for Widmore to speak before I asked. "You still haven't found her?"

Widmore sighed on the other end in his office at Johns Hopkins. "If I had, then she would already be at The Manor."

My breath caught in my throat. "You still think she's alive?"

"She's very powerful, Phoenix."

"But it's been so long, and no one has seen her." I started to pace between the antique, dark wood coffee table and burgundy leather couch. "If somebody found her, they'd turn her in to the police at least."

"You know as well as I that she can erase herself from one of our memories. It would be easy to extract herself from a Non-Enhanced memory."

"Not if they had a connection, remember she went into that coma when she erased her mom's memory." That had been the most stressful five days of my life. Well, up until now.

"I sincerely doubt that Talitha has made such a connection. It's only a matter of time before she shows up."

My pacing quickened. "But what if she's been kidnapped, or drugged, and someone has her, and they're torturing her?"

"If The Lab had her then they wouldn't still be watching me so closely that I can't come and see you every day, and I find it improbable that a Non-Enhanced would be able to capture her."

I stopped pacing. "But what if they did?"

"Phoenix, without Reed you are in charge of the group, and they need you to be strong. I know that it has been difficult for you, maybe more than anyone else because I depend on you so much, but right now I need you to keep your head at The Manor, and not on Talitha."

"That's like asking me not to breathe," I muttered into the receiver.

"I know how you feel about Talitha and trust me, I'm doing everything I can to find her," his voice turned into a whisper, "there is no line I won't cross to get her back to The Manor."

I held the phone in my hand, it seemed to be the only thing that was anchoring me to Earth. "I really want to trust you."

"And you should, after all this time Alejandro," my heart stopped when he said my name, my *real* name, "understand that I see you as a son. I would never betray you or any of the others. Your mother left you and your sister in my care, and I did not take it lightly. While I understand it's been quite difficult the past few years, I assure you that I will find Talitha and bring her home."

So much went through my mind, but what kept echoing in the background, no matter how much I tried to drown it out, was my fear that I'd forget her face. But, the truly terrifying truth was that I might be obsessively in love with Talitha, even though she'd never even held my hand, because my life had been such shit that a pretty girl smiling at me was enough to get unlimited devotion. Although the why didn't matter — Talitha had my heart, soul, and mind.

"Are you still there?"

"Yeah," I nodded, even though he couldn't see me, and clutched onto the phone as hard as I wished I could hold her. "Just promise you'll get her back."

"I promise."

# TALITHA
10/12/2020 3:45 PM

If I was smart, I would have done it while he was asleep.

We'd spent nearly twenty-four hours naked. Well, I did put on one of his shirts, and he put on a pair of boxers when we were beyond starving and he made mac and cheese. With Carl, there had been many firsts, including having sex in a kitchen.

*But I'd have to be insane to not wipe his memory, right?*

I needed to do it before he woke up and we spent another day screwing. But if I never again spoke to someone who remembered me, *then what was the point of not just turning myself over to Jonas?*

Granted most of our conversations revolved around what part of my body I wanted him to touch, but he also told me that he'd drunkenly admitted to Jenny that he didn't love her enough to propose. She responded by telling him that she'd been sleeping with her thesis partner for a year, so it didn't matter anyway. He also told me how listening to opera now tortured him, but didn't lessen his overall love of music that his tenor father gave him. He listened to all my favorite Justin Bieber songs, and Carl taught me all about the glorious band M83. Along with a brief history of indie music in general, with a highlight of Future Islands, Beach House, and Wye Oak—what he called the 'Baltimore Trinity'.

We watched *The Matrix* and *Blade Runner,* which he told me were 'guy movies' until I made him rewind and start them over again. Turned out that he read King's *Carrie* too, although he preferred *The Stand* and he promised not to tell me what happened to Katniss Everdeen before I read *Catching Fire* for myself. He even taught me about Daredevil and Electra, but he never asked me about being Enhanced like I was a comic book character.

That's why I didn't mind telling Carl about The Manor, the school Widmore built that was stricter than a military compound. Or about Jonas, the originator, the founder of Wakefield Laboratories, an Enhanced being I'd never met, who was more powerful than Widmore. Jonas was the reason there were so few of us left. I described my Enhanced friends, like Fidget the ginger-haired German with a badass punch and the ability to walk through a wall as if she were a ghost, the Mexican fire-and-ice twins, Phoenix and Frozenstar, who were both beyond narcissistic, and how each had a face that only boosted their egos, and Baltimore-born chess nerd Siren, who was forced into being a mute because his voice was hypnotic.

But it was when Carl showed me his sketches that the real trouble started, because that's when I fell for him. He'd been given the gift to make pencil on paper look crisper than the most advanced camera. Trees, the Inner Harbor, the Paris skyline, his mother smoking a cigarette, and me, framed by the Seine where we had our first kiss. It was as detailed as the memory that shone like a Las Vegas sign in my head. The pull to him was stronger than any addiction, but it was so much more than sex. Although I'd thoroughly enjoyed the vortex of passion he'd drawn me into, it was everything else we did in between. I'd only trusted him because he was Blue, and his majestic Azure proved a beacon to stick to, as I found myself so easily surrounded by his thoughts. Carl was a good person, possibly the best I'd come across, and it was at his very core.

I had planned on leaving that afternoon, replacing our time together in his memory with a visit to a distant cousin, or a weird decision to leave Ottobar and go build a house for Habitat for Humanity over the weekend.

But I wanted him to touch me again.

Not wanted.

*Needed.*

I looked over at Carl, his eyes still closed, shifting quickly side to side as he dreamed. With the tip of my finger, I brushed the brown curl falling in his face, and traced his jaw. His stubble rubbed against me like sandpaper. The hurt felt so good, and I couldn't help but kiss his unshaved face. I wanted to kiss every part of him, and have him kiss all of me. I thought better of moving down his body, and when I returned my head to the pillow, his light gray-green eyes were open and focused on me.

He threw me a grin, showing off his lone dimple. "Why'd you stop?"

"You were asleep."

"Great way to wake up." He mimicked me, moving his lips down my neck. "I'm glad you didn't leave."

"I probably should have."

He shifted his body so he lay on his right side. "Then why didn't you?"

I answered him with a kiss, pushing him down on the bed, and straddled him. The tattooed side of auto parts made him look half machine with the bolts and gears matching his joints, bars matching bones. That ink was an embarrassing-to-admit turn on. And I swear his six-pack had become more defined from all the sex we'd had. His muscles tensed as I rested my palm on his chest, his heartbeat quickening under the inked version. His mind started replaying last night in the background, as his hands made their way to my breasts, then down, matching my hips with his. I took him inside, and a shudder ran through me.

He gripped onto my sides as I rocked my hips back and forth. "Talitha." Hearing my name come out of his mouth was like the sprinkles atop the ice cream sundae of sex. He crushed his eyes shut and gripped onto me tighter. While I would have preferred that it lasted hours, rocking my hips taking him inside of me, the Sparkling of his Blue Aura began to turn Blinding White, so I knew I only had minutes left. I slowed down until I found my spot, once I did it only took a few strokes to meet up with him.

"Carl," I moaned once I neared the edge, completely in sync, about to jump off together.

When he finished inside me, he filled me with his Sparkling Blue, a million Azure butterflies swarming in my stomach. All his hopes, dreams, and the joy he felt when he was ten and hit that home run at the final game-winning championship flipped through his mind and lit up the darkest parts of me. The Swirling Gray Smoke that surrounded me lightened and turned Puffy and White like the clouds in the sky.

He sat up and wrapped his arms around me, his lips on mine before they traveled to my ear. "I want to keep you in this bed all day."

"Why do you think I didn't erase your memory?"

He threw me back onto the bed as we laughed, and kissed, tangled in his mismatched flannel sheets. "I didn't know anything felt this good," he murmured. The sun filtered into the bedroom, casting a glow on his face, and that, along with his Sky-Blue Aura, was enough magic for me.

"Me either." I pulled him on top of me, in the hopes that with just the right kiss he'd be ready again soon. Because I wanted him to go slow, make it last until the sunset, dragging it out until I couldn't take it anymore, and projected the both of us past the Milky Way. I wanted my entire being to ache tomorrow, to sweat out every toxin that could still reside inside of me, to give him all of me again and again.

My body pressed against his. I breathed in time with him, our beings existing only for the other. All consumed in foreplay, we had both forgotten about Widmore, The Lab, and most certainly everyone else in Baltimore. He was ready, and I was starting to boil over when there was a pounding at the door.

"Carl!" If I hadn't been vibrating on another plane, I would have felt Jenny's Jade Green Aura from two blocks away. "I know you're there because your car's here!"

I pushed Carl off of me and practically threw myself on the floor, grabbing for my clothes, not worrying to put all of them on, just to hide the evidence of my existence. I stumbled into the bathroom and he threw my sneakers in after me before I shut the door as quietly as I could.

He'd thrown on a pair of boxers and had his jeans zipped up when he walked to the door, his delicious abs on full display. But Carl's sex-god physique was blocked out by the Jade Green Aura pushing in through the openings in the side of the door before he opened it.

"Why haven't you been answering your phone?"

"I blocked you," Carl answered.

She pushed past him, the Jade Green Pulsating. I didn't have to take her off mute to know that she was looking for me once she found Carl half-naked, hair disheveled, with fresh scratch marks on his chest, and a hickey on his neck. I dressed as quickly as possible, which is when I realized that didn't have my bra. I put on Carl's t-shirt atop my long-sleeve one which covered the scars on my arms, snapped on my leather cuff over my barcode tattoo, and hoped that Jenny didn't find it.

"Where is she?" Jade Green Flickered, starting to turn Flaming Orange as she moved closer to the bathroom.

"Who?" All his Glitter was gone, and Deep Sea began to take over the center of his Aura.

"That girl you brought to the party. Everyone said she ran out right before Clint punched Joe for what he did to Tanya. Annie, right?" Her color stopped Flickering and her voice softened. "You didn't even hear, did you? Joe drugged like a bunch of girls and raped them, been doing it for years. Tom and I had already left, but I thought you were still there with that Annie girl?" Jenny didn't pause before she started rapid-fire gossip. "Gabby told me all about it. Tanya started freaking out when she saw Joe. Guess she remembered somehow and told Clint who beat the fuck out of Joe. The cops came and broke up the party, and no one has seen Danny or Joe since."

Carl's Blue Aura Darkened. "What do you mean no one's heard from Danny?"

"Just like I said, Gabby was going to take him home, but when the cops showed up, she ran off. And neither of you has answered your phone since. Thought maybe he was here," Jenny stopped talking as I finished lacing up my Chuck's. Her Jade Green Aura turned Pumpkin Orange, with Flickers of Red on the edges. "Is this that weird girl's bra?"

"What do you care?" His Blue turned Dark, like the center of a storm. "You cheated on me for a year." He scoffed. "Not that it matters since we were never in love. You're only here because you're miserable."

The Pumpkin deepened to a Burnt Umber and she hissed, "Who says I'm miserable?"

"It's obvious, you won't leave me alone, and now you're freaking out because you *think* I hooked up with someone."

"Did you?"

"It's none of your business, Jenny."

She threw my bra at him and screeched, "Well I know it's hers because she's as flat as a ten-year-old."

I sighed and opened the door realizing that I could no longer fight the inevitable. Both sets of eyes zeroed in on me, but I only looked at the Flickering Red Flame surrounding Jenny. "Just say what you're going to say."

"Excuse me?" She put her hand on her hip. "Were you, like, listening to us just now?"

"This isn't exactly the fortress of solitude, Jenny."

"Bitch, don't say my name."

Carl faced Jenny. "Don't call her that."

I waved my hand. "It's alright, I want her to get out all her negative energy before I erase her memory." Then I locked eyes with Jenny, who'd turned Bonfire. "Because I don't need to remember her either."

"Wait, you don't have to—" Carl began.

"This is what I'm talking about. I don't want people to know that I exist, and if you're not cool with that, I'll just wipe your memory after I'm done with her."

"Excuse me," Jenny's face pointed like a fish, "what are you doing here again?"

She started spewing color like Red Lava, sending her energy out, leaving a husk behind, but just to make sure she was as blank as possible I smirked at her. "I just got done literally blowing Carl's mind before you interrupted us, and I know for a fact that he won't ever think about what it was like to be with you anymore."

"What?" Her tone was like nails on a chalkboard.

"Carl wouldn't fuck you again if you were the last girl on Earth."

"Whore!" Jenny swung back her hand at the exact moment her Crimson Aura had turned Night Sky Black, and I stopped her hand with my own, giving me a direct line to her grey matter. I started by locating the original film in the movie of her life that played in her head. Next, I took out a razor and sliced out the cells that included me. If she hit rewind there'd be a few skips, but not enough to send off alarm bells. I was the only living creature doomed to remember every single moment of their life.

Before Carl could finish saying my name in the sentence, "Wait, Talitha, don't," I reset Jenny.

She returned to the Sunshine Yellow Aura that was at her core now that she'd been released of the jealousy she felt for me. She sat down on the edge of Carl's bed, which turned my Swirling Gray Smoke the slightest hint of Jade Green. I grabbed my bra from off the floor and shoved it in the pocket of my hoodie before I zipped up my jacket. A Flicker of Red rushed through me when I realized Jenny was right, I didn't need a bra because I had mosquito bites for breasts.

Carl pressed on his temples. "What did you just do?"

"She'll be thirsty when she wakes up, so get a glass of water for her." I looked up at Carl who'd returned to his Azure hue. "Just ask her what happened with Tanya, that's why she came over to talk to you, she was just distracted by me."

I pulled up my hood and started toward the door, Carl reached out and took my hand. "Where are you going?"

I shook free of him. "You gotta deal with whatever is going on between you two. If you want to be with her, it's none of my business. I'll wait at the bar around the corner, Rick's place, for an hour in case you still want to help me."

"What if I don't come?"

I shrugged, avoiding his face. "Stay away from me, and I'll stay away from you."

"Don't you want to erase my memory?"

I opened up the door, cold air smothering me. "Not if you keep your distance. Then we'll always have Paris." I walked down the steps to the sidewalk, out into the city, once again all alone.

# Talitha
## 10/12/2020 5:55 PM

Reed first brought me to the forty-year-old establishment simply called *Rick's* on my eighteenth birthday. It was a disgusting dive bar that only locals knew about. The brick-front building was a mile from the boundary of Carl's neighborhood, east of my beacon in Baltimore: Johns Hopkins. *Rick's* was a place you went to be left alone. Every surface was sticky, the dartboards were hung by pure imagination, and the jukebox had the most random selections that changed monthly. There was a booth full of Hazy Purple college kids taking a break from their study session, hoping the beer would level out the stimulants, a Strawberry Aura at the far end of the bar with divorce papers in front of her, clicking on her phone, and a group of old-timers in Shades of Sherbet near the front, playing cards with the owner. None of them would remember me once they walked outside. *Not that I'd have to erase much anyway*, I thought as I took another swig of my whiskey.

I sat on the stool that had the best view of the front door, and a mirror across from me behind the bottles of bottom-shelf liquor to check my surroundings. I always sat far from the seats in the middle booth that Reed and I had occupied all those years ago. I quietly hoped that he'd stopped searching for me on the other side. That he hadn't been driven mad trying to find me in the never-ending darkness that enveloped you once you died. I'd been there twice, and it had felt like a million lifetimes in one, trapped in the eternal darkness.

Now I only held on because if I died a third time, I knew I'd never come back, and there was no guarantee that I'd be able to find him. No promise that each of us hadn't been damned to a separate existence in abject horror of the nothingness. At least on this side, I could remember his laugh. Reed, with the power to heal, was too pure for this world, leaving me, a telepath that couldn't move things with her mind unless she was terrified, all alone. *So it shouldn't be shocking that there is no God, and that there's nothing but pain and emptiness when you die,* I contemplated as I drank.

My radar beeped and a Blue Flicker exited a rowhouse and hugged a Sunshine Yellow before one went left toward the Harbor, and one turned right toward me. I rubbed my face with my hands and refocused on the napkin in front of me. The Blue Sparked as it ebbed ever closer. I double-clicked the mute button so I could go through the bullshit plan I'd formulated over the past forty minutes.

"Hey, Rick." I nodded at the Lime Green bartender with the pudgy belly, gray overgrown curly hair, and a black t-shirt that bore an irregular amount of grease stains considering he didn't serve fried food at his bar.

"Yeah," he nodded back.

"You got a pen I can borrow?"

"Of course." He smiled and pulled at the pen wedged behind his ear and his Oriole's cap. "Never know when you need to write something down."

I let my eyes skirt over him, noticing how many more wrinkles he had on his hands, even a few spots that hadn't been there in months prior. Last winter he had a cough and I wanted to take him to the doctor, but that proved difficult when I was a stranger to him, not someone he'd known for half a decade.

His eyes caught mine, and they narrowed. "Do I know you from somewhere?"

"Just got one of those faces."

He smiled. "Well a girl as pretty as you," he began.

"You'd never be lucky enough to know," I finished.

He chuckled, but I could see his Aura start to turn Marigold Yellow at the edges while the center remained Lime Green. "How'd you know I was gonna say that?"

I leaned in and whispered, "Would you believe me if I told you I can read minds?"

He threw his head back and laughed. "Better watch what you say I might have to cut you off."

The bar door swung open and Carl's Bright Blue Swirled around him like marble as he walked toward me. It wasn't until then that I realized I'd been holding my breath, and when I did breathe, the air tasted sweet in the stale bar. I nodded toward Carl while keeping eye contact with Rick. "My designated driver is here, so can I have a double?"

Rick looked over at the Swirling Blue. "She with you, Carl?"

He pulled up the stool next to me and I almost smiled when I read 'I see dumb people' on his t-shirt. "Yeah, and I'll take one too."

"That good, huh?" I asked as I looked back down at the napkin, pen in hand dancing over the surface. I didn't want to look directly at him since I was pretty sure that my face was flush, because my heart rate had sped up now that he was next to me.

"It's just like you said." His eyes darted around, and he whispered, "It didn't hurt her at all, and she doesn't remember you. She was back to herself."

"I told you she'd be okay."

"And it's beyond over now just so you know."

I didn't say anything, just continued sketching on the napkin.

He put his hand on my knee. "After this drink you wanna go back to my place?"

"I'd really love to and if you want, we can spend the whole day together, and tomorrow morning we'll go our separate ways."

His dimple winked at me. "Why do I feel like you want to do something else?"

At first, I was embarrassed because I was blushing, until I heard, *she's so beautiful* over the airwaves that had gotten through mute somehow. I shook my head in an attempt to get his thoughts out and focus. "There's a reason Rick doesn't remember me, and I'm going have to erase his mind again today."

Carl looked over his shoulder at Rick. "Why?"

"I need to get to a man that works *here* because he can help me control my powers." I pointed at the rudimentary map I'd drawn on the napkin. "And you're going to help me do that."

"How?" He raised an eyebrow at me. "I'm not like you."

"And that's exactly why this will work. You're not on their radar, I checked, but I can use you as a walkie-talkie. We'll practice it tonight, with our clothes *on*," I stressed which made his Aura flicker, "and tomorrow morning you'll be safe to just walk up to him and I'll tell you exactly what to say. Once you tell him the code phrase, he'll give you an address and I'll be able to go there and check it out while you still have all those Flashing Reds watching him."

I bit my bottom lip for a second before I asked. "So will you help me get to Widmore?"

"Of course." He leaned over, looked at the drawing and tentatively asked, "Maybe you should just describe how it looks like and I'll draw it?"

# WIDMORE
10/13/2020 12:27 PM

The brisk autumns in Baltimore had a way of making me realize just how old I was as I hobbled from my office in Johns Hopkins to my VW Beetle in the staff parking lot.

The faculty has stressed for years that I acquire something modern, more comfortable in my old age. They didn't realize just how right they were, nor how many faces and names I'd used to teach at the acclaimed University since its inception. This University had brought Cordelia into my life. She'd been given the serum as a child, so I had seen her name amongst the hundreds of other children's names that had been injected across Europe, but we didn't speak until she came to Baltimore to earn her master's degree and I happened to be her advisor. While our relationship wouldn't be considered the most ethical even in the 1990s, it was the first time I'd been in love since my wife had died in the fifteenth century. And our courtship was far more ethical than that of Jonas and Lola—which in no way could be called a love story. While Cordelia and I were more epic than any of Shakespeare's characters, I kept her shut out of my mind until Jonas and I could find the formula for immortality. And the key to all of it was Talitha.

Although I couldn't 'see' the future, history does have a sick way of repeating itself, and humans were beyond predictable. Living eternally was a pleasure, a lonely venture, but any joy came to a halt when Talitha had escaped from The Lab. She'd ruined most everything I'd worked for by becoming too powerful for us to control, and dangerous as we were unaware of her allegiance. Now, almost every day was the same. Work, home, microwave meal, a glass of wine, sleep, repeat. The only deviation was to visit The Manor weekly to quell Phoenix who was slowly going mad over losing the unrequited love of his life.

Therefore October 13, 2020, should have been like any other, only today someone stopped me on my journey through the Homewood Campus, which was picturesque. Leaves in the trees matched in tone the red brick buildings that lined the green quad, including what students called 'The Beach': a spot of grass in front of the old clock tower. And on an afternoon like today, it was filled with students; although they were wearing sweaters and scarves, they still sat atop a blanket and quietly studied. Some speculated on the true intentions of the greatest artists of the Baroque era, and a group discussing the finer art of 'flow'.

"Mr. Widmore?" The young man that stopped me as I traversed around The Beach looked sorely out of place. His attire of leather, shredded jeans, and scuffed boots was more conducive to a biker bar. And no self-respecting young man would walk around unshaven as such.

"I'm more accustomed to being called *Professor* Widmore." I paused in the middle of the sidewalk that curved around The Beach. Students were a flurry around us, although too self-involved to notice the conversation. Foliage in heartwarming hues of tangerine and red apple proved more interesting than a tenured professor.

"Ugh, yeah, sorry." He scratched his head which had brown curls on the top, trimmed expertly on the sides, unlike his face. His posture and grooming habits reminded me of our primitive relatives.

"Is there something I could help you with, young man?"

His eyes scanned from left to right then zeroed in on me. "What can't answer but will reply when you talk to it?"

Taken aback I stuttered, "Where did you hear that?"

He asked again with the same forcefulness, "What can't answer but will reply when you talk to it?"

"An echo." I shifted my briefcase in my grip, my knuckles sore, as I tried to pry into the young boy's mind and found I could not. The process should have been easier than untwisting a bread tie, but even as I concentrated, I couldn't get past what appeared to be a layer of impenetrable metal. Fear began to creep in, but I banished it as best I could while grappling with a logical explanation. Carl flinched as I brought out a drill to open his mind up to no avail. Instinct told me it was Talitha, but she'd never been able to block out someone else's mind from my own. *Could she now*, I wondered, as Carl rubbed his temples with his index fingers for a moment.

His eyes shifted up and to the left as he murmured to himself, "Because the echo just says what you say, right?" Then his gray-green eyes met with mine. The tone seemed familiar, but I couldn't place it. "I'm Carl." He reached out his hand to shake mine. He had a tattoo of gears on his wrist peeking out from under his leather jacket. In my youth, we would have been matched for height but after a few centuries, one starts to find that gravity is quite powerful. "I have a friend that would like to meet with you."

I did not accept his hand, so it eventually fell to his side when I asked, "And why didn't she come and introduce herself?"

Carl shrugged and leaned in at the same time. "All the Auras, guess it's like system overload, and she says someone is watching your house at all times."

"Describe her to me."

The smile that took over Carl's face was enigmatic. "Blue eyes, short blonde hair, petite, or whatever." Then he blushed. "Really pretty."

"Talitha?" The name left my lips and floated on the air.

Carl nodded. "Where can she meet you?"

I instantly felt sheer terror that I would have to put my full trust in this young man that didn't look like he knew how to open a bank account and had a brain as unreadable as a tween novel. "I need more proof that she sent you."

Carl's eyes flickered up and to the right as if he were remembering something, proving my hypothesis that he wasn't special, Talitha was cloaking him. Carl muttered, "I can't say that I don't speak Spanish." His eyes moved some more. "I know I don't have to talk out loud, but this is weird having you walk around in my head." He closed his eyes and shook his head. "Okay, okay." When he opened them again they were as sharp as diamonds. "You used to have a friend in common, a healer. Years ago you told both of them that if they got into trouble they were to come to you and ask you that question, but if you still didn't believe me, I'm supposed to recite a line of a poem to you but it's in Spanish and I—" I didn't let the young man finish.

"*Las blancas estatuas que no tienen voz ni mirada.*" And my heart soared because I thought for so long that all had been lost, all my work gone because we hadn't let Reed rest.

The idiot, Carl, nodded at me and translated as if I didn't understand what I'd just said, "The white statues that have neither voice nor sight."

I brought the boy close to me, which was only slightly repulsive, being so close to what amounted to a roach, and whispered the address to a parking garage near the Harbor in his ear, knowing that Talitha was more aware than Carl would ever be. I couldn't help but smile as I began to scheme on my brisk walk to my car where I could think as loudly as possible until tomorrow night when I'd once again be in the same space as Talitha. First, I'd send the signal to Jonas for us to meet, then I'd have to steel myself against her once again. After all this time, there'd be no way to know how much more powerful she'd become, but I was determined to find out.

# Talitha
## 10/14/2020 12:07 am

"Thanks for meeting with Widmore." I lay in bed next to Carl. "The parking garage, you checked it out, and it's all okay?"

I smiled. "Yeah, no problem."

"And you really think you can trust that guy? He gave me a headache."

"He was just reading your mind."

His eyes widened. "Do you think he saw like everything we've done?"

I pressed my lips to his, Sparkling Blue intermingling with my Swirling Gray Smoke, until it looked like we were in a Glitter storm, which broke apart when I sat up. "I doubt he looked for that."

"Can you check? Maybe he moved something around and that's why I have a migraine?"

I rose an eyebrow at him as I put back on my t-shirt. "The sex didn't help?"

"Yeah," he sat up and put on his boxers, "but maybe you should still check."

I sat next to him, on the edge of the bed, my feet barely touching the floor. "You sure?"

"I want you to know everything that can keep you safe."

I brought my hand to the side of his face and dipped back into the bright white corridor in my head. His door was just to the left of the driftwood one that leads to my fog. Carl's was made of solid wood, but it was hard to tell what kind because it was completely covered with art. Whether it was a sticker from a band with their album cover, a postcard-sized print of Ansel Adams' landscape photography, a blueprint of the Eiffel Tower, or sketches of his own, together they created a mural that had no beginning or end.

The knob was in the shape of a boom box from the 1980s, and when I turned it, Future Islands *'For Sure'* started up. The playlist to his biopic was strictly indie, all with a nod to his favorite era. I went to the reel, hit pause, rewound, going not quite far enough so I could replay when he spent an amazing half-hour with his head between my thighs. After I checked out the parking structure near the Inner Harbor where Widmore and I were to meet before the last call, Carl practically ripped off my clothes before he gently made love to me for hours.

*C'mon Talitha, you can relive that moment soon enough.*

I flipped the filmstrip back, tracking Carl to when he parked his car and headed out to the Homestead campus of the University. Carl must have been nervous because he didn't make eye contact with Widmore as often as I would have liked so I could maybe crack into his head via Carl's memory.

He told me that his headache was beyond intense, but there were no fingerprints left on the film reel—mine were the first. Nor had anyone sat in the theater below the projector, as the seats were futons that creaked if they were touched. But there wasn't a sound in Carl's memory but the filmstrip winding through the reel with his soundtrack on pause.

No one had been here but me, and in truth that was more horrifying than if Widmore had burned the place down. I was the only one who could alter a memory, but Widmore was more powerful than me, and he would have at least viewed the footage on Carl's reel. Yet there was not a scratch, dent, or mark on a single frame.

I rolled the movie back to 12:07 AM on October 14, 2020 , and hit play. *'For Sure'* started back up inside his head right before I took my hand from the side of Carl's face. "He didn't read your mind." I picked my jeans off the floor and pulled them on.

"But he's like you, right?" Carl put on his t-shirt.

I nodded as I buttoned up my jeans.

"Is there any reason why he wouldn't?"

I shook my head.

"Then why?"

"Maybe he couldn't." My eyes scanned Carl up and down, and the hair on the back of my neck pricked up. *Maybe he's not all he appears to be*, but the thought rushed out of my head just as quickly as it entered.

"How?"

I shrugged. "My powers have been crazy since we met, and I want to protect you so maybe I'm doing it unintentionally."

"Another sign."

"Yeah?"

Fully clothed he murmured into my ear. "I think you got into my head."

I laughed and looked up at him. "Yeah, but I'm not anymore."

"You know you are," he took my face in his hands, "you have to know."

"Carl," I started but he interrupted.

"Threaten to erase my memory all you want for my protection or whatever, but until then..." He kissed me, and turned lighter and brighter the longer we made out. He'd nearly turned Pure White when I knew that was no return and in a few more minutes neither of us would be able to stop. Even though we had just put on our clothes back on.

"Take me to Rick's first." I laced my fingers with his as we left his bedroom.

"Then come home and get naked?"

I laughed as I pulled open the door. "You sound pretty confident."

He locked it. "Just hopeful."

"I can't believe that's your favorite movie." He shook his head from the stool next to mine.

"Like you wouldn't love to fly on a huge dog through the sky and save a princess?"

He shrugged. "I mean yeah when I was a kid. I like *The Neverending Story*, but I would have thought you'd prefer *Eternal Sunshine of the Spotless Mind*."

"Never heard of it." I held up my glass to Rick, the bartender, who brought me another.

"This guy finds out his ex erased her memory of him, and he tries to do the same thing," his eyes held me, "only he realizes too late that he wants to remember, even the bad parts."

I looked down at the dark wood of the bar. "Sounds shitty."

"Talitha, you're the first person I've had a connection with that I can't explain. You make me feel things that I haven't since my parents died. And you're just going to make it like it never happened."

I bit my bottom lip as the truth bubbled to the surface. "I'm not sure how easy it will be anymore."

"Why?"

"We've shared too much, I shouldn't have taken you in two of my memories, and now I've been in a few of yours." I shook my head. "I should have done it before the party, but I can't do it now."

"Because you're in love with me?"

I nearly choked on my drink. "Don't even say it."

"But that's what it is, you told me when we met that it was too hard if there was a real connection."

I gripped the glass. "If I was able to make my mother forget about me I think I can take care of a guy that's got a crush."

He threw me a smirk. "You don't want to do it, that's it, right?"

I bit my bottom lip before I murmured, "Shut up."

"You act all tough," he nudged me with his knee, "but you got it for me."

"We've known each other five days, not enough of a foundation for a romance of the ages."

His dimple deepened in his right cheek. "I think the lady protests too much." He laughed. "Or however it goes. I might not be the smartest guy, but I know you feel the same way."

I rolled my eyes. "I could go to a childhood memory of anyone in this bar, doesn't mean we're soul mates."

"What about what you showed me?"

I tossed my head back to let the shot of whiskey coat my throat. "You mean when I took you to meet my dead boyfriend and then proceeded to cry about it on your couch?"

His dark eyelashes fluttered over his gray-green eyes, his Aura moved like the waves of an Ocean. "The one after that. After the party, can't tell me you've taken anyone else there."

Carl was right, I'd never even taken Reed to August 13, 2008, although I told him what my father had done because I didn't want to be called a liar claiming to be a virgin who didn't bleed their first time. But tonight, I didn't want to think of Reed, much less my father. "So?"

"So maybe we did it backward and shared all of our baggage first." Carl shrugged. "And maybe I don't completely understand what you're going through, but that doesn't mean that what I'm feeling isn't real."

I didn't want to get too heavy tonight seeing as soon I'd be in the presence of a telepath that would attempt to dismantle the wall around my grey matter. So, I changed the subject. "Is that really your favorite movie?"

His gray-green eyes sparkled, and I took a deep breath as he agreed to join me back on the surface and not in the depths of emotion. "*Say Anything*, that's my favorite movie."

"Never heard of it."

"It came out when our parents were kids, it was the first movie I saw in English, so it was a pretty big deal. But it's about this guy, Lloyd, and he's a nice guy, you know the kind that doesn't get the girl. And he's totally fallen for Diane, and at first, she's into it, but then she dumps him and gives him a pen."

I ran my index finger along the rim of the glass. "And let me guess he makes some grand gesture, and they live happily ever after?"

"Well, he did stand outside her window, with a boom box, and plays the song they listened to the first time they first hooked up. But it doesn't work until her dad gets put in jail."

"Whoa, wait, her dad gets put in jail?"

A grin covered Carl's face. "Aha now you want to see it."

"So, what you're going to play *Hit My Line* outside my window so I don't erase your memory?"

He scoffed. "I know you better than that, I'd play your favorite song."

"And you know which one it is?" My cheeks hurt from smiling.

"I know that Justin Bieber has quite the catalog, but you've mentioned one, in particular, a few times." His eyes caressed me, from my leather jacket to my Chucks. "Still don't get how a girl who looks like you listens to Justin Bieber."

For a second, I kept the story to myself, guarding it against exposing my soul any further to Carl. But when I got caught in his eyes, I found the words came so easily. "Remember when I told you that Widmore got super pissed when he found Stephen King's *Carrie* in my room? Which was so stupid because it's not like I'm like her."

"Guess you didn't have Prom either."

"Nah." I shook my head. "But if there was, then Micha would have been the DJ. Micha, Fidget and I were inseparable." For a beat I recalled us giggling at lunch together, passing notes in class, making friendship bracelets like we were normal teenage girls. "Fidget bunked in another room, but Micha and I would spend hours talking past curfew. She's the one that had Justin's CD, and she could make electronics work just by touching them. We listened to that stupid CD like a million times. Widmore took it after The Lab kidnapped Micah, but I could still go back into my memory and hear it. And I'd pretend that he was singing to me whenever I was lonely or scared, which was nearly all the time." I let my eyes move over Carl, hoping it didn't sound as pathetic to him as it did to me. A girl so depressed she'd conjure the voice of a popstar for comfort. I literally shrugged the feeling off. "Plus, you know, I was fifteen and he's pretty hot."

"So, I got some competition?"

"He's married to a model, and I'm," I waved my hand over my body, "as flat as a ten-year-old," I murmured, remembering what Jenny had said to Carl when she found my bra in his bedroom.

"Boobs are overrated," he responded succinctly. "I'm more of an ass man." His eyes charted down my anatomy. "And I'd have to say you have the best one in Baltimore."

The muscles in my cheeks hurt from smiling. "That, right?"

Carl's hand reached up to the side of my face, tucked a lock of hair behind my ear. "Looking at you, it's like looking at the sun."

"What?"

"So beautiful it hurts."

I wanted to say something sarcastic or point out that I was covered in scars so deep that even Reed, a superpowered healer, couldn't make them fade. Instead, I let my skin burn under his touch, concentrated on the space between Carl's shoulder and neck, wanting to rest my head on it and breathe him in. With Carl, I'd made a million mistakes. Every moment I was in his presence was just putting him in peril. But I knew for a fact all he was thinking about was that if he had it his way, the date would never end. Just as I was trying to navigate my intense feelings for a Non-Enhanced when our future could only include pain, the song on the jukebox changed and I couldn't help but laugh.

"You do that?"

Carl nodded at Rick, who nodded back from the other end of the bar playing a game of hearts with the only other patron. "Told him to play it after your third drink, that way my chances of taking you home were pretty much on lock."

I smiled but refused to admit defeat.

"Wanna dance?" His eyes were wide, like a puppy in the window of a pet store. He pulled me to the center of the empty bar. He gave me a twirl. "So, I get it right?"

"Close enough." I smiled up at him.

Justin Bieber explained all the ways he'd be the best *Boyfriend*, and it brought me back to 2012 when I'd dreamed about dancing with Justin to this song. But Carl proved to be an exceptional choice for guys to dance with. I stood on my tiptoes to kiss him. It was the kind of kiss worthy of a litany of childhood dreams of falling in love, his hand cradling my face, mine lost in his hair. It was so wonderful that I stopped paying attention to any Auras that might be lingering on the block. Completely muted everyone and everything.

"So, am I your boyfriend now?"

"Well, I do like guys with tattoos," I murmured in Carl's ear.

Carl's hands and lips were everywhere before he unlocked the front door. I couldn't remember craving anyone this bad. Not even Justin Bieber. The blistering desire to have Carl shove me against a wall and be anything by chivalrous was overpowering.

I let my jacket fall to the floor as I walked back toward his bedroom. "Do whatever you want to me," I whispered to him.

"What?" His hands stopped taking off layers of clothing and his brows furrowed down at me.

I peeled off my shirt, then started to unbuckle his belt. "Do whatever you want to me. No limits."

He kinda chuckled and his Aura wavered. "Shouldn't we have a safe word?"

"*Stop* should work." I pulled off his shirt and started kissing his tattooed chest as I pulled him into the bedroom.

"Okay," he said but his Aura started to turn like a typhoon.

"It's not a trick, Carl. Seriously, do whatever you want."

His eyes took me in, and I saw flashes of every sex position flare in his mind. Each more enticing than the last. "Lay down."

I expected scratches, bite marks, and bruises. Wanted them. Instead, Carl moved over me slowly, like a feather falling from atop a building, the tips of his fingers gliding along every square inch of me. His tongue followed along so slowly, like honey.

"*Tu as un goût si doux,*" he murmured, and I read his mind for the translation: "You taste so sweet."

"You're teasing me," I moaned reaching down to touch him.

"Talitha." His lips were inches from mine and our eyes locked. "I want to make love to you."

"You don't have to like I said, I'll do whatever." I scratched my nails along his side.

He trembled atop of me, his Aura Glittering and turning a Bright White in the center. "I don't want to just do whatever with you, you're not just someone I fuck. I'm in love with you."

"Carl," I groaned but not because of what his hands were doing.

"You don't have to say it," he kept his eyes locked with mine. "Just tell me if that's okay?"

I nodded.

His mouth turned up in half a smile. "Say it. Please."

I ran my hand up to his tattooed side and brought it up to his chin. "Make love to me. Please."

He sunk into me, and my breath caught in my chest. My eyes instantly crushed shut as my body sang.

"Look at me," he murmured as he found his rhythm, slowly moving inside of me.

I did, and somehow it was as if I were even more naked. He'd cracked me open and found a diamond he swore was there. It might have been hours or minutes that our eyes were locked, our hearts beating as one, each inhale and exhale matched. The heat in the room started to rise, as did the tension inside of me, like pulling on a string, causing me to vibrate from the inside out. I could hear the seagulls, feel the sun hitting my skin, my eyes closed again as I began to drift off into the depths of the Ocean of pleasure Carl had brought me to.

"Stay with me."

My eyes shot open focusing on his, the energy inside me rising. "I might break something."

He kept with his pace. "Good thing I don't own anything then."

The lights flickered above us, but they stopped when I started to conjure the Ocean again, until Carl pulled me out of the water when he demanded. "Be here, with me."

The energy that filled me found its way out by turning on and off the lights throughout the house. I slammed the door to his bedroom. Jolts of electricity surged through the room and fear washed over me because the last time I let all my power out, I killed a building full of soldiers. I tried to fall back into the safety of the Ocean, creating another plane of existence that wouldn't draw as much attention as flashing lights and slamming doors.

"Talitha, stay with me."

"I don't want to hurt you." The windows in his bedroom shook with my words.

His breath hot on my skin. "You won't."

Carl's bedroom door opened and slammed shut again and again as he murmured, "*Je t'aime*," in my ear.

I let my energy fully flow from my hand and into Carl and his skin glowed like a firefly, which freaked me out, so I sent my energy out into the room, which made his skin dim back to normal.

Every light in his rowhouse turned on, brightening to a nearly blinding, the bulb in his bedroom shattered. All the doors in the house opened and closed in rapid succession, straining the lock on his front door. His record player turned on, blaring *'You and I'*, all the windows shook, and the appliances in his kitchen turned on. Even his broken blender.

But before the glass from the lightbulb crashed to the floor, each piece froze in midair, all the doors in the house stopped slamming, and the record stopped spinning. The only movement was our bodies, and my lungs as I shrieked in pleasure, Carl's skin brightened along with the strength of my voice as we climaxed together.

Just as everything had stopped as the orgasm took over my being, everything started up again as we fell back to Earth. Glass fell to the floor, the doors slammed shut a final time, the appliances quieted, but the record started spinning again making *Washed Out* our soundtrack. Sweat coated our bodies, and it was then that I realized I was crying. Not hard sobs, but enough of a release that I didn't light up the whole street.

Carl's face turned to the broken lightbulb on the floor. "That was crazy, huh?"

I turned his face back to me and held it in my hands, but couldn't form words.

"You okay?" His thumb wiped my tear-stained cheek.

I gulped for air as I pulled it all back in, letting the lights dim and the doors stopped rattling. "I told you I would break something."

Both our faces turned to the lightbulb on the bedroom floor. "That's not a big deal," he muttered.

"I thought I might hurt you."

"You didn't." Carl pressed his lips to mine. For a while we kissed, still wrapped together, until he rolled off of me, lay his head on the pillow so I could stare at his handsome face and his one dimple.

But the memory of the last time I let myself release all my energy bubbled to the surface. Hundreds of bloody soldiers littering the floor as I made my way out of The Lab. The faces of every soldier I'd murdered with my telepathy morphed into Carl's.

Unaware of my inner turmoil, Carl sat up, reaching for his boots, when in the background all I could picture were his dead eyes, red pooling underneath him. "Stay here, I'm going to clean that up, then maybe take out all the other lightbulbs."

I sat up so his back pressed against my chest as I murmured, "I'd lose it if something happened to you."

He brought my hand to his lips. "Me too."

"Seriously," I felt hot tears streak down my cheeks as I forced the image of hundreds of dead Carls out of my mind, "if something happened to you because of me, I'd never get over it."

"Nothing's going to happen to me."

"I don't want you to forget me. Ever."

He smiled. "I could never forget you, even if it is your superpower."

"And I love you too." It wasn't until the words left my lips that I realized how true they were. "I love you so much, Carl."

I pulled him back on top of me before he could clean up the glass, kept him enraptured with me until he was ready to go again. He went harder and faster, which made me scratch his *Washed Out* record, which I could tell by his Aura upset him more than he let on.

I helped him clean up, then we sat on the couch and watched his favorite movie. Although we didn't get past the first time '*In Your Eyes*' played. But that time we went to the Ocean of pleasure my mind created so I didn't break his T.V., which had started to shake halfway through.

# Widmore
## 10/14/2020 1:37 AM

"You know what you must do then, Gustav?" Jonas tented his fingers on his desk deep below the Earth at Wakefield Laboratories in New Jersey.

"Once I get her to control her abilities, I'll alert you and you'll kidnap her from The Manor," the words rushed out of my mouth, extinguishing the memories of the little blond-haired girl that loved climbing trees and collecting flowers.

"And if she refuses to work with you?" His body squared with mine.

"I'll send her and the others out on an errand, and you'll capture her."

"And it will be up to Eight Fifteen if she ever leaves The Lab again."

I shifted in the chair that matched Jonas' in style, but was nearly a foot shorter. "But you won't take the others, or hurt Carl?"

It could have been mistaken for a smile, but it gave me the same feeling as hearing a crash in the night when you knew you were home alone. "Such a big heart, so easy for you to fall in love. Thought you would have learned after what you had to do to Cordelia."

I could still taste her on my lips, see her gray-green eyes, and feel her alabaster skin. It had been twenty-eight years since I'd last seen Cordelia, still tangled in sheets when she asked me to stop injecting women with the serum. Stop trying to replicate the formula for immortality that was lost in a fire. She wanted me to move back to France, start a family, pay bills, pretend to be Non-Enhanced. Talitha wouldn't exist if I'd gone with Cordelia that day; instead, Talitha might be the key to creating an all-powerful Enhanced being.

And once I found the right ratio for immortality I'd unblock Cordelia's mind, inject her so we could be together forever. Literally. Then I'd have a family with her, *because what was the point of having offspring if you'd outlive them all?*

"Not love, just don't see a reason for such waste. And the others can still give us data," I insisted.

"Oh, Gustav, you were always a softie." He stood up and moved over to me as he spoke. "But you may keep the others. They can't accomplish much more than a pack of matches, karaoke machine, sledgehammer, and ice machine. My beloved, Lola, is already stronger than all of them, and I still have yet to approve the third evolution that I'm going to test on her."

There was a knock at his office door and in entered two of his enchanted soldiers, each holding an arm of a twenty-something in a black hoodie with the image of a man with a hawk on his shoulder on the front. His light hair looked greasy and had bloodstains on the left temple, illuminated by the bright lights above as the officers pushed him to his knees on the ground in front of Jonas.

"Gustav, let me introduce you to Danny Turner, a friend of Carl Anderson, the Non-Enhanced that Eight Fifteen has been spending so much time with."

The boy, Danny, was shaking and wringing his dirty hands as he whimpered, "I told you everything I know."

"Well, would you mind repeating it for my dear friend?"

Danny looked up at me. "Carl, known him for years, ever since he moved from Paris with his parents. Work at the same bar, live in the same neighborhood, he's really good at drawing and stuff."

Jonas cut him off with a sigh. "We're not looking to *date* Mr. Anderson, we're interested in the girl he brought to the party. You remember what party I'm talking about correct? The one that my people picked you up from and brought here?"

Danny feverishly nodded. "You mean Annie, right?"

My heart sang. *If we have Talitha, we're one step closer to the formula.*

"You're not a quick-witted breed," Jonas murmured, "yes, the girl we've been asking you about for a week is who we want to discuss."

Danny shook, sniffled, then continued his story, "Carl bailed on me at the Cold War Kids show, and the next day he brings this chick, with blue eyes and blonde hair named Annie to the party. She said that he saved her from some tool that was hitting on her and they spent the whole night talking."

"So that's where they met, at some bar?" I asked.

He sniffled again, but there was still snot mixed with blood dripping down his face. "Yeah, I mean, he hasn't had anyone serious since he dumped Jenny."

"Tell Gustav what happened when your friend Joe came to the party," Jonas said.

"That prick isn't my friend, and I don't know how sick you must be if you've been beating the shit out of me, and haven't done anything to him," Danny's voice was as firm as his body was shaky.

Jonas's smile had so many teeth it reminded me of a shark. "I have a plan for Joe, just as I have a plan for you. Now keep talking or I'll simply have the guards shoot you right here, right now."

Danny pivoted back to me, words flowing like water. "When Joe came in, it was like a glitch in the matrix or something, because a screen popped up in my head and started playing this movie. A really fucked up one, where Joe was raping all these girls. But I couldn't just *see* it, I could feel it." His face dipped down, and his voice shook like his body, "I could *feel* what he did to Tanya."

I didn't need an explanation that yes, Talitha's powers had increased, because at the mere presence of someone she could put a memory in another's mind. The question now: Was it intentional?

"What happened when you saw the memory?" I asked.

"Tanya's brother kicked the shit out of Joe. Everyone could see it too, and I saw Annie freak out and run out of the party. Carl chased after her. But I couldn't stop them, all I could see was what Joe did to those girls." His voice quieted at the end. "That's still all I can see."

"Now you know as much as I do." Jonas got my attention. "But I expect for you to find out more during your training with Eight Fifteen and proceed as discussed."

Talitha was more powerful, unable to control herself, and we didn't know her allegiance. But soon we would know, and hopefully, she'd be the key to the next phase. She could be the answer to everything and get me back Cordelia. I'd just have to make sure that she was loyal to me above all else, even Carl the Non-Enchanted who seemed as dangerous as a Daddy Long Legs spider.

"Thank you for your service," Jonas said as he waved his hand at the glamoured officer on Danny's left.

Before the boy could blink, much less plead for his life the officer pulled out his revolver. Danny fell on his right side before I heard the bullet leave the barrel. Red oozed from the side of his face which had busted open, expelling tissue, bone, and goo.

"Nice to see you again, Gustav." Jonas turned to me smoothly. "Will you have Sabine call the janitor to clean up this mess on your way out?"

# Talitha
10/14/2020 11:57 PM

"Just because I can't erase your memory doesn't mean you have to come with me." As I said the words, I could still see Carl's dead eyes replacing those of the soldiers I'd killed.

"Can't or won't?" His elbows were on his knees and his hands were folded under my chin, our faces level.

"Does it matter?"

"Yeah, if you're asking me to go meet up with a bunch of superpowered strangers."

I didn't have to take him off mute to read his mind, his Aura said it all as the tones of Blue wavered and deepened in the middle. He wanted to protect me, but he couldn't, and he didn't know how to prepare himself for the heartbreak of me leaving him. But I would not let the image of him dying in a hundred different ways become a reality.

"I'm in love with you, Talitha. So yeah, it does matter. To me."

"It's been nice."

"Nice?" His voice squeaked like a mouse.

"You have to know what you mean to me, but I don't even know what I'm doing," the words rushed out of my mouth, "I've been running so long, and I don't know what happens if I stop."

"You'll be safe with the professor though, right?"

"I know he can teach me to control my powers so I'm not just breaking lightbulbs and making you light up like a flashlight."

"And what would you do, if you could control your powers?"

My eyes drifted back down to the floor. "There's a reason he didn't want me to read *Carrie*."

"So, you're saying you don't want me?"

"No, that's not what I'm saying." I shook my head, wishing I could get him to understand he'd be better off forgetting about me. "It's just that I know one day they'll get me again, and right now I'm not sure I could get out. So how can I ask you to come with me when I can't keep you safe from The Lab or my friends?"

"Why would your friends hurt me?"

"I'm not saying they will, but they're probably pissed at me. When I broke out of The Lab, I didn't wait for them. There was so much going on, but I could hear them in my head. They were crying out for me to save them too, but it was like an out-of-body experience. Fidget was almost through the wall when I left, but I'm too far away from wherever they are to read their minds now. They're going to feel betrayed when they see me, and I don't want Frozenstar to freeze you and shatter you with a hammer."

His Aura Darkened to Navy. "She could do that?"

"She could, but most likely she'll try and sleep with you."

I suppose he was imagining an angelic Selena Gomez, as I'd described Phoenix's equally vain twin-sister, because he asked me, "Frozenstar's the hot one, right?"

I hit his knee with my own. "If you think I'm bringing you just to hook up with her then you can fuck off."

"There's not anyone else, Talitha, not while you'll have me."

"I know, I can read your mind, remember?"

"Then take me with you." He took my hands in his.

"Carl, if you come with me, you're probably going to die in some messed up way," my voice shook at all the possibilities of Carl's Aura dimming forever, "and I'll never get over it if something happens to you."

"I get the point, but what's to say I don't get hit by a bus the day after you erase my memory? Or mugged? Or aliens come down to Earth and make me one of their slaves? I don't know how to explain it, but I know I'm supposed to be with you."

"The Lab killed Reed, and he had to power to resurrect," I felt hot tears run down my cheeks, "they'll kill you just because you're with me. They won't even care that you're like them. I can't lose another boyfriend."

He couldn't help but smile. "I'm your boyfriend?"

It must have been infectious because I grinned in return. "That's what you took away from this conversation?"

"We all die, Talitha. I just want to do it next to you," he kinda chuckled as he corrected himself, "Not that I want to *die* next to you. Well unless we were old and in bed. But yeah, I want to be with you. Forever."

"Forever probably won't be very long."

"We could have a hundred years and it wouldn't be enough, and if you're too scared to even give us a chance, then maybe you should just turn yourself in."

It was those words that got me, because he was right, either of us could die at any moment, never to return to this plane of existence. And I wanted to spend every moment that I had left in this life with him, just like I knew he wanted to with me.

I brought his hand to my lips and kissed it. "I'll be yours if you'll be mine."

His Aura lightened to Blinding White, nearly the tone I'd turned his skin when we were having sex. "I'm yours."

# Talitha
10/15/2020 1:56 AM

Carl was whistling, but I didn't read his mind to figure out the song. "Quiet, I need to concentrate."

"Sorry," he mumbled.

Without a word, I tugged on Carl's arm, drawing him toward the parking garage a few blocks south of the Inner Harbor. We were surrounded by lovers, tourists, and college students taking advantage of the clubs and bars in the heart of Charm City.

Carl broke the silence, "He's telepathic like you?"

"That's like saying pasta is your favorite food when there are so many types. Some people even think risotto is pasta."

"Pasta is totally my favorite food."

"So, I converted you from pizza to mac and cheese?" I smiled up at him and he smiled back.

"Guess so." He opened the metal door at the north corner of the concrete structure. "But he can move stuff with his mind. That's what he's teaching you, right?"

I walked through the open door and started up the concrete stairs, each of our steps echoing around us. "Yeah, and he can read minds from oceans away, locate a person based on a picture alone, enchant humans to essentially be his servants, and I have no idea how old he is."

"What do you mean?"

"Back at The Manor, we found pictures of him back in the sixteenth century when he lived in Europe, and he looked exactly the same."

Carl scoffed, "Kinda sucks to be immortal but look so old."

"He can change the image of him in your mind and make himself into John Cusack if he wanted to."

"He's a shapeshifter?"

"No, he's always an old man." We'd reached the top of the stairway. "But when you look at him, he'll look like someone else. Like he's wearing a mask. But underneath the mask, he's still him. Plus, he can't change his Aura, so he's never tricked me."

"Can you do that? Mask your face?"

I shook my head as I pulled on the door that opened to the roof of the garage. "Was working on it, but it takes a lot of energy."

The air was still, but I could feel the Professor before Carl and I walked to the edge of level seven. "Talitha," my name floated on the wind behind me, and like a magician, Gustav Widmore appeared. His Aura moved around him like bits of Ash, unlike any I'd seen before, although it had the same tornado movement as my Swirling Gray Smoke. Wrinkles had wrinkles on his paper-white skin, with eyebrows so overgrown they could be confused with an animal living on his face. He hadn't aged a day since I'd seen him last when I was eighteen. He looked at least a hundred. His coat was plaid, in rainy day shades like moss green and slate. As he stepped toward us, he seemed to lean a little more to the left than I last recalled.

"Hello, Professor Widmore."

"I never thought I'd see you again, not after what happened." His dark gray eyes wavered over Carl and landed on our interlocked hands. "I see a lot has changed since we last met."

"Yeah, you can say that."

The streets around us began to explode with people as the bars offered their patrons a cup of coffee to go as they shut down. Some meandered out of the club waiting for a ride, some would stroll along the Harbor, but for now, no one was coming to the parking garage. Their chatting and laughter floated between Widmore and me, it seemed to get louder until he flicked his head to the side, and then even I couldn't read the minds of the people on the street. That's when the breeze took over, a chill that started on my face and sunk to my Chucks. I couldn't explain it to anyone, because I didn't understand it myself, but the energy in the air between Widmore and I hung heavy. Literally. Lightning flickered in a sphere that hovered between us like a spaceship. Widmore took control of the spaceship of energy, flattening it into a movie screen so we could communicate through it.

Widmore flipped through every memory he had of me and projected it on the screen. He paused on a few of me crying on his shoulder when I first came to The Manor and had nightmares about my father; Reed's palms glowing over my torso, sucking out all the water inside; all our classes together where he tried to teach me to be like him, and the heartbreak of Reed and I leaving. *You were my favorite,* Widmore gave the thought an outline of magenta, so I'd be drawn to it. The lights on the street dimmed as I turned off the screen and pushed him out of my head, careful to board up the weakness he'd found.

"Where'd you two meet?" His Aura Flickered, just on the border. I'd never known him to ask a question in which he didn't already have three countermoves to. His Ash Aura slowed in its twirl, which told me this time was different.

*Can he not read Carl's mind?* I kept that thought private as I shrugged and verbally answered, "Ottobar."

"How very...romantic." His eyes hung on Carl for a moment longer until they locked with mine. "Suppose I shouldn't expect you to spend an eternity alone."

"Thanks?"

Widmore knocked on the wall around my mind and I opened up a window a quarter of an inch so his neon magenta thoughts could peak through, *I meant it sincerely, I'm sure that Reed would not want you to be alone. Now, can we begin discussing you coming with me to The Manor?*

"I'm not going anywhere without Carl," I spoke aloud rather than returned the sentiment mentally.

Widmore mentally sighed. *Talitha he is a Non-Enhanced, therefore we can't bring him with us.*

"Fine, great seeing you again." I turned back toward the staircase, pulling Carl with me.

"Talitha!" Widmore called out, my name echoed on the concrete walls of the parking structure.

"What!?" I didn't mean to do it, but when I groaned back at Widmore the lights along the Harbor grew brighter. And I could hear the sounds on the street again as a flurry of noise and sound filled my head. Widmore's mouth hung open slightly, as he now knew I was more powerful, and my abilities were connected to my emotions and just as uncontrollable. I'd overpowered an immortal telepath without even trying. Widmore didn't move from his position, but his Ash Aura turned Yellow in the center.

He was scared.

I pivoted back toward him, only then realizing how hard I was holding onto Carl's hand. As I returned focus to Widmore, the lights along the water dimmed, "What?"

"You can't run forever." The Gray Ash around him smothered the Yellow at his center.

"I've outsmarted them for over two years."

"Yes, you can erase their memory of you. But how are you going to camouflage Carl?"

"I'll take him into my fog."

"Merely smoke and mirrors to Jonas." Widmore's smile verged on a sneer. "Even if that were possible, you'd take a Non-Enhanced into the very core of you? Talitha, that is not the girl I remember from my school."

"Yes, it is," my voice shook, and the lights on the Harbor tremored with it. "That's why I left, and unless you can give me another reason to come with you other than because I might die then I'm gone."

"I'll give you four."

"I'm waiting."

"Frozenstar, Phoenix, Fidget, and Siren."

My Aura started to Whiten on the sides. "They're all with you?"

"Yes," Widmore reached out to me, "and they're waiting for you to come back home Talitha."

"I'm not going anywhere without Carl."

Widmore's eyes ran over Carl. "You have my word that he'll be protected."

"What good is your word?"

"Has your trust receded in me so deeply since we've been apart?"

"I will protect Carl against everyone, including you."

I could almost hear the wheels turning in Widmore's head; his eyes held me as if we were in love and he telepathically told me: *I promise, on Reed's memory, that you nor Carl will see harm. And once the rest of The Manor has met him, we'll have a vote.*

"A vote?" I asked aloud.

"Majority rules, and if he's accepted," Widmore's gaze moved to Carl. "If that's alright with you."

Carl turned to me and without opening his mouth he asked me, *It'll be okay, right?*

*Just don't let go of my hand*, I mentally responded as I gripped onto Carl. *I'll take you into my fog if I need to.*

*I know you'll keep me safe.* Carl's thoughts were the same Azure as his Aura.

*Always*, I responded with the ease of a whisper to Carl. "Okay," I nodded at Widmore, "we'll go with you, but if they don't vote my way then we're both leaving."

"As to be expected." Widmore motioned to a town car behind him. "Shall we go?"

"Looks the same."

"Why would I alter its appearance?" Widmore polished his glasses across from me in the town car.

Which I silently thought was hilarious because I was pretty sure his vision was better than mine. "Maybe because you had the opportunity to create something new, and you made a micro version of the school two hours north of where it was before."

He pushed his glasses up the bridge of his nose. "Is my lack of creativity a problem, Talitha?"

"Just funny how much you like things to never change." I rubbed my thumb on Carl's palm as he sat next to me.

"If you'd seen as many pathetic excuses for beauty when it comes to the building one resides in, then you'd appreciate Neo-Gothic architecture as much as I do."

I rolled my eyes as the chauffeur opened up the door for us, and Widmore, Carl, and myself got out to gaze up at The Manor. Although it was a quarter the size of the building that I attended while in school, the plot of land The Manor 2.0 took up was roughly the size of a football field.

"You're right," Carl mumbled next to me, "it looks like a mini-British Parliament with a nice backyard."

I looked up and over at him and smiled. "Thankfully no politicians."

The structure was more out of place than bell peppers in a Maryland crab cake. It appeared to have been built ages ago in Europe and only transferred here by Widmore's exceptional abilities. This was partially true, because much like masking his face, most of The Manor wasn't in the physical world, but something Widmore projected in our minds. The Manor rested in the otherwise empty forest, miles from the nearest bus line, and even further from the Metro Rail that we'd used to leave Baltimore and enter the country. A cool autumn wind circulated through the remaining auburn, crimson, and amber-colored leaves that still clung to the tree limbs and wrapped around me. I hung onto Carl's arm as Widmore started up the stone steps to the three-story structure with narrow windows that came to a point at the top reaching up into the sky.

"Very astute, Mister..." Widmore waited for Carl to finish the sentence, but Carl was too enamored with the iron inlay in the stained-glass window above the thick wooden doors. A visual of the Milky Way, including moons, began above us and rippled out into every window on The Manor. The planets seemed to move and stars shone, although it was just a trick of Widmore's mind.

"Anderson," I answered Widmore on behalf of Carl. "His name is Carl Anderson."

There was a twitch in the muscle under Widmore's eye, and for the second time since we'd been reunited, I felt like he was hiding something from me.

"How'd you find everyone again?" I asked as the door opened and we were greeted by a blast of hot air along with the warm chestnut wood that was polished to near incandescent. The staircase that rose up in front of us had familiar swirls and loops. A hand-tied, oxblood-colored carpet with golden embellishments that appeared to be flowers squished underneath my muddy boots.

"They found me, just as you did, Talitha." Widmore took off his trench coat. Instead of someone coming to hang it up for him, the outerwear glided over to the coat rack by the front of the door. It hung amongst several others, including a baby blue puffer, a tan corduroy flannel-lined coat, a floor-length duster with bright red lining, and a blue jean jacket with black leather accents and dozens of buttons with everything from a drawing of Marvin the Martian to the sentiment Eat The Rich.

I dedicated the layout to memory. To my right was a living room, with several leather couches, a fireplace, a record player, and a bar stocked with top-of-the-line alcohol. Which was a happy addition from when I was in high school at The Manor. To our left was a formal dining room with a solid wood table and a dozen high back chairs, past that was a kitchen that appeared to be made strictly of gleaming stainless steel with accents of black marble. Basically, the place looked like where Edgar Allen Poe would live if he hadn't drunk himself to death hundreds of years ago.

"How'd you do it?" Widmore's eyes held me expectantly.

"Do what?"

"I couldn't even get into The Lab to save you. It's as if Jonas has multiple telepaths that helped design the building, making it impossible for me to open."

"Everything was locked down on a timer. When the timer was up and the doors opened, they were there waiting." The memory flashed to the forefront of my mind. Voice ragged from screaming Reed's name, haggard breathing, mind completely gone as the soldier's eyes lost focus on me and turned to their friend. "I made them think that the guy to their right was me about to attack, so they shot at him, and the ones that didn't kill each other, I twisted their necks until they cracked. The doors were programmed to open in a pattern that I already knew so I just walked out."

Carl's Aura Flickered Navy as I realized I hadn't told him specifically how I escaped The Lab. It was one thing have an abstract understanding of escaping from an evil corporation, but another to hear me describe how I'd killed hundreds of soldiers as if I were making toast.

Behind Widmore's eyes, something shifted. And without entering his grey matter, I knew he'd seen the slaughter of the soldiers firsthand as the memory of blood staining his shoes popped up to the front of his mind. "You were there?"

Widmore nodded. "They found me first, and I wanted to see it for myself." The iron gate between me and his mind reformed with twice the thickness, but it didn't seem to matter. Now I could read him just as easily as he could read me.

"Was anyone left?"

"You made quick work of everyone there, Talitha," Widmore's tone was tempered. "My question is, how did you do that? There were so many soldiers, all trained and fully aware of your abilities, and you'd never been able to enter more than one mind at a time."

I shook my head. "I don't know, I just did."

The tips of his fingers began to tap on the brick wall that I'd erected around my memory. "You have no control?"

I poured a layer of concrete in front of the bricks. "No."

I made sure not to turn to Carl, who I knew was thinking about Paris. The food, hours of talking, and the rain soaking us through as we made out. I always had control in Carl's memories, between creating more bottles of wine to drink, the ability to drive his grandfather's Jaguar, or when I made the sunset last twice as long when we went to the French Rivera. I didn't contemplate the why, simply appreciated the new memories I could create in Carl's old ones.

But if Widmore knew I was lying, he didn't give it away with a single facial tick or a word.

"You can leave your," Widmore scanned our black leather jackets that, although we both had before we met, appeared identical, "*outerwear* here, and we'll all meet in the living room."

As we hung up our jackets, Carl's hand ran along my arm, and he laced his fingers with mine. "You're not going to leave me alone with him, are you?"

I smiled up at him. "Scared of an old man?"

"Every time he looks at me, I get a headache."

"You'll get used to it, he's just reading your mind."

"Just please," his tone wavered and his Aura Deepened in the middle, "don't leave me alone with him."

I ran my hand through his hair, brushing it out of his face. "You'll never be alone again."

He smiled down at me. "Okay."

"C'mon." I tugged on his arm as we made our way to the living room. "You can meet my friends."

# Carl
## 10/15/2025 9:29 AM

*Holy shit, what did I get myself into?* Images of my imminent demise filled my brain as Talitha directed me to the parlor. *Everyone here can kill me, right?*

*I'd never let that happen*, Talitha pushed the thought into my brain, which gave me the same sensation as if she were whispering in my ear. We stood in front of the fireplace, which was so big it could have held an entire oak. *There's no line I wouldn't cross to keep you safe*, she insisted.

*Me too*, I thought, knowing she'd hear it. And there wasn't much else she could hear in my empty brain other than my heartbeat, which I swore was louder than the cherrywood grandfather clock that reached the ceiling and rung once on the half-hour. Although she didn't directly compare The Manor to a prison, beyond the obvious ornate decorating, this place had never been a home for her. She swore it was safer than escaping Baltimore because Widmore would teach her to control her powers. And after hearing how she killed those soldiers in The Lab, I was just as invested that she learned to control.

Her four superpowered friends came in all at once, Widmore waiting in the background as if he were a painter observing his setting.

"Litha." A caramel-skinned guy in a red tracksuit, shaved head, and a chain with a crucifix walked up to her. He threw his arms around Talitha tearing away her hand from mine.

He pulled away from her just enough so that he could murmur to her, but I was close enough to hear every word. "I've been so worried about you." I remembered Talitha describing Phoenix as 'an uptight cholo' so I guessed that's who was holding onto my girlfriend's hand and whispering, "I thought of you every day."

*Jesus Christ, the guy that can light me on fire has a crush on Talitha,* I realized. I might have failed Chemistry in high school, but after years working behind a bar, I understood body language and what it meant that Phoenix's bottom lip quivered before he brought up Talitha's hand to kiss.

"You don't have to worry about me." She took a step back, lacing her hand with mine. "This is Carl." She looked up at me and nodded toward him. "This is Phoenix."

Phoenix looked me up and down, his eyes dark, nostrils flared slightly before he faced Talitha. "Why'd you bring him?"

"Carl's cool, you can trust him."

"Why should I?"

An eyebrow arched on Talitha's face. "Because he's with me now."

"He's with you?" Phoenix's lips formed a point. "Like he's your boyfriend?"

"Yeah, and I don't get why you're pissed about it."

"Reed was like a brother to me." Phoenix clenched his fists and snarled at me, "and now that he's dead, you're just fucking some random guy?"

The lights flickered above us, and Talitha squeezed my hand and inserted instructions into my mind, *whatever you don't let go of my hand, I'll take you into a memory if I need to.*

"Phoenix!" A girl with long dark hair, glittering with pieces of white and silver grabbed onto Phoenix's shoulder and pulled him back. She was dressed entirely in pale blue, a skin-tight shirt, and sparkly leggings under a leather mini skirt. Talitha was right, Frozenstar was hot. Like so hot I couldn't take my eyes off her. Even though I knew her brother could set me on fire and my telepathic girlfriend accidentally killed people when she got emotional.

"All of you calm down." Widmore seemed to appear in the center of the room as if he were magic. "Let's take a moment to get acquainted then we'll have a vote, and majority rules."

The Professor's words brought the tension in the room down, but Talitha's hand still gripped onto mine. Phoenix nodded at Widmore then faced Talitha. "Sorry, I'm really glad you're back." He turned his attention to me. "So what's your story?"

I shrugged. "Just some guy from Baltimore."

"Quite the conversationalist." He kept his eyes steady on mine.

"Maybe I just don't want to talk to the guy that's being an asshole to my girlfriend."

Phoenix gritted his teeth. "Funny, too."

"Chill, man." The freckled girl who moved from the back was about Talitha's size, and a mess of long red hair fell over her left shoulder, while the other side of her head was shaved. Talitha had spoken about Fidget, the superpowered strong woman, most of all, thus she was easy to recognize. "You really think she'd bring some freak to The Manor?"

A lanky, dark-skinned guy looked over the top of his coke bottle glasses at me but didn't say a word. He wore a polo buttoned up to the collar, pressed trousers, and his polished loafers tapped out a beat on the floor.

Fidget tilted her head toward the silent Siren. "He thinks you're cute."

I felt an eyebrow raise on my face. "Thanks?"

Fidget's eyes widened as Siren's shoe tapped again and he made a range of gestures with his hands, a kind of sign language I'd never seen before, which made Fidget laugh. "Now he's wondering what music you like to listen to."

"Don't sing for him unless you want to find yourself in a bed of roaches, Siren," Talitha responded, as the superpowered prep winked at me.

I felt all the blood rush to my face, and it didn't improve when Frozenstar, a girl that had curves to rival a rollercoaster met her eyes with mine. Her hand remained on her twin brother's shoulder when she cooed, "Carl, it's a pleasure to meet you."

"Yeah," I cleared my throat because the word seemed to get caught in there, "nice to meet you guys too, Talitha's told me a lot about you." My eyes lingered on each of them as I said their names. "Fidget, Siren, Frozenstar, and Phoenix."

Although when I stopped at Phoenix, his nostrils flared again. "How can I trust this creep around my sister?"

"Like I said, he's my boyfriend." Talitha gripped my hand. "I didn't bring him here to hook up with Frozenstar."

Frozenstar said something to her brother in Spanish, then turned to me and smirked for a beat before I looked down at the floor.

"Why didn't you save us when you escaped?" Phoenix asked Talitha.

"You should have waited for us," Fidget mused, and the group nodded.

"I wasn't in my right mind after Reed died, but I'm still the girl you knew all those years ago, and I'm back now. But you all need to know before you vote on whether Carl can stay or not, we're a package deal."

Fidget's voice was so quiet I could barely hear her. "You'd just stay out there? Alone?"

"She wouldn't be alone," I insisted.

Phoenix's face contorted until it was distorted, his mouth started to open when Widmore lifted his hand, "I'd have to speak on behalf of all of us, that we'll accept you Talitha, but if you want a Non-Enhanced to live with us we'll need more reassurance than your word before our vote."

"I'm not sending my best friend back out into the world so Jonas can catch her. Here she's safe." Fidget straightened up. "And I don't need anything but Litha's word. I vote they stay." Siren made a checkmark in the air with his index finger which Fidget interpreted. "Siren agrees."

Phoenix shook his head. "You might be in love after knowing a guy for a few days just because you saw his Mom take him to kindergarten or whatever, but that's not enough for me. I need more if I'm going to sleep in the same house as him."

Talitha scoffed. "You're afraid of Carl when you can conjure fire?"

"I'd never use my powers against a Non-Enhanced." His eyes moved over to me. "Unless they leave me no choice."

An avalanche of words erupted, their questions like the point of a needle, and while I know she wanted to protect me, there was an answer that I knew they'd accept. After all, it was the first words she'd ever spoken to me. "I'm Blue," I said loud enough for everyone to hear.

Talitha gave me a death grip, *information is power, stop giving it away*, she mentally chastised me.

Phoenix's eyes doubled in size and charted me before he turned to Talitha. "He is?"

She nodded.

"But you told us that Reed was the only person you'd ever met that had a Blue Aura." Widmore drew closer to me.

"He was." Talitha's eyes danced around me. "Until I met Carl."

"What else can he do?" Widmore asked, his eyes zeroed in on me, and I felt a sharp pain in the back of my head where it met with my spine.

"What do you mean, what else?" Talitha asked.

"It's just quite a coincidence," Widmore mused as a woman with gray hair tied up in a bun, dressed as if she had just walked out of the nineteen fifties, with her black circle skirt and white lace-trimmed apron, walked into the room.

"Breakfast is served." She bowed at us.

"Who's that?" I turned to Talitha.

"One of the enchanted humans," she answered.

Widmore's gaze moved from me and landed on Talitha. "Let's eat and we'll have a private discussion afterward, then a final vote at dinner?"

"What about Carl?"

"No one will harm him while we speak, and you can read my Aura and tell if I'm lying."

Talitha took in Widmore before she agreed. "Okay."

## Talitha
10/15/2025 11:55 AM

"I'm so happy that you came back to me, Talitha."

"Spent this whole time in Baltimore trying to figure it out." I squeezed Carl's hand. *I'd still be running if it wasn't for you*, I pushed the thought into Carl's mind, and his Aura Shimmered.

Widmore's hand rested on the bronze doorknob of the third bedroom on the right on the second floor of The Manor. "If you get another vote this will be your room."

I arched a brow at Widmore. "Does that mean I already have yours?"

His Ash Aura Swirled. "You've always had my vote."

I took a step in, the plush, wine-toned carpet squishing under my sneakers as I moved into the room. Like the rest of The Manor, it was covered in tones of oxblood, burgundy, and merlot with accents of gold and bronze. A four-poster bed made of dark wood with deep navy sheets verging on black was soft to the touch as I ran my hand along it. I stopped at the bedside table when I found a book that used to belong to me. The weight of it was so familiar in my hands, each word cherished more than the last, even though I'd completely forgot about the Girl on Fire. I'd hidden *The Hunger Games* in my mattress and hadn't taken it with me. Even when I could have gone to a bookstore and stolen them, it never crossed my mind. I'd only come out of my depression from waking up next to a dead Reed by searching for Justin Bieber videos on YouTube. After that, I'd been running from the Flashing Reds that seemed to swarm me at all times as I tried to figure out a way to get to Widmore.

I flipped through the pages, and they fell open to a photograph that I forgot I'd used as a bookmark. Even though I literally remembered everything, I'd tried to forget my mother's smile, that way it didn't hurt as much that I couldn't see it anymore. Our eyes were bright blue and focused on the camera. I had a matching blue bow in my bright blonde hair, which complimented my mother's navy dress. I was holding a stuffed white bunny, and the large hat with a bow tilted on the side of my mother's perfectly curled blonde hair let me guess that this picture was taken at Easter. I stared at my mother's face, trying to recall the sound of her laugh when I was interrupted.

"I'd kept your things." Widmore stood in the middle of the room, while Carl leaned against the windowsill looking out at the backyard and surrounding woods.

I shut the book, leaving the picture inside and set it back down. "Why, when you took away anything else I had?"

He sighed "If this is still about *Carrie*, I apologize for not wanting my only telepathic charge to have an obsession with a story in which a girl kills all of her classmates."

"It always felt like a cage because you never let us experience anything."

Widmore's eyes moved off of me, and over to the closet door with a full-length mirror on the doors. "I brought some of your clothes as well."

I held my breath as I remembered the one article of clothing I was obsessed with as a teenager. The dress was the color of a Bluebonnet, with white polka dots. It had a Peter Pan collar, cap sleeves, a circle skirt, and a hundred tiny white buttons that ran up my spine. When I opened the closet and found it hanging there, I couldn't help but pull it out, and rub the fabric between my thumb and index finger.

I didn't have many options to choose from when I decided once and for all that I was going to lose my virginity to Reed, but he'd told me it was his favorite dress of mine. A month before my sixteenth birthday, I went to Reed and confessed my undying love for him. That to me, he was the only reason that I kept going, and that I didn't care that he was two years older. I didn't just want him. I needed him. The memory came forward and I could feel Reed's hand running down the side of my arm.

"It's not that you're too young, Litha," Reed's voice trembled, "it's that once I'm with you, that's it, forever."

"Promise?"

He did with a kiss, and we didn't say much else as we continued to make out. I didn't care if he'd been with other girls, didn't want to ask him if the rumors were true about him and Frozenstar, because now he would be mine and I would be his. He'd fumbled with the buttons on the back when in truth he could have just pulled it over my head, but it felt amazing for his lips to caresses the skin he exposed with each button. Reed had been so gentle, soft like a concerto as he made love to me. We spent the evening in each other's arms. The next day I'd swear to Micah that I could still smell him, even though the sheets had been changed.

Months later I'd have the polka dot dress on again, and he came out to me as I read about Katniss out in the woods. His face was coated in tears. There'd been a hurricane in the Dominican Republic, the house he'd grown up in had flooded a week ago, and they'd only just found his mother's body. She'd been dead too long for him to resurrect her even if he could get back home.

"Litha, don't ever go where I can't find you, because if I couldn't bring you back," he held me in his arms, shaking with sobs, "I don't want to live a day on this Earth without you."

And he didn't.

Back then tears turned to kisses, to Reed laying me down on the forest floor. He barely had time to unzip his jeans as I pulled him on top and hiked up the polka dot dress. I needed to have him inside of me as soon as possible. There was nothing sweet about it, only raw emotion as he thrust harder and harder, my shrieks of pleasure waking all the creatures in the forest. His lips on mine, our hands interlocked above my head, the way he crushed his eyes shut when he filled me up as I danced on the edge of ecstasy. Neither of us even took off our shoes and for some reason, it had been the most erotic experience of my life.

Well up until October 14, 2020.

"Matches your eyes," Carl said from behind me as I held the polka dot dress.

And even though it made no sense, at that moment I felt like I was cheating on both of them. Betraying Reed by falling in love with another, and betraying Carl because I was using my superpowered memory to relive my dead boyfriend making love to me. While Carl stood in front of me, my body was tingling as I remembered Reed. The mere fact that I could love Carl was disgraceful to the memory of my first lover, protector, and greatest friend. The first man I loved echoed all around me. But he was gone. Carl was alive and with Widmore's training, I would become strong enough to keep all of us safe. I hung the dress up and pushed it to the back of the closet, behind the unfamiliar pastel-toned t-shirts, lightly distressed jeans, and a few pleated wool skirts I suspected Widmore had his enchanted human servants purchase for me.

"Not my style anymore." I got on my tiptoes and pressed my lips to Carl's.

# FIDGET
## 10/15/2020 1:55 PM

"So you really think he's Blue?"

"Talitha wouldn't lie about that."

"You read minds now too, Fidget?" Her dark almond eyes took me in, strands of tinsel shimmering in her hair, and when Frozenstar set down her arm in between us, my skin somehow warmed at her frigid touch.

"No, but Widmore does, and he wouldn't let a human stay here if he was going to cause trouble."

She rose an eyebrow at me on her cinnamon bronzed skin. "He certainly is trouble."

I sighed as I shifted away from her, falling deeper into the plush sofa in the library reserved for texts written in German. The first edition of *Catch-22* closed in my lap. "I don't have to be a telepath to know he's into Talitha."

She tilted her head to the side. "You saw him looking at me though."

"Everyone looks at you like that." I pulled my legs under me.

"*Everyone?*"

"You know you're so hot, it gives girls an eating disorder."

She leaned forward. "Are you one of those girls?"

"Stop now." I picked the book back up and put it between us.

"That's not usually what you say to me."

"What does it matter? You just sleep with me to pass the time."

Frozenstar pushed the book away and leaned closer to me. "That's not true."

"It's my fault anyway, we've been hooking up for a decade and you won't even tell your brother that we're together."

I hit the nerve without even trying as she straightened up her back. "We're not together."

I threw the book at her, stood up, and walked through the wall before she could follow me. I got to my room, the door was always locked, and sunk through the wood like most people walk through a beaded curtain. I turned on my stereo, Best Coast came on, but it was interrupted by the doorknob to my room being frozen and broken with a kick.

"I don't have to tell Phoenix anything," Frozenstar continued, as if I hadn't walked out, slamming the door behind her.

"Why? Because being twins is another one of your superpowers?"

She laughed, a sound so rare, but so beautiful that it would make a person wait around for a decade in the hopes that they'd hear it again. "Everyone already knows that we're fucking so why do I have to give anyone a replay on what we do together?"

"Because it would be nice if I was worth talking about."

"What?"

I walked up to Frozenstar, she was taller than me, and her curves were perfectly placed, as was every other part of her anatomy. "I'm not worried about Carl at all because I know what Talitha and Reed had. She wouldn't just screw some random guy, she picked someone that I know she can't wait to tell me all about. Once Widmore is done testing Talitha to see if she's stronger, I know for a fact she's going to find me and tell me all about it. Where they met, what it felt like the first time he kissed her, what he did that made her fall in love with him."

"I've told her all about you. How shocked I was when you kissed me first, because you could have had anyone, and you picked me. When I couldn't take it another moment and had to pass you that note before hand-to-hand combat class. I told Talitha about our first night together, when I fell in love with you. And I didn't tell her because I wanted everyone to know that you were mine, I told her because I was yours." Her mouth started to open, but I shook my head. "You don't have to say it, I know you don't feel the same way, and I've come to accept that. But I can't be with you, especially now that I'll have an actual relationship shoved in my face in half an hour. So just go." I motioned toward the door.

"It was Tegan and Sara," she muttered.

I pivoted so quickly my long, red hair hit me in the face. "What?"

"That band you listen to, with the twin sisters."

"Yeah." I don't know why, but the muscles on my face started to hurt as I think I was on the edge of laughing at her.

Normally Frozenstar had the stature of a Victoria's Secret model, but now her arms were crossed, shoulders slouched, and eyes unable to hold onto mine. "You, Talitha, and Micah were always talking about music, and you were always obsessed with all that weird riot girl stuff that I thought was just so stupid."

My smile had fallen to the floor. "I hope this starts turning sweet really soon."

"I started listening to them, because, well I didn't really know why at first. But I knew that you liked them a lot, so I thought maybe I just didn't get it. So I listened to them for like hours, and I was thinking that I was right and indie music sucks."

"Like Cardi B is better?" I muttered.

"But then I heard the song *Nineteen*, and it was like they were talking to me. I thought that I could treat you like crap because you didn't matter. But when I heard that song, I knew you did. You mattered more to me than any guy or girl I'd been with. That's when I fell in love with you." Her eyes skirted mine. "I just never told you."

Usually, I always had something to say, but now I didn't have a single word that I could form. Her bottom lip quivered as our eyes met, and I felt all the blood rush to my face right before I leaned forward and kissed her, fully succumbing to my addiction known as Estrella Ramos.

Her lips were soft, tender, but strong. At first touch, her skin was so cold that it caused a shock, but the longer we kissed, the more my warmth seemed to wash over her. She pushed me back, and I fell onto my bed. Her face hovered above mine as her hand went up my shirt. "This okay?"

I so wanted it to be okay, to not care that Frozenstar had sex with anything that had a pulse, and only treated me sweetly when we were alone. All I wanted was for her to pull off my jeans and bury her face between my thighs until the sun came up tomorrow, then we'd switch, and I'd do the same for her.

"Please," she murmured as she kissed my neck, her thumb circling around my nipple, "let me make you cum."

"Frozenstar, I don't think…" I began, but her hand made its way down my stomach.

"Don't think, Nina."

The sound of my name, my *real* name on her lips is what did it. A name she only called me when she desperately wanted to fuck me, and every time I let her have me. All of me, only to get nothing in return. I grabbed onto her hand and pulled it off of me. "I don't want to," I mumbled as I sat up.

She was next to me, her lips dancing on my skin. "All you have to do is lay there, babe, and I'll take care of you."

"I said no." I pushed her hands off of me and stood up, moving over to my stereo and switching the song to *Wasted Time*.

"You're seriously saying no to me?"

I sighed. "I know you've probably never heard it before."

"No," her tone turned as cold as her skin, "I haven't, and I didn't think it would happen after I told you I loved you."

"You just said that so I'd sleep with you. If you really loved me, then maybe you'd ask me how I felt after seeing my best friend after over two years."

"We already talked about Talitha."

I turned around to face her, standing in the middle of my room, arms crossed over her chest, which somehow made her breasts look even more perfect. "You mean when you insinuated that you were gonna screw Carl?"

She rolled her eyes. "You know I was kidding. I like my men a few shades darker anyway."

"The go find one of them." I started back toward the door, but before I could sink through it, Frozenstar grabbed onto my arm.

"Nina, I really do love you." Her almond eyes took me in, as mesmerizing as a kaleidoscope.

"I love you too, Estrella, but I don't trust you." I yanked my arm back and went through half a dozen walls just to be free of her.

# Widmore
## 10/15/2020 2:00 PM

"Don't try to bend the spoon, bend yourself." My high back leather chair felt like a cloud. Before me, a solid oak desk, the size of a pool table, held the day's papers from Paris, Tokyo, Rome, Berlin, Los Angeles, London, and Baltimore.

Across from my papers, Talitha slouched in a jade green velvet chair. "Did you get that from The Matrix? Changing my name to Neo?"

I sighed. "I'm sure that I have no idea what you're talking about."

Talitha rolled her eyes. "If I were immortal then I'd spend some time catching up on some movies."

"I'm not immortal, Talitha, I just age very slowly."

She rose an eyebrow at me. "You know your Aura flickers when you lie, right?"

"So, your powers have increased but you have no control?" I felt a twitter of excitement spark in my stomach because I was one step closer to getting to Cordelia with the formula for immortality. All I had to do was make sure she was strong enough for Jonas to get her to break into the CDC, who'd been working on the formula nearly as long as Jonas and I had been trying to replicate it.

"Yes." She crossed her arms over her chest. "Like I already said a hundred times."

"You'd have to know this was coming, that I would want to find out how you were able to stay away from The Lab for so long."

"My telepathy is not all you're interested in though, is it?"

I saw no reason to draw out our conversation when she already knew where I was going. "How did you come upon this Carl Anderson?"

"I already told you."

"I understand that you trust him because he has the same Aura as Reed, but I need to know everything about him."

She grinned, the kind of facial expression you'd expect on a child that had broken a rule and knew they'd get away with. "You can't read his mind." It was a statement, not a question.

And I returned it with my own. "And you can."

Instead of exerting the confidence that she seemed to exude ever since she walked back into my life, her shoulders fell, her mouth turned down, and her eyes held onto the carpet. "So, what does that mean?"

I stood up, buttoning up my suit jacket as I did, and walked from behind my desk, a foot away from Talitha. "Considering his age, I don't believe he's been given the serum, or he would have exhibited something by now. Besides, Jonas would have brought him to The Lab."

"That's what I thought." She bit her bottom lip. "So it's got to be something I'm doing, right?"

I looked out the window that took up the entire wall to the left of my desk. It had a view of the Tahitian sunset, complete with palm trees and birds. I could practically hear the calming sound of waves lapping on the sand.

But it wasn't there.

Nor were the walnut bookcases on the far side of the room, with copies of every work by Shakespeare, Neruda, Camus, and Balzac. The wallpaper with bronzed geometric shapes atop a black background had never been crafted or adhered to a wall. While the carpet appeared to have been hand-dyed and placed in such a way it gave the viewer the effect of the rolling grass on a moor in tones of bone and dust, it was not real. I could create an intricate room, including the tempered glass in the

Tiffany chandelier that hung above the desk. While Talitha and I were able to interact with the daydream, this room had no blueprint, hallway that leads to it, or a door from which to exit. All of it existed only in my head, save Talitha and the spoon, and took as much effort as a sneeze to create. "It could be your telepathy shielding him from me, but we would have to wonder what it means that his Aura is Blue."

"I can believe that I'm somehow cloaking his mind from you, but there's no way I could alter an Aura." She shook her head. "That's like changing someone's soul."

"You might be amazed at what you're able to do, Talitha. After all, you weren't sure that you'd be able to erase yourself from your mother's memory, and now you could show up at her house and she wouldn't recognize you."

Her bright blue eyes met with mine. "Then when does it stop? When can I just be me?"

I extended my hand, turned it palm up, and with the briefest thought I conjured fire. The flame was black as the night sky, not a multitude of oranges, reds, and yellows like Phoenix's. "I don't know how hot it is, because I've yet to touch it to someone's skin. Don't want to kill someone when we don't have a healer anymore."

Talitha's posture turned ridged. "Why didn't you try when Reed was still in school?"

"Because I've only been able to do this since he died." I made a fist which put out the flame. "So I can't tell you when it ends, because it still hasn't ended for me. My powers have evolved just like yours. Doesn't happen to many of us, only a handful of students that have attended The Manor over the years became more powerful."

"But Jonas killed all of them before they could kill him, right?"

I nodded.

"And I could wake up with laser vision one day and cut Carl in half?"

I nodded.

She sighed. "Well, then what are my options?"

Without moving a muscle, I slid the spoon from the center of the desk and let it hover in front of Talitha. "You will learn control."

"I told you I can't move things like that, it only happens when I'm really emotional. Like someone's trying to kill me." She returned to her slouching position and murmured, "or during sex."

"Well we most certainly won't be going through either of those scenarios, so you'll have to concentrate and bend the spoon because otherwise, you will end up dead," I said the words as a warning, but I wasn't sure if it was for me or her. I knew that I'd have to tell Jonas that she was more powerful. The least I could do was give her a few lessons before I essentially turned her over to The Lab. There was no other way around it, no matter how attached I'd become to Talitha, she'd been created to be used as a weapon. And her time to do as she was intended had come. She knew it to be true, although I wasn't sure if she truly understood the lengths that Jonas would go to control her. "You know what they'll do to you?" I continued, "Shave your hair again so they can attach those electrodes to your head. Don't they usually begin by showing you some rather violent images?"

Talitha's nearly invisible eyelashes fluttered, and she nodded.

"They'll have you at their side during any interrogation, poke and prod at you at their will." The spoon between us began to shiver. "Of course, they'll try and get you to crack at the very least by beating you. Some of those soldiers have been alone for a very long time, and you are a very pretty girl, and before you had Reed to protect you. Now, you're all alone and unable to bend a spoon, much less kill your attacker."

Her eyes narrowed at me.

"Last time when you refused food, they force-fed you didn't they?" I took a step forward and leaned against my desk. The spoon rattled between us. "After all, you're no use to them if you don't have energy, but Jonas will make sure that you're never strong enough to get out of there. His cruelty will know no bounds to break you."

"I get it." The spoon started to curve to the left. "Are you going to help me or just remind me how royally fucked I am?"

"This is how you save yourself, with a spoon, and if you're lucky they'll just shoot Carl in the head, but you remember how creative they are." I leaned in and dropped my tone as I continued. "Was Reed ever able to heal those scars on your body that were left by the chainsaw when the soldiers killed you that second time?"

The spoon didn't just bend, it crumpled like a piece of aluminum foil, and fell to the ground. "I won't let them touch Carl," she muttered not giving herself a moment to relish in the fact that she had just done what a moment ago she thought impossible.

"He's literally powerless." When the words left my mouth with a nonchalance to them, the lights above us flickered. The thing was the spoon did exist, just as Talitha and I exist in a physical plane. But the lights didn't. She was powerful enough to make the lamp that I'd created in my head flicker, yet she was still a novice who couldn't control the flow of energy that flowed through her. That was the moment that surprise turned into fear. There had been a handful of students that had come through The Manor and their powers progressed as they aged, the energy that fed their abilities seemingly knowing no bounds. For years, Jonas and I believed that Reed was one such pupil, with limitless power that we were able to control because we held Talitha captive.

Turns out we were wrong the whole time, because I could sense the power surge inside of her, attempting to boil over, and her allegiance was unknown.

"I'm telling you now Widmore, if they touch Carl then I won't need another lesson from you because I'll blow the whole place up."

"You'd sacrifice yourself for a Non-Enhanced?"

She nodded.

There was a tug in my heart because I remembered what love felt like just at the start. How the world was only the other person, everything they did was equally magical and revolutionary, and a kiss was akin to an existential crisis. But I knew that Jonas would never let her kill herself because he'd created her just as he had all of us. Therefore, our lives, deaths included, belonged to him alone.

"Then I think we should get a few more spoons, Talitha."

# Fidget
## 10/15/2020 3:47 PM

As the peacemaker of the group, it was decided I'd speak to Carl first, and I left Phoenix in the foyer as I walked through the French doors to the expansive backyard. He'd been sitting under the biggest White Oak in the backyard ever since Widmore had taken Talitha into his office. The buttons on my jean jacket clicked with each step my boots took toward the unknown entity.

"Hey," I called once I'd passed the tennis court that Widmore would enchant to be a swimming pool, or even an ice rink, depending on the season.

Carl lifted his rectangle-shaped face, gray-green eyes set on me, a single curl falling on his forehead like Superman. "Hey."

"Can I join you?"

He shut the sketchbook and set it on the ground to his right and nodded to his left. I tucked my legs underneath me in case I needed to bolt, and lay my hands on my lap, not sure if he knew just how lethal they were.

Carl grinned at me, which shockingly charmed me. "I was hoping it was you that came out to talk to me."

"Why? Because you think I'm the least scary?"

"I know you can't set me on fire, but Talitha told me that you're really strong, and can like..." but his voice faded off and I didn't feel inclined to add, *can move through solid objects that aren't made of metal.*

"Wouldn't want to give my best friend's boyfriend a concussion the first time I meet him," I quipped, letting the wall that I kept between me and everyone else slip just a bit.

"Appreciate that." His gray-green eyes flittered on me like a butterfly. "She talked about you a lot. And Micha."

The whole world crashed around me when this stranger said Micha's name, and I wanted to hit him, but I responded with a smile. "Reed used to call us the trifecta, but we always knew who he put in first. She went to The Lab voluntarily because they wanted Reed. She sacrificed everything to be locked away and tortured, just to be with him."

"She never told me that," Carl's voice floated away on the breeze.

My words followed after his when I added, "There will never be two people more in love than Reed and Litha."

Siren and I had shared a cell at The Lab. All of us had been tested, they'd have me fight men four times my size, but to test Reed's abilities at reanimation, you have to kill someone. The whirling of the chainsaw still haunted my dreams, and I wondered if it kept Talitha up at night. If she still felt the metal tear at her skin every time she touched the scars that covered nearly every inch of her body. If she couldn't forget the faces of the soldiers that cut her up into a dozen pieces as Reed was forced to watch. And what it felt like to be dead for over a day as Reed used his powers to make her whole again. Surely Carl had seen the memory of torture on her body, but if Carl knew the story of her scars and still came, then maybe he wasn't something to be silently feared, but an ally. "If you want to be with her, you'll never be able to leave The Manor. Ever."

Carl shook his head. "You might have known her longer, but when's the last time Talitha did what she was told?"

My eyes met his. "Then they'll get her, and they'll kill you on site."

As if she knew we were discussing her, the French doors which connected the foyer to the backyard opened, and Talitha walked toward us. She put on her leather jacket, tugged her beanie over her short blonde hair, and although I locked my eyes with hers, I continued talking to Carl.

"It will piss me off if they hurt Talitha because she's trying to save you. And I break things when I'm pissed." I acted cooler than I felt as I stood up, not letting him respond, and met my friend halfway between the doors and the bench by the birdbath.

# Phoenix
## 10/15/2020 4:00 PM

I quietly waited for Talitha in the foyer after Fidget had walked out to talk to Carl. I heard her gentle footsteps and watched the outline of her body coming toward me when I called out, "Litha."

She stopped, her hand on the handle of the French doors that led out to the backyard. "Phoenix."

The sound of my name on her lips drew me from the shadows into the light next to her. "Every day I felt like I was dying without you."

She rolled her eyes then threw me a grin. "You're always so dramatic."

I didn't interpret her tone because that might break the thin illusion I held onto that she might love me too, and I continued solemnly. "I burned Reed up with The Lab. He wanted to be buried back home," my voice cracked at the end as guilt gripped hold of me, "I promised I would take him back to the Dominican Republic."

Her hand fell from the doorknob as she took a step closer to me. "He never told me that."

Reed had been more than a friend, a brother, and that's why my affection for Talitha had been completely platonic. But now he was gone, and I was here. "Guess he figured the only reason he'd be dead is if he couldn't bring you back."

She took my hand and squeezed it, which felt better than if I'd gotten a kiss from KAROL G, a million dollars, and a lowrider. "He'd want us to go on, Phoenix, not dwell in what we've lost."

"Easy for you to say." I pulled my hand from hers, caught between my desire to kiss her and yell at her.

"What the hell does that mean?"

I nodded toward the *gringo*, Carl. "You've already moved on."

"If it were the other way around, I wouldn't want Reed to be alone."

"It's not just that." Fury ate at my stomach. "You belong with your kind."

"Are we so different from Non-Enhanced?"

I lifted my palm, let it fill with a bright red flame, a hint of steel heat in the center. Then closed my hand, killing the fire. "Can your *novio* do that?"

"No, but he can feel pain, loss, and I know he loves me just as much as Reed did," Talitha insisted. "I can't help who I love, and if you're my friend then you'll vote to let us stay."

I wanted to tell her that she shouldn't be with Carl simply because he wasn't me. That my every waking moment revolved around her. That I needed to see if she tasted as sweet as I'd imagined all these years. Promise to give her all that I had in this life.

I had to tell her.

Now.

And maybe then she'd realize how right I was about our destiny.

Instead, all of that got caught in my throat, and what came out was, "I'll tell Widmore, that I vote you stay."

"Thanks." And for a split second, I thought she might kiss me, at least on my cheek. Instead, she squeezed my hand, turned, and walked through the French doors into the backyard, leaving me with a broken heart.

# Talitha
## 10/15/2025 4:14 PM

"I'm sorry I left you there," I mumbled into Fidget's shoulder, her red hair covering my face.

She patted me on the back. "I understand. Reed was dead, and you couldn't control yourself."

I nodded, gulped, as Fidget gave me another squeeze before she stepped back, her smile filling up her face. "Tell me everything."

"Everything?"

"Yeah, like about being on the run, and how you met." She looked over my shoulder at Carl. He was sitting under a tree on the other side of the yard, sketching.

"The Flashing Reds had been chasing me for I don't know how long," and so the story began. While I'd only known Carl for a week, I still had over two years to tell Fidget about, so I picked out the highlights and shared them with her. After a while the past and present found their way to each other.

Fidget looked back over at Carl. "You really love him, don't you?"

"Yeah, I do."

"You said he's Blue, right?"

I nodded.

"Maybe he's a healer too?"

I shook my head as I sat down on the bench in the backyard under the weeping willow that still clung to its yellow, orange, and red leaves. "He's twenty-seven. He would have exhibited by now if he'd been given the serum. Widmore agrees."

Her eyes held onto Carl for a second longer than I liked as she sat next to me. "I just want you to be careful."

"Don't worry about me."

"Became kind of a habit." Half her face turned up in a smile as she faced me again. "*So*," she stretched the word and her Aura Lightened to the same Copper as her hair on the edges, "is it true what they say about guys? You know, like if they have big hands, and feet or whatever?"

"Don't have much to compare it to."

"Neither do I."

I threw her a smirk. "Since when do lesbians have an interest in a guy's size?"

She tossed it back. "I don't want to see it or anything, just curious."

I fell back into the memory of Carl making love to me in the very early morning hours as I gave my friend as many details as I felt okay with sharing. "He's very proportional."

She giggled like we were little girls. "Proportional?"

I giggled back but didn't add any more details, I wanted to keep my beyond exceptional sex life to myself. Especially that I could make his possessions float in midair and scratch his favorite records.

As if she knew I hadn't been forthright with Widmore, Fidget said, "I just want you to be safe."

"I think we'll be safe in the backyard of The Manor."

"You think?" Her green eyes moved to Phoenix, who walked out of the French doors. He threw me a nod, letting me know he had cast his vote so Carl and I could stay. Fidget continued talking while the object of conversation was too far away to hear. "When the guy that loves you can conjure fire and he's jealous of your new boyfriend?"

"Phoenix loves me, but he's not *in love* with me."

"He's been talking about you nonstop, getting you back, even more than me."

"Reed was like a brother to him."

"And that's precisely why he didn't say anything back then. But now?" She shrugged.

I cast my eyes over at Phoenix, who sent out a flame from his index finger to set the falling leaves on fire turning them to ash. It was something I'd seen him do a hundred times, a habit of the bored pyromaniac, but this time a chill was sent down my spine because Phoenix's eyes were fixed on Carl as he used his powers to set the leaves aflame. I didn't necessarily mean for it to happen, but Phoenix must have sensed that I was staring at him from across the field. Our eyes met and I couldn't help but open his mind as one would open a can of soup.

The door to his memories appeared in the bright white corridor in my mind. Technically he had two doors; one was a rusted screen that was holding on by pure imagination rather than screws. I turned the knob on the second one, with bright yellow paint that had chipped, exposing the wood underneath. I didn't have to take more than a step inside his mind before I heard my voice murmuring, "Phoenix."

Although I didn't remember the casting call, I was the topless lead in the movie that played on the screen in his head. Phoenix was holding me, so tenderly, "Litha."

I pulled off his shirt, and in Phoenix's daydream I licked what I must admit were an exceptional pair of abs. My skin was void of scars, his tongue massaging me as he lay me on his bed and started pulling off my jeans as I continued to repeat, "Yes, Phoenix, yes."

I turned back toward Phoenix's door, leaving my bright white corridor, and returned to the bench next to Fidget. She finished her thought, unaware that I'd been somewhere else, "I don't know what he's going to do, especially since Carl is Non-Enhanced."

I looked down at the grass beneath our feet, still clinging to life as autumn took over, concentrated on my breath after coming out of a sex dream that made me feel... Well, it made me feel a lot of things. Yes, it was a compliment to have someone fantasize about you. And yes, Phoenix, much like his sister, was the definition of attractive with his caramel skin, muscles, and based on what I'd seen in his mind, he'd be a very giving lover with me. But Phoenix didn't notice that I broke into his grey matter as his eyes moved back to Carl and he kept burning the leaves. Phoenix didn't know that I knew he loved me, didn't even know that I had read his mind. But he did hate Carl, and I was in love with Carl, who was completely helpless against a jealous man that can conjure fire. *I'll always make sure Carl's near me. I won't let on to Phoenix that I know about the crush, and I'll take Carl into my fog if I need to,* I decided. Because there would only be one man that would know my body like that, and it was Carl, who was totally unaware of all of this as he sketched under the tree.

"You're blushing like crazy," Fidget broke into my train of thought, also unaware that anything had transpired.

"It's just cold out here."

She laughed. "I'm a ginger, so I know what it looks like when someone is blushing."

"You're right, okay? I didn't think Phoenix felt like that, but I guess he does."

"You just read his mind?"

I nodded, but my eyes held onto Phoenix's Neon Orange Aura that started to dim on the sides as Frozenstar's Milky White broached his. She sat next to her brother under the tree by the tennis court. Frozenstar's eyes locked on Fidget, and her Aura started to Sparkle on the edges.

"Are you two still..." I began.

Fidget's Aura Darkened in the center. "She'll lavish me with attention, then screw anyone remotely attractive that Widmore glamours to work at The Manor."

"So nothing's changed?"

Fidget's Aura lightened back up to Orange Dreamsicle. "She didn't even ask what it was like to get my best friend back, just tried to hook up with me."

"Tried?"

Fidget started picking at her cuticle on her thumbnail, the nervous tick that was the reason Widmore named her as such. "Told her to fuck off."

"You deserve better, Fidget. Like someone that will actually admit you're dating."

Her eyes shifted. "Talitha you know how it is, we're in a bubble. And you're not gay. And I don't like blondes."

"Baltimore is full of hot brunettes."

She shook her head. "Widmore wouldn't allow it."

"No one ever caught me. I basically turned myself in. So, if you want to go somewhere and try and meet a girl that isn't a total bitch, then I'll be your wingman."

"My wingman?"

"Yeah, and if I see any Flashing Reds then I'll just take you in my fog and we'll come back to The Manor."

"But isn't it still hard for you, to be around a bunch of people at once?" Blood filled up her nailbed, which she promptly put in her mouth to stop the flow.

"Not like it used to be. Besides, Widmore is going to make me stronger and teach me how to control my telepathy."

"Well, you don't have to use your powers to get me laid."

"Everything's going to be different now because Widmore might live forever, but what happens if he doesn't?" Fidget connected her eyes with mine as I continued. "All they could do was chase me, but now that I'm back and can learn to control my powers, I know I'm going to be just as powerful as him one day."

"Talitha," Fidget shook her head, "none of us expect you to protect us from Jonas."

"But they want me, and when they find out—" but I halted my words because I hadn't been completely transparent with Widmore.

"Find out what?"

"You know I told you it was raining in the memory where Carl and I first kissed?"

She nodded.

"It soaked us, the rain. Every time I go into his memory, I can create a new memory. It's like I'm making an alternate universe or nearly altering time." Although I could barely admit it to myself, much less Fidget, I was interested in just how I could push my limits.

"Holy shit." Her mouth turned up in half a smile. "Could you talk to anyone in the memory?"

I shook my head.

"Do you think it's happening because of Carl? Like his Blue Aura changed you?"

"If it means I'm powerful enough to fight Jonas, then that's all that matters."

# Phoenix
## 10/15/2020 4:14 PM

Whenever I was stressed, bored, or angry I'd come outside and sit on the bench under the largest tree behind The Manor and set the falling leaves on fire. I'd been scowling at the *gringo,* wishing he was one of those leaves that I'd set on fire, when I got the feeling someone was watching me. I turned my head to the right and locked eyes with Talitha. They were the clearest blue, her skin was the color of cream, and I couldn't help but imagine what it tasted like.

In my imagination she pulled off my shirt, licked my abs, and moaned my name. I lay her on my bed, started to pull off her jeans, my mouth moving down her glorious skin as she pleaded with me to continue. My fingers were inside of her, feeling how wet I made her, when a branch broke, bringing me from my sex daydream back into reality. The erection that had started to create a bulge in my jeans as I thought of making love to Talitha vanished just as quickly as Frozenstar walked up to me.

"Everyone loves Talitha more than me." Frozenstar slumped on the cold iron bench next to me as her gaze filtered over to Fidget and the object of my obsession.

I shook my head. "Fidget doesn't love her like that."

"You do."

"Doesn't matter what I feel." I slouched next to my sister. The sun had started to set as Talitha and Fidget continued to talk. Carl, the thief of a beautiful woman, was still sketching. I pulled my eyes from all of them and set them on Frozenstar. "She's happy, that's what matters."

Frozenstar chuckled. "Like you wouldn't fuck Talitha so hard she'd forget about that Non-Enhanced loser if you had the *cojones* to take her for yourself."

Anger filled me, and I let out all the steam I'd allow when I nearly growled. "Don't talk about her like that."

Frozenstar sighed, ignoring my pain because it didn't directly affect her. "Fidget doesn't get it, when we're together that means something, but if I'm with someone else, it's just sex."

And as usual, I stifled my inner turmoil and concentrated on my sister's trauma of getting rejected by Fidget, even after a confession of undying love. "You get Fidget's point though, right?"

"That I'm a heartless bitch?"

"No, you just don't believe in monogamy, and that's a problem for her."

"I'm not forcing her to only be with me forever."

I smiled at her. "And you'd be okay if Fidget was with someone else?"

"If it's just sex then yeah, it's fine."

"It wouldn't bother you to know that another girl touched her, kissed her? Wouldn't keep you up at night, wondering if she made Fidget cum harder?"

Frozenstar arched a dark eyebrow at me on her cinnamon-colored face. "Don't talk about her like that."

"See, what you want is unfair. You can't have it all and give her nothing."

"But I love her," Frozenstar's voice shook, "I really do."

"Sometimes that's not enough."

Her attention once again went to Fidget, whose copper hair had turned neon as the sun started to set. Talitha seemed to have a glow around her body as if she were an angel, or if I could see her Bright Shining Aura.

"Remember when we were little, Alejandro? And Papa would take us out to the beach to look at the stars?"

"Yeah, Estrella." I smiled at the memory of the still air wrapping around our small family as the waves washed on the cliff our house was built on.

"You think maybe he's still watching out for us?"

I fingered the crucifix hanging from my chain. "Yes."

"Do you think he still loves us, even though we're freaks?"

I didn't want to tell her that I asked myself the same question. Wondered if either of them knew what we'd turned into. *Did we even resemble the children they knew in Mexico?* "Of course he still loves us."

Her face cracked, but she was still so beautiful. There was no proof that her physical appearance was part of her Enhancement due to the serum But either way, she used it to her benefit. Only I was immune, still able to see the knobby-kneed girl that had the grace of a donkey. Not the girl with looks that got every man and woman to do a double-take. And it was that girl, the one so unsure and unconfident, that came through when she quietly asked me, "Do you think Jonas will come here, now that Talitha's back?"

"I won't let him take you."

"You can't promise that." If she were able to cry, I think a tear would have fallen on her face, but with a core so cold, at best ice shavings would fall down her cheeks.

"I'll never let them hurt you."

"But even together, we're not strong enough, and what if they have me and Talitha? Would you even pick me?"

"Of course."

She turned to me. "Really, you'd pick me over the girl you've loved forever?"

"Would you pick me over Fidget?"

She shook her head. "That's not the same thing, you're obsessed with Talitha, and Fidget is…" But she didn't finish her sentence.

I smirked at my sister. "You can't even say girlfriend, so I guess you would pick me then."

She punched me in the side. "Maybe I'll just leave you both. Tired of having you tag along all the time anyway, *hermano*."

"You'd save me, just like I'd save you."

"Even if it was between me and Talitha?"

"Yeah, because Talitha doesn't need me to save her." A leaf fell, and before it hit the ground I turned it into ash. "She's going to save all of us."

# CARL
## 10/15/2025 10:38 PM

I assumed that Widmore would make the 'vote' for Talitha and me to stay a big deal. Instead, he simply nodded at Talitha from the head of the table right before the glamoured housekeeper set a slice of pot roast smothered in onions with carrots and potatoes in front of me. Although, they're both telepathic, so maybe they had a conversation that no one else could hear. After dinner, Fidget invited Talitha and me to listen to some records in the study, but instead, Talitha directed me to our new bedroom, where we showered and got into bed.

"Do you regret coming with me?" Talitha shifted under the sheets next to me.

"No." I breathed her in and she smelled like roses, which made me wonder if I did, too, since we'd both used the same shampoo.

"You gave up everything for me."

"Wasn't that much."

She grinned. "You're the worst at taking a compliment."

"I wouldn't call giving up a shitty job at a bar and an empty rowhouse in Baltimore for a room in a country estate a sacrifice."

She propped herself up on her elbows. "Oh so that's why you came?"

"That and the sex is amazing." I pressed my lips to hers.

"Carl," she breathed my name, "you think that's gonna get you laid?"

"I know you want to." My thumb ran along her hip.

She grinned and her smile lit me up from the inside. "You can read minds too, huh?"

"Told you I got a headache today." I leaned in to kiss her again.

Her tone softened to a whisper. "You said it only happens when Widmore is looking at you, right?"

"Yeah, it feels like he's putting an ice pick next to my skull and pounding on it."

The tips of her fingers glided across my hairline. "It's because he can't read your mind. Hopefully, he'll stop trying now and they'll go away."

"Really, but isn't he super powerful?"

She nodded.

"Then that can't be possible, right?"

Through the tips of her fingers, she brought the image of us kissing in Paris in the rain, spending hours in memory of Christmas Day with my parents, everything in my house levitating as I made love to her. Reminding me that nearly every day since we'd met, her powers had expanded, and she had no control or understanding. I felt my heart fall to my stomach. "What's it mean?"

"I don't know. Just make sure you're always near me, okay? In case anything happens."

"I thought we were safe here."

"I told you that you'd never be safe, but if anything happens while we're here, I can take you into my fog if I need to."

I didn't have to read minds to know that something besides a lab that wanted to test on her might get her back. Earlier in the day, Phoenix had burnt ten pounds of dead leaves while staring daggers at me, so I could only assume that I shouldn't be alone with a guy that could conjure fire and lusted for my girlfriend. "Talitha, I feel safe with you."

"Me too." She kissed me back.

Wanting to escape from this creepy Victorian house filled with superhumans that might kill me I said, "I'm thinking of a place, somewhere nearly as pretty as you. Take me there."

She grinned at me. "Close your eyes." Her fingertips charted my temples as she dropped us into the middle of one of my memories.

I could smell the flowers before I opened my eyes. Before us stretched acres and acres of lavender, its deep purple hue shifting slightly as the breeze from the mountains behind us glided over the surface of the plethora of bushes. Bees floated around the gentle petals atop the fuzzy stems that bent along with the wind. They sneaked in past the clouds that moved quickly across the sky. On the horizon, there was a break in the field, of which we were in the middle, and a trail that led to my house. The small structure, which looked more like a barn than a house, had been crafted in stone and mud by my great-great-great-grandfather hundreds of years ago.

She'd taken us back to the 16 of July 2016, the last summer day I would be in France with my parents. I looked over at Talitha; the sun made her hair so bright it was nearly blinding, and her blue eyes had doubled in size as she took in the splendor of a landscape turned lavender. The tips of her fingers brushed against the soft petals.

"It's beautiful." She smiled up at me, her cheeks starting to turn red, and I didn't know if it was from the sun or if she was blushing. Either way, she was so much more stunning than the South of France.

"Yeah," I nodded, listening to the birds chirp around us, the chickens behind the house, and got high off the soothing aroma that infiltrated my lungs like the hook of a Washed Out song.

She put her hand to her forehead as if she were saluting me, but I knew she was blocking the sun out of her eyes so she could look up at me. I took a step to the left so I could cast a shadow on her before she asked. "Where are we?"

"A commune called *Valensole*, in Provence."

She threw me half a smile. "Your accent is hot."

I smiled back and responded in French, "That's why it's called the language of love," and I knew I didn't have to translate because I could feel her presence in my mind.

"Is this your family's lavender field?"

"Yeah, there's a field of sunflowers too, on the other side of the house, it's been in my family since like Napoleon."

"Which one?"

I shrugged. "The famous one?"

She giggled. "So wait. You're rich?"

"I mean, all of this is technically mine, if that's what you're asking."

"So back in the real world, you didn't have to live in Baltimore, you could have lived here?" She spun around. "Why the fuck didn't you do that?"

"I might have been born in Paris, but Baltimore is home." I shrugged as the wind wrapped around us. "I thought maybe one day when I'm old or whatever. There's a family that's lived here just as long, that's their house." I nodded over to a modern estate, which had been built in the past twenty years and was constructed of predominantly glass. "So, it's not like the flowers are going to die."

"You just brought me here to see something pretty?" Her fingers weaved with mine.

I nodded. "I can show you my room and you can laugh at how emo I was."

She cocked an eyebrow at me. "Was?" Then she cast her eyes at the horizon, past the lavender, at the end of the dirt driveway was an electric car.

"Race ya." Talitha tilted her chin at me.

"What?" I laughed.

She playfully shoved me in the stomach and bolted off through the lavender toward the farmhouse. Talitha darted through the field of flowers, the stalks as tall as her. I ran after her, and long before the farmhouse doubled in size on the horizon, I'd caught up with her. My Docs hit the gravel road fifty meters before Talitha, who protested, "No fair, your legs are longer."

"You got a head start."

"Yeah, like two seconds."

Before I could say anything else, the front door of the farmhouse opened and out walked my parents. My father opened the back of the car to throw in the lone suitcase they'd brought. My mom rifled through her purse as she called back inside the house, "Carl, would you please hurry up? You don't have to bring back all those band t-shirts right now, we'll be back for Christmas."

I don't know if Talitha felt the knife go through the center of my heart as my mother promised me a Christmas that would never happen, but she squeezed my hand.

Dad got in the driver's seat, pulled out the map, always trying to find a quicker route when there wasn't. Mom pulled a cigarette from her purse, with the flick of her wrist a flame ignited from her lighter. She inhaled, holding in the nicotine, only to release it out slowly as her gaze moved along the horizon. My mother's gray-green irises scanned over the flat ridge of Mount Ventoux, atop the hills of the valley, filtered through the lavender. And with a turn of her head, she took in the vast pillar of yellow that had been created by the millions of petals from the sunflowers that rose toward the bright blue sky. But they didn't stop on me, her only child that was standing inches from her face, nearly choking on the smoke that plumed out of her mouth as if she were a dragon. My mother's dark hair hung at her shoulders, a dimple in her cheek that matched mine, and of course her eyes. I'd forgotten just how dark her eyelashes were, like soot. And her bright red lipstick that would leave a mark on my face when she'd kiss as I left for school. Now, she left that mark on the filter of her cigarette.

I'd told her a hundred times that smoking would kill her and I'd been so very wrong.

"She reminds me of a movie star," Talitha mused. "You know, like from one of those old black and white movies."

I smiled, even if I felt so very sad. "Yeah, she was obsessed with Romy Schneider."

Talitha arched an eyebrow at me. "Who?"

Before I could go into French cinema history, the door to the house opened with a bang. "I'm ready," an eighteen-year-old me sighed as he put his headphones on over his offensive amount of curly brown hair.

My mother's face lit up as she turned to teenage me. "Did you have fun, *mon petit chou*?"

Teenage me scoffed, "Don't call me that."

My mother hooked her arm around my teenage self's arm, pulled me toward her, and pressed her lips against my forehead, leaving the tale-tell mark of crimson lips. "You'll always be *mon bébé*."

"Gross, Mom." My teenage self pushed her away, smeared the mark with the sleeve of my hoodie, pulled out my phone, and started the playlist. I could hear M83 even though the headphones existed only in my memory. If I could, I would rip the headphones off teenage me, shake some sense into him, let him know what's about to happen, and how even nine years later the guilt will live on. Instead, the end of the trip happened as it had, and always would. I got into the backseat of the car, caught between a suitcase and my backpack. Mom would take one last glance at the landscape as if she knew she'd never return, and Dad would drive off toward the horizon.

"You, okay?" Talitha asked, eyes wide, sides of her mouth turned down.

I nodded as her hand came up to the side of my face, wiping away a few stray tears that I didn't realize had escaped past my stinging eyes. "Sorry, I thought it would be cool to show you the farm, but instead I just showed you that I'm a complete asshole."

"Carl you were eighteen." She took my face in her hands. "And trust me, your mom knew you loved her."

"Really?"

"Look, I know what it's like, wishing you could go back and change it. We can come back here every day for the rest of our lives, but you'll never have a new memory with her. Never get the chance for one more day." She got on her tiptoes and pressed her forehead to mine. "We might be in the past, but this is our now, and if anything, what you just saw should let you know to really live."

She was so powerful that her words mended my broken heart. "I love you. And not like some stupid love song. I *really* love you, Talitha."

Our lips locked, and my hands couldn't help but run along her hips, one of them started to make its way up her t-shirt when she stopped me. "I was promised a showcase of an emo teenage boy's bedroom."

I laughed, took the four steps to the solid wood door with a copper, lion-faced door knocker, the handle in its mouth. My fingers interlocked with hers. "C'mon."

# Talitha
## 10/15/2020 10:38 PM

Every memory of Carl's that I'd entered had been a technicolor dreamscape. But it wasn't until this one that I truly felt like Dorothy, not realizing I'd lived my life in black and white, only to see color for the first time. The wood gleamed in the light that filtered in through the windows, all of which had a view that belonged on a postcard. Lavender flowers as far as the eye could see, with mountains on the horizon reaching up into the sky, which had begun to turn from blue to shades of pink, copper, and gold as the sun started to set.

The kitchen had a cast-iron stove, a table with six matching chairs, all made of wood and carved with intricate swirls, and the head of a lion adorning each high back chair. Leather, fur, and comfort were the words that I'd use to describe the living room, with the simple decor of a table, chairs, and sofa pointed toward the window, looking out at the sunflower fields. An acoustic blond-wood guitar and filled bookcases proved the only entertainment to be had in front of the brick fireplace.

My fingers glided along the neck of the guitar. "You play?"

"Not since I was eighteen."

I threw a smile at him. "You're full of surprises, aren't you?"

He threw it back. "This coming from the girl that can read minds?"

Down the hall, I found the bathroom, which had been modernized enough that it had a rainfall shower and bright white tile from floor to ceiling. The tub, with claw feet, was positioned at a window as well, so as one soaked in bubbles enraptured with the aroma of lavender, they could gaze upon the fields it came from. Carl directed me through the second door down the hallway. The solid wood motif and large expansive windows continued, but it was hard to tell if the wood held the same splendor because it was entirely covered in band posters. M83, The Mountain Goats, BØRNS, Washed Out, Beach House, Future Islands, and of course Cold War Kids, the band playing at Ottobar the night we met, were all highlighted. But there were even more stickers, concert ticket stubs, and flyers adhered to the wall. I wasn't sure if each was placed by pure chance, but the pattern of colorful paper gave the effect of waves in the ocean washing over the walls and ceiling. But what drew my attention was a poster of a scantily clad Ariana Grande on the back of his door.

I laughed. "Is this for real?"

He grinned. "Like you didn't have one of Justin Bieber?"

I bit my bottom lip. "I never really had a room that I could decorate."

His smile faded away. "Oh, yeah, sorry."

"Don't be." I squeezed his hand. "Because I would have had a whole wall dedicated to him."

Carl's eyes darted to the left, over my shoulder toward his bed with its comforter thrown on haphazard. *"Mon Dieu,"* he cussed in French.

I followed him with my eyes as he picked up a tan, leather-bound notebook, about twice the size of a cellphone, and he flipped it open to the first page. His Aura flickered from Soft Blue to a Dark Navy. "I left this here, and never got it back." His finger traced the words etched in a loopy cursive hand, which I translated from French when I read his mind. *May all your dreams come true, and if not, then create them -love, Maman Christmas 2013.* He flipped through the pages, and I saw flashes of sketches of faces, a few pages of just eyes, hands, and even one of himself that had been shadowed so perfectly, it looked as if it were a photograph and not pen on paper.

"Can we take this back?" He shut the sketchbook and faced me.

I shrugged. "I've never tried, because technically this isn't real." I motioned toward the sketchbook.

"Then how come I can touch it?" He dramatically turned through the pages. "How can this not be real?"

"I told you, this is all inside your head, not something tangible."

His shoulders slouched. "So you're saying what happened between us in Paris wasn't real?"

"No, that was, but everything else there wasn't."

"Then how'd we eat, and drink all that wine, and feel the rain?"

"I told you I don't know. I'm just different since we met."

"Then why don't we try? I'll just hold onto it when you're taking us back to 2020, back to The Manor."

"I don't want to test my limits." I gripped onto his t-shirt. "Not with you."

"Why not?"

"Because I already lost someone." I looked up at him, his gray-green eyes enrapturing me. The sunset reflected the most majestic tones into his bedroom, but not even the rolling hills of lavender could rival Carl's Azure Aura when it Sparkled. "And I can't lose you." I wrapped my arms around his neck and said the words I'd been so afraid to say before. But maybe now with Widmore training me, I could keep Carl safe. "I won't make it through losing you, Carl, because I love you too much."

"*Tu es le soleil, la lune et les étoiles mon amour.*"

"What's that mean?"

"You're the sun, the moon, and the stars, my love." He pressed his lips to mine and made my heart skip a beat.

We quickly became a flurry of discarded clothes. But once we fell onto his bed his mouth and hands moved over me, smooth as silk. He worked slowly. Appreciating every inch of me. Caressing, kissing, his tongue lingering around my thighs until I begged him to keep going. When he sunk into me, the rest of the world halted. He didn't have to ask for me to stay with him because I couldn't leave him mentally when he had fully possessed me physically. His hips rocked softly, our lips were always near the others, and when my energy started to bubble over the stereo turned on. *10,000 Emerald Pools* started playing and when Carl's tempo matched up with it, the lights started to flicker. And I couldn't be sure if it was the bed, or the ground itself, but everything started to shake when Carl thrust harder and harder. But I didn't worry about the fact that I was making things in a memory move. Nor did I contemplate what I might be able to do if I could control my abilities. All I could think about was how good it felt to have Carl inside of me.

"Don't stop," I moaned as the door to his room slammed shut, opened, then slammed again. A door that didn't really exist but in Carl's mind.

He laced his fingers with mine and stretched my hand above my head, pushing into me so deep the energy that flowed through me threatened to melt my brain. Instead, I released it, shaking the dresser against the wall as all the clothes were strewn around the room as if by a ghost. Carl's grip on me tightened as he moaned, "*Je serai toujours à toi,*" into my ear.

I didn't ask for a translation as we held onto each other as we reached the peak. My Aura filled with lightning, crackling around us. Usually, I would have let the energy flow and continue to toss around everything in Carl's memory. But I worried I might literally tear down the house. Without thinking of the implications, I pushed the energy out of me and gave it to Carl. Just as I'd concentrated my energy on the spoon in Widmore's office, or all those soldiers that I'd killed, I siphoned my power and directed it into the very center of my boyfriend's being as if he were a solar panel and I was the sun. My bubbling energy flowed out of me like water from a firehose. Carl's skin turned so bright it was blinding, and both our Aura's crackled with lightning. After a few strokes, the flow of energy inside of me leveled out between us, and all the objects in his room stopped moving as Carl absorbed my telekinetic energy. Although the music kept playing.

For a moment I was worried I was hurting him by infusing him with my powers, but from the noises Carl was making, and the look on his face, he seemed to be enjoying himself. He gripped a handful of my hair and groaned something in French in my ear as he filled me up, continuing to thrust for a few beats even after he was done. We kissed for a little while longer, as we murmured '*I love you*' in our native languages, then he rolled off of me and lay his head on the pillow next to me. Carl's breathing became less ragged. His hand continued to glow, though not as bright, as he stroked my cheek. "So you turn guys into glowsticks when you have sex with them, but don't think you can bring a sketchbook back."

"It's only happened with you." I kissed him, refusing to analyze what I might have done to him by sending my telepathic energy into him, nor congratulate myself on controlling my power. His glowing skin started to dim while his Aura Sparkled Blue. "But okay, I'll bring back your sketchbook if you answer a question."

"Yes, we can do it again." He gave me a peck as I giggled.

"What'd you say to me in French?"

"I didn't say anything in French."

"You always speak in French during sex."

"It's only happened with you." He grinned. "What'd I say, and I'll translate."

"*Je serai toujours à toi.*"

"I'll always be yours."

"I know, but what did you say?"

He laughed, showing off his lone dimple. "That's what it means, *Je serai toujours à toi.*"

"Teach me something else."

"Like what?"

"Something useful."

He thought for a minute, then said, "*Combien pour un hôtel pour passer la nuit avec mon petit ami?*"

He made me repeat it until my accent was perfect and I asked, "What's that mean?"

"How much for a hotel to spend the night with my boyfriend?"

I laughed at him. "That's useful I guess."

"Or," he brought his hand to the side of my face, "*Je t'aime plus que les étoiles n'aiment le ciel.*"

"And that?"

"I love you more than the stars love the sky."

"*Je t'aime plus que les étoiles n'aiment le ciel,*" I murmured as he wrapped his arms around me. Once again it started with his hands, then his tongue. I straddled him, and this time the moment I felt my energy begin to bubble I automatically pushed it into Carl. Not a single object in his memory moved, but Carl lit up brighter than Paris at night as I transferred my energy to him. So, I'd learned control, but had no idea what long-term effects Carl would have after being pumped full of telepathic energy.

However, it didn't seem to trouble him, considering he got me started up for a third time that night.

# WIDMORE
10/16/2020 7:45 AM

Jonas raised an eyebrow on his ebony-toned face as we walked the cold, steel halls of The Lab deep underneath the rural roads of Maryland. "So Eight Fifteen knows you can't read Carl's mind?"

"It seems very clear to me that Talitha can easily communicate with Carl through his mind, and I know that she's not only been in his memory but has taken him into hers," I answered as Jonas stopped in front of a door.

He snapped his fingers, and the door opened to a room much like a jail cell, with concrete walls, a metal toilet, and a cot with a threadbare gray blanket. Yet, it was void of a prisoner. Or at least, it seemed to be, but I could hear soft mental murmurs, a girl's thoughts in Korean, repeating, *not again*. I knew of only one Enhanced being who had the gift of invisibility. And when Jonas snapped his fingers again, Rose appeared, cowering in the corner of the cell. I'd met the now eighteen-year-old Korean girl years ago, when she was found at an orphanage in London. She'd become fast friends with Lola, the super-strong Enhanced being whom Jonas claimed to love. And although I couldn't read Jonas' thoughts, I predicted that Rose's presence was some punishment for Lola. Rose's sallow skin was bruised, crusted blood covered her hairline, and she was clothed in the same teal scrubs every Enhanced being wore while staying at The Lab. Only hers were torn and stained with various bodily fluids.

Jonas stood in the center of the room, his back to Rose. "And?"

"Talitha told us that his Aura is Blue."

"Like One Eleven, her dead healer boyfriend?"

"Exactly," I continued. "But I could find my way into Reed's mind easily. There's no evidence to support that Carl is a healer." I muttered the last bit to myself, "honestly, he's so dim I can't believe that he is a topic of discussion at all."

"You've told me that ever since she met this Carl, Eight Fifteen's powers have increased. And he's got a Blue Aura? You don't think this needs to be discussed?" Jonas chuckled. "Not sure why I have you, or anyone else for that matter, when I have to do everything myself anyway." Rose's whimpers increased in volume, which made Jonas narrow his eyes before he bent down and leveled his face with hers. A long, dark, bony finger with a sharpened nail brushed a lock of long black tangled hair from Rose's tear-stained face. She shivered and brought her knees to her chest as Jonas whispered to her. "Now stop with that; you'll be home soon enough. I just need my betrothed to stop telling the authorities that I raped her. It's become a nuisance killing everyone that she tells."

"You did, though," Rose's whimper turned up to a screech. Her British accent was evident when she hissed, "you're a bloody pedophile rapist—" But her words halted when Jonas snapped his fingers a third time.

Bone protruded out of her wan skin as Jonas telepathically shattered her femur. Blood spattered on the walls, her wails of agony echoing around us. Jonas grabbed onto her face, closing her mouth. I knew Jonas' snarling threats were beyond distasteful, but all I could hear were Rose's very unselfish thoughts. *At least if he's hurting me, he's not hurting Lola.* Rose grieved for her friend's future, as did I. However, I couldn't help but fear for Talitha's immediate future more than Lola's, because Jonas was obsessed with Lola. If he would defile and torture the best friend of someone he wanted to marry, what would he do to Talitha, whom he saw as a threat? I pushed that thought aside, concentrating on the fact that if I trained Talitha, we could use her in the fight to recreate the formula for immortality.

"Lola is mine," Jonas insisted to Rose, "and until she can come to terms with the fact that I alone control her body, mind, and soul, I'm going to keep you here."

My stomach turned as the Rose nodded, tears streaking her face, but Jonas was unfazed as he turned back to me. "We need to bring Eight Fifteen and Carl in immediately."

"No." I pushed the images of a bloodied Talitha out of my brain. "You told me that if I gave you updates, then you'd let Talitha stay at The Manor."

"Talitha," the word rolled in Jonas' mouth like a marble. "You see her as more of a daughter than a specimen, and that is all she is. A test subject. A weapon to be used against anyone who goes against us. And you need to do as promised, Gustav. Send her out into the world so we can capture her while keeping your identity and allegiance to me a secret, then we can use her to break into the CDC and get their formula for the fountain of youth."

I clenched my fist. "Lola's abilities are increasing just as quickly as Talitha's, and you plan on injecting her with the third evolution of the serum already. She's already beyond capable of breaking into the CDC. So why bother with a girl that can alter a memory when Lola's super strength will be more useful as a weapon?"

Jonas' eyes zeroed in on my knuckles, which flashed white. "Lola is to be my wife in a few years, to rule beside me. Talitha can either be a weapon, or there's no reason for her to exist. And Carl?" Jonas scoffed as he waved his hand over Rose, and a cast appeared on her leg. "He's not worth the energy it takes me to kill him, and I'll have my glamoured officers take care of him. And I'll drag Talitha out of The Manor myself if you don't get her in the city by tonight."

"How do you expect me to do that? She just showed up, and I never let any of my charges leave. Won't she suspect something if I give them a night out on the town?"

"She didn't come back to be locked in a cage, but to be protected." Jonas grinned. "She blindly trusts you, or she would have left Baltimore years ago. All you have to do is have a fight and offer her the olive branch of a night out."

"You can take Talitha, but only Talitha. Please."

"Such a softie in your old age, when, if I recall, you were the one to tell Machiavelli that it is better to be feared than loved."

"Not soft, just don't see the purpose in killing the few charges I have left."

"If you're so worried, tell her to make a copy of herself and implant it into her friends' minds. This copy will be able to have some basic interaction and make her friends and Carl believe she's with them while we capture the real Eight Fifteen. The telepathic trick that she'll send with her friends will lead them to safety and they'll see no harm from us. Eight Fifteen is who we want anyway." Jonas' nearly black eyes focused in on mine. "We'll keep an eye on Carl once he's back in Baltimore. He might come in use if we need to get Eight Fifteen to cooperate and go to the CDC."

I could still hear Rose's whimper as Jonas directed me out of the cell and locked the door with a snap of his fingers.

# Talitha
10/16/2020 9:15 AM

"I presume that you found your accommodations up to par, Talitha?" Widmore asked from the head of the breakfast table.

I couldn't help but giggle. I swear I still smelled like lavender, and the image of a glowing Carl on top of me flashed through my mind just as Widmore gave me a swipe with his eyes. I put up my neon sign that read 'Stay Out' as I stuck the prongs of the fork into the scrambled eggs adorned with crème fraiche. "I'll be sure to give it a five-star review for all the other orphaned mutants looking for a place to stay."

Carl chuckled next to me and nearly spat out his orange juice, which made me giggle more.

"You know how I detest that word," Widmore grumbled as he stirred his tea. "And what on Earth is so funny?"

I rolled my eyes. "Don't start with that 'we're the superior race' shit."

"Then how else could you explain your gifts?"

"Tragic irony?" I nibbled on a slice of bacon.

"How can your abilities be called tragic?"

I scoffed, "Doomed to remember everything when I can free others of their horrific memories, which I then have to take on as my own?"

He leaned in, his voice steady and low, while Fidget sat across from

Carl pouring copious amounts of ketchup on her plate. "But imagine what you could do."

"I guess you're right," my eyes flitted over Carl, "if I can have more nights like last night."

Carl started to blush.

"What are you talking about?" Phoenix pulled out his chair across from mine and poured himself a glass of orange juice from the carafe. "My room is right next to yours, and it was so quiet I thought you both had left."

"We didn't spend the night here."

"Then where did you spend the night, Talitha?" Widmore asked.

"Where was it?" I muttered to Carl.

"Provence," he said with an accent that made my skin tingle.

I turned to Widmore. "What he said."

"How could you have gone to memory in the South of France if you've never left the continental United States?"

I shrugged. "I took us into Carl's memory."

Widmore's Gray Smoke Aura began to surge, just like mine did before I went into my fog, "Why do you continue to go into a Non-Enhanced's memory?"

"That's kinda like, my thing."

"You're able to spend an entire evening in a memory now?"

"Yeah, so?" I shrugged.

His Aura Flickered Yellow in the center; he was frightened of something. "Anything else you'd like to share about your abilities?"

I threw him half a grin and popped into Widmore's mind, *Holy shit, are you scared of me?*

*Don't be ridiculous*, he mentally responded.

The lights flickered above us; everyone but Widmore and I looked up at them. *Then who did that?*

*A light show, Talitha. You really shouldn't feel as if you've outwitted me just yet. I still have so much more to teach you.*

Then it happened. He slid into my memory of last night like a snake that found a crack in the wall and got a handful of still shots. He saw Carl and me running through the lavender. The sunset from the view of Carl's bedroom. And Widmore knew how Carl tasted just before I ejected Widmore from my memory. *Pervert,* was the last thought I shoved into Widmore's head, then let a steel shield fall over the brick wall around my gray matter. Everyone at the table was murmuring, but I couldn't make out the words, because Widmore's light eyes held me as the Gray Smoke Aura around him swirled at double speed.

"Where is it?"

I didn't lie and pretend that I didn't know what Widmore was talking about because I'd been just as shocked that I'd been able to do it. Carl had begged me to bring the sketchbook back to 2020, and after a night of ecstasy, I couldn't say no to him. I don't know how it worked, but Carl held the book in one hand and gripped onto mine with the other as I directed us back to the endless white corridor in my mind and then our bed at The Manor. A secret was something hard to keep around an immortal telepath, so even without words, he'd pinpointed the location of the object I'd been able to bring from Carl's memory into our present reality. Widmore dropped his cloth napkin atop his plate, pushed his chair back, and started toward the stairs. I chased after him, and even though he was hundreds of years old, he beat me to the bedroom. With the flick of his wrist, the mattress on the four-poster bed flipped, exposing the sketchbook.

"Don't," I pleaded.

With a snap of Widmore's fingers, Carl's sketchbook flew across the room and landed in his wrinkled hand. I found that I couldn't move a muscle, as if he put me in a block of ice. When he faced me, a smile covered Widmore's face. "Do you realize what this means, Talitha?"

With a flick of an eyebrow, Widmore released me from the telepathic block of ice so I could say. "Doesn't mean anything."

Now everyone was standing just inside the doorway as Widmore held up Carl's leather sketchbook. "You were able to bring something from Carl's memory into the real world." He took a step closer to me. "Imagine what else you can do inside someone's memory?"

"I don't want to."

A few more steps closer. "Want to what?"

"Whatever you want me to do." Now it was my turn to take a step toward him. "If you force me to use my powers, then you're no better than those fuckers at The Lab that tortured all of us."

Somehow the old man's face became whiter than a sheet. "That's what you think?"

"It's one thing to teach me how to move stuff with my mind, but it's another to push me to see how far I can go."

"But don't you want to see what you can do?"

"If I could, I'd give it all up so I could be normal."

"Talitha," Widmore sputtered. "That's blasphemous."

"*We're blasphemous,*" I nearly screeched the words. "Jonas made us this way. Just because you've lived long enough that you're too powerful for him to capture doesn't mean that I want to be in some war."

"A war?"

"Why else would he make us?" I turned back to my friends. "Phoenix can light someone on fire, Frozenstar locks you in ice, Fidget can move through walls, and Siren can torture with his voice." Then I looked back at Widmore. "And me, who can trick a human into killing his fellow soldiers. What else would be the purpose of making us, than to start World War III, and I'll have no part of it." I reached out to Widmore. "Now give me the book."

The ends of his mouth curled. "Why should I?"

The lights flickered above us.

He chuckled. "Like I said before, you can't scare me, Talitha."

"This will."

Before Widmore could say another word, I went to the long white corridor in my head and searched for his door. It was made of steel, concrete, and a hundred locks, but all I had to do was touch the door handle to open it. His movie theater, aka brain, was musty, like an old bookstore, and as I suspected when I made it to the projection room, there was more film than I'd ever seen. Tin canisters stacked as high as I could see, some covered in dust and spiderwebs, with cells that were so brittle a mere thought could turn them to dust. *Edge of Seventeen* played inside the projection room; the decor matched the era as well, with shades of avocado and mustard. But I didn't give myself time to wonder why he was such a big fan of the nineteen seventies.

Reels were stacked so high and tight there was barely enough room for the three-legged stool that was next to the projector. I hit pause on his projector, the bio pic of his life that was playing on the screen froze. I took the spool of film out of the projector, setting Widmore's present aside as I inserted the oldest reel I could find. I hit rewind, the film started to spark, and Stevie's voice faltered on the second chorus. A sign of a man that didn't ponder the past often.

I turned the film by hand; it was so brittle that I worried the memory might dissolve from the oils in my hands. The memory had to be over half a century old, and was verified once I saw the house that Widmore lived in. A hut, really made of stone and mud, that was in the distance from a grand castle surrounded by sprawling fields. Widmore looked in his early twenties with dark brown hair with a slight curl, a jaw that could be used for geometry class, and a handsome face devoid of wrinkles. His trousers were stained at the bottom from dirt as he tied up a lone horse in front of the hut. Three children rushed out, all wearing clothes made of the same burlap type fabric that Widmore's clothing was made of. Sans buttons and zippers, I wondered how he got it on when I noticed the sandpaper-soft bows on his shoulders as he picked up his daughter. However long ago this was, Widmore and his children would tie their clothes on and had no running water, which explained the aroma that shrouded me as I stepped closer to Young Widmore, who spun around his daughter in the air. She giggled as her gray skirt spun in the air, her boots appeared to be made of hide, and were tied to her tiny feet. She, too, had dark curls but had eyes as bright and wide as a doll.

Whatever language they were speaking, I assumed it was French, although only a few words sounded slightly similar to ones that Carl had spoken. *Widmore's so old even the French language has evolved since he became immortal,* I realized as a woman pushed aside the hide from the narrow opening in the front of the hut. She was holding a book, with a quick scan I assumed it was the Bible, considering the ornate cross on the front. A chicken followed after her and I knew why: Widmore's wife was the in-person interpretation of a storybook princess. Her smile was bright, her chocolate hair braided and away from her face, save the few tendrils that escaped and brushed against her milky skin. Her cheeks were cherry red, a smile so bright it nearly camouflaged her crooked teeth.

*Guess braces weren't a thing in medieval times,* I pondered as Widmore set his daughter back onto the ground and moved over to his wife. He murmured something that I couldn't translate until I read Young Widmore's mind, *Isolde, you are the sun and the moon.*

She returned with, *And you, Gustav, are my earth.*

I watched them long enough to see them share a meal. Although, I couldn't identify the lumps of protein that Isolde ladled from the cast iron pot above the fire and set in a large polished wooden bowl in front of her family. After a quick prayer, they each pulled off a piece of the fresh loaf of bread Isolde had removed from the fire as well, and used it to spoon the mush in the bowls into their mouths. There were no napkins, although there was little slosh of either the dinner or the unidentified deep purple liquid in each of their mugs.

While it was odd to travel back in time, what was stranger was seeing Widmore smile. This was a person I'd never seen before, and for a second, I wondered if in fact Widmore wasn't truly immortal, because he was once this man with a family and now, he had not even a trace of this joy and an aged body.

*A part of him is dead, and can only live on here, in this movie reel*, I realized as I paused the movie. With the gentlest touch, I took out the frames I found, then wound what was left back on the spool. I tucked the extracted footage in my pocket before, stood up as I returned the present back onto Widmore's projector and was about to hit play when a canister that was devoid of dust caught my eye. I reached out just to the left of the projector, chastising myself for not noticing the canister that he kept so close first. However, I couldn't spend much longer in Widmore's memory or they'd notice my leaving, but I memorized the name written in black marker across the piece of tape adhered to the top of the canister. I returned the memory back and hit play on Widmore's bio-pic so the present would be displayed on the screen in front of me.

Back in my bedroom at The Manor, Widmore stood about five feet from me, still holding Carl's sketchbook when I returned to October 16, 2020.

"I'm still waiting to be scared by you, Talitha." He had a Cheshire smile that mocked me.

Which I returned with my own. "Were you married before?"

The smile didn't disappear, but it started to fade. "Before?"

"Before Jonas injected you with the serum?" My grin became more pronounced as his gray eyes flicked to the left, rewinding his reel, and finding that fifteen years of his life was gone. It had been replaced with the classic song on repeat, so at least Stevie's enchanting voice would bring him solace. My bedroom grew dark and cold as Widmore tried to recall his wife's long locks, her voice, and her name.

"What about your children?" I took a step closer, the tension in the room rising. "Was it twin boys and a girl, or twin girls and a boy?"

"That's beyond cruel, Talitha." His words were so soft I almost didn't capture them.

"Isn't that what you wanted? For me to see what I could do?" I reached for the sketchbook. Only then did I see tears streaming down Widmore's face. "And now I know that you might try to hurt me, but I can take even more from you."

He gripped the book as he hissed. "You've already taken my family, what else is there?"

"There was another woman from about thirty years ago, and you called her Cordelia?" Widmore's eyes widened larger than a saucer as I continued to whisper, "You had so many reels, but there was only one that you seemed to revisit. Didn't have time to get too deep into the memory, but I know you loved her." I ripped the sketchbook from his hands. "And no one will ever love you as Cordelia did again, so don't make me take her away from you."

I didn't wait for Widmore to respond, much less ask for his wife and family back, before I turned back to my friends. Each of them was still as a statue. All their Auras had a Yellow center—they were scared of me, too. But none of them mattered to me as much as Carl, whose Aura held a steadfast Azure. We locked eyes, and I handed him back his sketchbook.

He didn't open his mouth, just thought, *Thank you.*

And I responded in his head with, *Je serai toujours à toi.*

After our fight, Widmore took me to his office and practically tossed me into the green velvet chair across from his desk, and I shouted, "You have us locked in a cage here, too."

"Are you insinuating that I'm no better than the men that sliced you like an animal to watch Reed heal you?"

"Almost," I hissed the word, remembering the blade piercing my skin so deep that I couldn't heal myself. Reed became Frankenstein, and I became his monster.

"I'm so strict to keep you safe," Widmore's voice became a murmur. "I want to keep you all safe."

I leaned forward in Widmore's nonexistent chair in his absent office. Everything about Widmore was fake. All I could hope was that his desire to keep us safe was not as inauthentic as the environment in which he thrived. "When I met Carl, I hadn't been living, not really, for so very long, and now that I am, I can't go back."

"Reed is dead because of your desire for freedom."

"No, Reed is dead because Jonas is a sick and twisted psychopath with a God complex." I shook my head. "I can't go back to the way it was, and if that's not cool with you, then Carl and I can leave."

"And go where?"

I shrugged. "Guess we'll figure that out."

"So, you're going to spend the rest of your existence on the run?"

"Better than being a prisoner here."

Widmore looked at me from over the top of his glasses. "And what could I do to get you to stay?"

"Stop telling me what to do." My Gray Swirling Ash Aura was filled with Fiery Red.

He nodded. "I got that already. What else?"

I rose an eyebrow at him. "What are you offering?"

His Aura shifted, but I was so filled with fury at the time I didn't catch it until I replayed this conversation much later. "An evening at a club in D.C. might be something we can try."

"Really?" I let my guard fall, the three layers of concrete shielding my grey matter from Widmore began to falter.

"It's a Thursday night; the clubs won't be that full. I believe that you're strong enough to protect your friends, correct?"

I sat on the edge of my seat, like an eager student that had the right answer. "I can bring them into my fog."

"Have you brought five people into your fog before?"

I cocked an eyebrow at him. "You want me to prove I can do it before we go?"

"No, I trust you, Talitha." A smile covered his face and had the same effect as having a warm blanket wrapped around me. "I just want to make sure that this is something you want. It will be very dangerous." He started fiddling with the newspapers on his desk as his Aura Flickered so quickly I missed it the first time because he'd wormed into my mind and slightly glamoured me.

"I'm bringing a guy that can burn the whole city down if we need to." My Aura had returned to the Swirling Gray Smoke as I nearly chuckled, filled with a confidence that Widmore gave me.

"If the Flashing Reds find you," Widmore built a screen in my head, and visually directed me as he verbalized his plan, "Make a copy of yourself, and insert it into your friends' memory reels. Go into their movie theater tonight if you need to, just like you did with mine when you found my wife. Give the copy some basic functions in the minds of your friends and Carl to direct them away, and *you* run the opposite way, directing the Flashing Reds away from the group. The Flashing Reds will chase after you because you're the most powerful. If you make your friends think you're with them, then they'll escape to the safety of The Manor, giving you the opportunity to escape into your fog, and I'll come to find you."

I nodded. "Sounds like a perfect plan."

"When one has lived as long as me, they have plenty of time to plan. You understand that you might have to sacrifice yourself?"

As I nodded, a Pastel Yellow began to overpower Widmore's Aura. In hindsight, I should have interpreted it not as a fear for what might happen, because once the night was over, it was as if he'd predicted the outcome. But at the time, I was beyond cocky, powerful enough to make someone in a memory real. I had infused my boyfriend with telepathic energy without hurting him. Hell, I'd even stolen memories from Widmore himself and was now able to shield myself from him. If I'd been smart enough to see past myself, I'd have seen that Widmore wasn't afraid *of* me but afraid *for* me.

But at the time, I was simply exhilarated for a night out, not contemplating how odd Widmore was acting.

# Phoenix
## 10/16/2025 9:55 PM

Talitha's laugh from the far end of the Metro car sounded nearly as beautiful as a sunset looked, only she was smiling at that *pendejo*.

"*Cálmese*," my sister murmured into my ear.

"I'm fine."

Silver and light blue glitter clung to her dark eyelashes as she rolled her eyes. "I'm just worried you're going to set *estúpido* on fire."

"Not when he's that close to her."

"Guess you're not as dumb as I thought." Frozenstar got up from the bench we occupied as the car slowed down to a stop.

"What do you know about it?" I huffed as I stood next to her as the doors opened.

"We're twins; I know what you think before you do."

"No, you don't." My teeth gritted as Carl's hand moved down from the small of Talitha's back to her butt. I couldn't get out of the Metro car fast enough. Bodies pressed against us, locals going out on a Thursday night to clubs and bars, and the occasional tourist complaint about how much they had to walk.

"I know once guns started going off at The Lab," Frozenstar

matched her pace with mine, "you started screaming her name and banging on the door."

"I thought she could get us out." I looked toward the escalators that rose up out of the concrete tunnel and to the busy street.

"*Mierda*, you didn't even know it was her getting them to shoot each other." Her dark eyes locked with mine. "You can lie to yourself, but you can't lie to me. You have to tell her how you feel."

"She's happy." I shrugged as we exited the Metro station, stepping off the top of the escalator and carving our way to the 9:30 Club through the crowd. *I can't remember the last time I was around this many people*, I thought as the wind tunneling through the buildings wrapped around me. Part of me was euphoric, to be out of the Manor and out in the real world. However, that part was battling with the keen fighter that I'd transformed myself into after being imprisoned by either Widmore or The Lab for nearly my entire life. *Everyone around us could be a potential enemy and should be treated as such*, the voice inside my head kept reminding me as Frozenstar and I traversed through the streets. While my heart told me, *this is what normal twenty-six-year-old men are doing with their evenings.*

"So, you're okay with a stranger making love to your girl every night?" My sister's question brought me from contemplation back to reality.

"*Cállate la boca*, shut the hell up." I turned left and my sister kept up with my pace, although I sped up half a step with each passing minute, unaware that the rest of the group lagged so far behind us.

"You know The Lab will come back for her, and you can protect her, but Carl can't," Frozenstar's voice was low and fast as the group caught up with us. "You know I'm right, and sure she might be happy, but it's not practical to be with a Non-Enhanced."

We were the first in our group to make it to the 800 block of V Street, although there was already a dozen or so people waiting for their turn to enter. Neon lights flashed each time the door swung open, but only the bouncer got the blast of heat as everyone else wrapped their jackets tighter around them. I was the only one impervious to the cold. "If she's with us, then she's safe."

"You need to tell her before it's too late," Frozenstar insisted.

Talitha was close enough now that I could take her hand and pull her to me. But Carl's hands were all over her. In my head, I replaced them with my own. Talitha would kiss me back, rub on my bald head, wrap her arms around me, and beg me to fuck her. She'd tell me that she'd be mine forever because that's what I'd give her. Forever and ever and whatever came after that. I forced my mind to clear as her blue eyes danced over me, still smiling at whatever Carl had whispered. Talitha usually kept everyone on mute, but her cheeks reddened. Our eyes met, and I felt a sudden pain in my temple. But the sharp edge dissipated just as quickly as it came. DJ Khaled played from the speakers above us, and Justin Bieber started singing just as the line moved, and my sister essentially pushed me inside.

# Talitha
## 10/16/2020 9:55 PM

We swayed as the Metro moved beneath the city. I could feel Phoenix's eyes on me, hear his sister tell him to calm down in Spanish, but steered clear of their thoughts as I concentrated on my boyfriend and his utter lack of knowledge of pop music. "What do you mean you've never heard it?"

"I swear I've never heard it."

"How is that possible, that I've heard Justin and Ariana's duet and I've been either a prisoner or on the run for the past six years while you haven't?"

He smiled down at me. "Just lucky, I guess?"

I laughed as the Metro stopped, and Carl pushed through the crowd to make space for me to exit. The moon hung above us, yet was barely visible through all the light pollution once we made our way up the escalator from the underground and onto the busy city streets of D.C. Usually, my mind would have been on overload. Yet, it was easy to turn off everything else and focus only on Carl. I was a ship lost at sea, and he was my lighthouse on the horizon. "So, you just admire her assets?"

His hand squeezed my butt. "I think you have some similarities to her."

I laughed as he leaned down and kissed me. Cars honked, people chatted, and even Fidget called out for us to hurry up, but I spliced *Stuck With U* into Carl's mind, giving us a soundtrack to our make-out.

He tucked a lock of hair behind my ear. His hands were cold, but not nearly as cold as my cheek. "You're right. It's a good song."

I grinned up at him. "I'm always right."

"Talitha!" Fidget stomped her foot behind me. Her Aura had turned Crimson. "This was your idea, and the rest of us want to get laid tonight too, so if you could keep your mind clear long enough for that to happen…"

Siren was behind her; his Aura matched Fidget's in tone with his arms crossed over his chest. "Sorry," I muttered as I took my arms from around Carl's neck and followed them to the line outside the club.

"When we get back to Baltimore," Carl bent his head down to my ear as Phoenix and Frozenstar came into view at the back of the line, "I'm going to strip you naked and kiss every inch of your body."

"That a promise?" I started giggling at first as Carl and I made our way to the 800 block of V street and joined the twins at the end of the line. I felt the joy fill my body until Phoenix's jealousy rattled in my head, forcing himself off mute. In his thoughts, Phoenix's hands moved over me. Each was finding their way over the few curves I had, ripping off my clothes. And in his fantasy, I begged him to fuck me. Phoenix promised me forever, and ever, and whatever came after that. The hair on the back of my neck stood up, and I felt all the blood in my body rush to my head as I banished Phoenix from my mind. I might have pushed him out too hard because Phoenix brought his hand to his temple and winced. We locked eyes, and before he had a chance to think my name, I ejected from his thoughts and poured concrete over my grey matter just as the song playing in the speakers outside of the club changed.

"Wait, isn't this Bieber too?" Carl chuckled as he pointed up at the speakers hanging above the front door of the club. "I swear I've heard him more since I met you than in my entire life."

"You're welcome." And I laced my fingers with Carl's after the bouncer stamped my hand and I pulled open the glass door and entered a whole new world known as the 9:30 Club.

The ambiance was just as vibrant as *The Mother We Share*, the song that played inside the club. The club was full of life, a far cry from the sad tan brick building that gave no sign as to the fun inside. Five hundred prisms' worth of color reflected on every surface, including the stage right in front of us that housed a local DJ on Mixtape night. Each Aura from the dancing people bounced back, rattling inside my head like there was a mirror in the center of my brain. Each of the hundreds of Auras ranged from Neon Green to a Deep Burgundy that nearly matched the leather that adorned the couches that lined the club's perimeter.

Carl nodded at me. "Whiskey neat?"

"Yeah, make it a double."

He cocked an eyebrow. "You, okay?"

I nodded. "Just trying to, you know, see everything all at once." Which was true, as I stretched out my mind as you'd do with a sweater that was accidentally put in the dryer. Expanding my vision beyond Carl's worries and Phoenix's continued dream of fucking me, I mentally traveled up into the atmosphere. Each Aura acted like a blink on my radar, allowing me to create a map of a five-block radius that I could view as if I were a bird. Which at current was void of any Red Flashing Auras, and the exact tone of Royal Purple that the Feds had.

"Take a sec." He nodded toward a corner that was devoid of people. "I'll meet you there with your drink."

I squeezed his hand before I made my way through the crowd and went into the bathroom to splash some water on my face, only now realizing what I'd promised to everyone. It hadn't been that hard when it was just me, but now I had to keep an eye on five other people, two of whom couldn't stop thinking about how bad they wanted to fuck me. All I wanted to do was put everyone on mute, come down from the sky watching the block, and just make out with my boyfriend. *No matter where I am, I'm in a cage,* I contemplated as I looked at myself in the mirror. My eyeliner had smudged, and it only made me look slightly less like a raccoon when I wiped it away with a paper towel. Strands of hair stuck to my forehead, my pupils had started to turn from light blue to red. I wore only black. The only color beyond my eyes were the ruby studs in my ears, yet another bit of brightness competing for attention.

I closed my eyes and took in a deep breath, and when I exhaled, all the colors stopped moving and filed themselves very neatly in my brain. It was as if I'd finally found the page numbers and was able to collate the documents and store them correctly in amongst everything inside of me. When I opened my eyes, the colors started to move again, but now it was more like a game of chess; between their thoughts and Auras, I knew what the next three moves of everyone would be. Which is why I not only knew whose Baby Pink Aura was waiting from me on the other side of the door, but what he wanted to say. I tried ignoring him, simply walking past, back toward the corner that Carl was moving toward with my drink.

Phoenix shifted to the left, blocking my way out of the narrow hallway from the lady's room to the dancefloor and bar. "Litha, can I talk to you?"

"I already know what you're going to say, but you're too late."

"How can that be when I've known you for sixteen years?" His hand reached out to touch me, my body reacted like he had flames on the ends of his fingers, and my back pressed against the wall as he continued, "Litha, I've been in love with you for sixteen years."

I shook my head, but his emotions ran so high I couldn't block out flashes of the past sixteen years that ran through his mind. Each smile I sent his way he interpreted as a promise, each hug an invitation, and now with Reed dead, my return proved to Phoenix that we were destiny. Phoenix's mouth found my ear, "Every woman I've been with, I pretended she was you."

I wanted to sarcastically say, *'that's romantic,'* but instead, I found my body reverted to the third and less-mentioned basic instinct: freeze. Phoenix pressed his body into mine, his breath on my skin, the lights from the club glittering off his chain and shiny shaved head as Lil Baby flowed through the speakers. Phoenix had more hands than an octopus. One gripped onto my butt, another with a fist full of hair, another running up my thigh, and the tips of his fingers grazed just above my belly button. A stranger would have assumed we were lovers, but my soul was being crushed the tighter he gripped.

"Please stop," I murmured as my Swirling Gray Smoke seemed to dissipate rather than strengthen, as if Phoenix were extracting my energy.

The center of his Aura Bubbled Black, like oil pouring out of his chest. "I want to be more, I need to be more." His chocolate eyes charted my face.

"I can't."

"Because of Carl? He'll never understand you." He rested his forehead on mine, his hands still moving over me. "Not like I do."

"Just stop, okay?"

"Are you going to make me go my whole life without making love to you?"

A switch flipped in my head, and my Aura rebounded at full force. "You're asking to rape me?"

The Black Oil in his Aura started to free flow, his hips dug into mine. "I'd never do that."

"That's what you'd have to do because I'm never going to sleep with you." The energy inside of me formed into bolts of lightning and sparked in my Aura. The bolts took over when I nearly growled, "I don't love you, Phoenix."

"Yes, you do, Litha."

"I'm not sure I even *like* you anymore after this."

"I'll love you enough for the both of us then," Phoenix murmured before he stuck his tongue in my mouth.

It happened so suddenly I couldn't have stopped it if I wanted to. Which I didn't because I wanted to hurt him, make him feel as trapped and scared as I was. I would protect him from the Flashing Reds because Phoenix was Enhanced like me, but as he sucked on my bottom lip, I lost any compassion I had for him. A light, as bright as the corridor in my head, lit up between Phoenix and me. My energy pulsated, but instead of gently infusing it into him as I do with Carl, I let it push against Phoenix. He was thrown against the wall leaving a dent in the plaster. Phoenix righted himself, his hand shot up to the back of his head and cussed in Spanish. With the flick of my chin, Phoenix's attention was brought to his crotch because I'd used my telepathy to kick him in the balls. I clipped out the frames in any of the clubgoers' memories that involved Phoenix as I trudged back through the crowd. Back to the Blue Aura waiting for me in the corner. Without a word, I took my drink from Carl's hand, tilted my head back, and let the whisky drain down my throat.

"What's wrong?" Carl asked.

I took his drink too, not sure what it was, and drank it as well.

"What happened?"

"Nothing." I shook my head and turned back toward the bar. "I need another one."

He held onto my arm and pulled me back. "Talitha, you're shaking."

"Some asshole kissed me." The moment the words left my lips, I instantly wished that one of my superpowers was the ability to lie to Carl.

"Someone kissed you?" His gray-green eyes doubled in size.

*Jesus Christ, I'm so stupid*, I thought. "Don't worry, I used my powers to get him off of me."

"Who was it?" His brows furrowed, then his eyes left mine and charted the club.

I took his chin in my hand and moved his face back to mine. "Please just let it go. I don't want to erase you kicking some guy's ass out of everyone's memory."

Every muscle in his body was tense. "I know you don't want me to get into a fight, but I can't just let this go."

"Carl, forget it." I put my hand to his temple.

"Don't erase my mind because we're fighting." He pulled away from me. "And I'm not going to let some creep get away with assaulting *my* girlfriend."

I nearly pushed Carl against the wall with the bolts of electricity in my Aura. "So, it's not because of my honor. It's because I'm your property?"

"No, no, no." Carl shook his head frantically, his voice so soft I might have been hearing his thoughts. "Talitha, I know I can't protect you from The Lab, but after what you showed me, with your father. I want to protect you from guys like that."

His Blue Aura swirled with mine like custard removing all my anger. "I know."

"Just point the asshole out and let me be your knight in shining armor."

"I took care of him, and I'm safe with you now." I brought my hand up to his temple.

His head snapped back. "*Don't* erase my memory."

"I'm not. Just come with me for a second."

He didn't move, just kept looking at me. It broke my heart a little because I could hear the thoughts in his mind weighing what his next move should be.

"You trust me, right?"

He tilted his head down and brought my hand back up to his temple, giving me the opportunity to empty out the club in his mind.

There wasn't a single soul, not even my friends, but the music continued to play, although I was the DJ now. While the dance floor appeared empty, all the lights continued to refract rainbows all over the space. I took Carl's hand and pulled him out to the center of the dance floor. I put his hands on my hips, my arms draped around his neck, and turned on the music to *The Night We Met*, the most romantic non-Justin Bieber song I could think of on the fly.

We swayed side to side wordlessly to the song until the bridge when he asked, "You're okay?"

"When I'm with you." I would have wallowed in his Ocean Blue Aura longer if I knew that all of this was about to end.

I rested my head on his chest as we danced, not realizing then how often I'd return to this exact moment, the very last in which I felt safe. To remember what it was like to be held by the only living creature that I knew would never betray me. Carl was not just my North, but the whole damn compass. At the time, I was at the peak of joy, so calm I could hear Carl's beating heart with my ear pressed to his chest.

Or I was until I realized that wasn't Carl's heart, but the thoughts of the Flashing Red men rattling in my head.

# Talitha
10/16/2020 11:57 PM

"Follow me," I insisted as I brought Carl back to reality, and just as quickly pulled him to the front of the club and out the door. The Flashing Reds made a right, so we turned left down an alley, and I set off a signal, like pulling a fire alarm that only my friends could hear. Once I got all their attention with the telepathic text message of *'they're here',* I made a map of the area appear in my friends' minds, with an 'X' where Carl and I stood. The Chemical Brothers halted mid-song and Siren had the opportunity to display his power, forcing any Non-Enhanced that weren't already running away at full speed to flee. The sound that Siren emitted was a mixture between a baby screaming, guitar feedback, and an injured animal wailing as it clung to life.

Carl's hands rose to his ears. "Jesus Christ, what is that noise!"

"It's Siren, come on!" I yanked on Carl's hand and brought him to the back of the building.

Fidget was the first at our side. As she walked through the walls of the club, she pulled Siren behind her, who promptly became a mute again once outside.

"This way," I commanded as we ran through the alley to the next block. I can't explain it, even now, but I could feel the power rise inside me, a slow burn that started in my brain with trails of electricity sparking inside and filtering down my body.

The Auras of every club-goer became muffled by the Flashing Reds. Frozenstar crawled out of a bathroom window. Phoenix was right behind her, and their stride fell in line with the rest of ours.

"Here." I stopped short in front of an abandoned and graffitied office building with all its windows boarded up. A metal chain with a rusted lock kept us outside until Frozenstar raised her hand above the rusted metal, her palm emitting an incandescent glow which froze the metal. With a snap of my fingers, the lock and chain shattered into shards of ice and we were inside. I didn't take time to check out the dark abandoned room full of cubicles, just rushed my friends inside.

The Flashing Reds were one hundred feet behind us.

Siren made it past the threshold before Carl slammed shut the door and the boys started pushing desks, chairs, and even tossed a few ancient computers in front of it.

But the Flashing Reds were closing in.

"Fuck," I muttered, barely remembering the last time I ate. Even if I felt a surge of energy fill me up because of fear, it wouldn't last long if I had no fuel.

"Where are they?" Frozenstar cried.

"Widmore was right, they're going to get us." Fidget started biting her nails.

Siren, Carl, and Phoenix turned to me, the last of which nearly snarled when he said, "You promised you'd keep us safe."

I reached out my hand to Phoenix, because even if I currently loathed him, we were the same and I had to protect him from the horde of Flashing Reds that were just outside the door. "I can do it." And I knew I could bring them into my fog, even if I'd never done it before. The power building up inside of me told me I could. "Close your eyes," I added.

When they opened their eyes, we were in the bright white corridor with an endless number of doors. The five of them were circled around me when they started questioning me.

"Holy shit, where are we?" Fidget whimpered.

"Did you kill us?" Phoenix gritted his teeth.

"Why can't I feel the floor?" Carl asked.

"I can't," Frozenstar started to hyperventilate, "catch my breath."

"Everyone shut up," I insisted, and their minds fell silent. Well, all except Frozenstar, which made me roll my eyes. "There's no air in here." I pushed my way through the group and rushed over to the door made of driftwood, which I flung open, and nodded my head toward. "C'mon, through here."

"What the fuck is that?" Phoenix's eyes had doubled in size as he looked at my fog, a thick gray smoke with bolts of electricity that randomly sparked.

"It's like the center of my brain. We'll be safe here."

Carl came forward and was the first to step in, and once inside he almost immediately disappeared amongst the dense atmosphere. There was a mutter, and all their Auras Sparked Yellow in the center, but they all followed Carl inside. I'd never had anyone in my fog before, much less five people, and their thoughts swirled loudly. They were all highly concerned about how we had begun in the real world being chased by cops, what was up with the endless hallway of doors, and if the swirling fog was poisonous. I knew I'd never be able to get them to shut up completely, nor would I be able to put them on mute, so instead I stretched my mind even further. The fog began to clear, and they could see we were still in the abandoned office, just shielded. They grappled with the fact that we were in another dimension of sorts, behind a one-way mirror, and just about the time their minds began to settle everything went to hell.

There was a boom and the furniture that the boys pushed against the door blew out at us. A chair should have impaled Phoenix, a table leg snapped off right where Fidget was standing, and a computer came crashing down on my head. But in my fog, we were protected, dissolving the objects before they could touch us. No implement of death would be able to break through my fog. Red Flashing lights penetrated the room, moving like trained military men making sure that every inch of the room was clear. Without having to say a word the five of them huddled around me. Carl stood on my right side, while Phoenix was on my left.

"Is this how you see the world?" Carl murmured as the Feds walked in coated in their Deep Purple Aura.

I nodded, then put my finger to my lips, not because the Deep Purples or Flashing Reds could hear them, but so I could concentrate. As the soldiers now moved into the center of the room after finding it clear, their Flashing Red Auras tried to break into my fog, but they were stung with a bolt of electricity, unable to find the source. The men didn't realize it, but it would be impossible for them to come into my fog, now with a membrane strong enough to encapsulate us. As long as I could keep it up, we'd be safe. I felt the surge inside me waver as the thought, *I need to eat soon,* crossed through me. The soldier's mouths were moving, so I took them off mute, and their conversation began to play out as if there were on a speaker above us.

"No one's here, sir," Flashing Red said to his boss who had entered the space. He had an Orange center that vibrated out to Neon Red.

"You're telling me you let a bunch of mutant terrorists get away?" Boss' Aura began to glow Stop Sign Red. "You know one of them could burn down the entire Capital, and another could walk through The White House walls like a ghost, so I understand why you're scared, but all we want is the blonde girl."

Flashing Red holstered his gun. "But didn't she kill all those soldiers?"

Stop Sign Red smiled, and I felt the hair on the back of my neck prick up, the electricity in the fog began to rise, causing so much static that all our hair began to float against gravity. "That's why we're going to knock her out first." He tapped on Flashing Red's helmet. "If she's unconscious, then being able to get into someone's memory isn't much of a superpower."

Carl laced his fingers with mine and squeezed.

The Flashing Red team filtered out of the warehouse. Stop Sign Red's eyes scanned the space, and for a while lingered on me as if he could see through my fog. I waited until the Flashing Reds and Deep Purples all moved to the end of the block, heading West back toward the Metro. Which left the bus station open for us. It was slower, but then we could head to Metro Center right before it closed and make it back to Baltimore. That's the plan I telepathically shared with my friends and

Carl as we returned from the fog, through the endless white corridor, and back to the abounded building in D.C.

My friends ran off using the directions I'd telepathically given them. And while Carl thought his fingers were laced with mine, it was a trick of the mind. I did what Widmore instructed, and sent a clone of myself with my friends. The Flashing Reds would follow the real me, who'd be easy to track because I'd be using my powers. *They only want me, so if I'm not with them then they'll be safe,* I thought to myself as I ran right while my friends went left. Once again, I ran through the streets of a metropolitan city all alone, being chased by those that wished to hurt me.

Three blocks away, I found a fire escape and began to climb up to the roof of the warehouse. I'd wait until my friends made it to the bus station safely, then the real me would follow them back to The Manor. But I wasn't used to keeping so many people in my head at once. All their Auras mingled as one, their worst fears of being returned to The Lab ignited in their brains and making it nearly impossible to put my friends on mute. So, when I was a quarter of the way down the fire escape, I heard the thoughts of the Flashing Reds before I saw their Auras, I was so distracted.

I jumped down and ran in the opposite direction of the sound.

My feet found it easy to recall my pace once again, speeding away from the Flashing Red lights that swarmed the building, trying not to read their minds to find out what they had in store for me. Although I couldn't do it, because the Flashing Reds kept reminding themselves that they *had more drugs than the Mexican Mafia and that's what will keep us alive.* Each carried two syringes filled with enough tranquilizers to kill even the most addicted pop star. All the Flashing Reds were tittering about the man that I was going to meet, a man that they'd only heard of, and I could tell by their excitement that whoever it was didn't need any drugs to control me.

I tried to focus on the map of the world in which the real me was inhabiting, not the copy that was still holding Carl's hand as they made it onto a bus headed toward the Metro. But that proved difficult because I wanted more than anything to be with him for my last moments. *Almost makes me jealous of a telepathic trick.*

The copy of me smiled at Carl and kissed him one final time and, whispered, 'I love you', knowing that he was safe. To conserve energy, I dissolved the clone while the real me continued to run through the back alleys of D.C. as the Flashing Reds surrounded me. No matter which way I turned, I would end up running directly into their trap. I made three lefts and went right back up the fire escape that I'd come down, because I had no other choice but to backtrack.

Four flights up and I crawled through the window of an apartment and rushed through the floor, using my telepathy to open doors and push aside residents until I reached the North side of the building. Once I reached a window on the far side, I was able to jump down to the roof of a 24-hour laundromat. It had only now occurred to me to reach out to Widmore, but when I turned on the walkie-talkie inside my head that leads directly to his and screamed inside of it, all I got in return was static. Which scared me even more, because he promised to never turn it off.

I sent off a flare that would be like a fourth of July firework display in Widmore's head, typed a dozen frantic telepathic text messages, but did not get a single response. But I didn't have time to worry about why he wasn't responding to me, because as I made it to the edge of the roof, I realized the Flashing Reds were below me. They'd surrounded the building, and I could see the Deep Purples make a radius outside of them.

"Fuck," I muttered then closed my eyes and went to the endless white corridor. I ran to the driftwood door, pulled on the handle, but it didn't open. I pressed the bottom of my sneaker against the wall, gripped the handle with both hands, and pushed my leg hoping to get the door to my fog open.

I hadn't eaten for hours and exerted so much energy already, I couldn't get into my fog.

Without a choice I returned to the roof. No matter which side I went to, Flashing Reds were below it, but they didn't breach because they'd been instructed not to. Someone else was there, and I felt a tremor through my body because he was not surrounded by Yellow, Green, Red, or even Black. Nor could I read his thoughts. There wasn't even a Shimming hue of Crystal that I'd seen before in people that were about to die. Whoever was walking up the stairs toward me had no Aura, and all the Flashing Reds turned Brighter than a Christmas tree. It was then that I realized it was over. Whatever they had in store for me, I knew it was about to begin now, and I didn't have enough energy to get into my fog, so what little hope I did have for my salvation was gone.

I'd been running for over two years, and now I was caught.

Then the man with no Aura, someone I'd only ever seen in my nightmares, joined me on the roof, jumping down from the same window I'd used. His skin was as dark as Reed's, he was nearly as tall as Carl, dressed in a three-piece gray suit, with eyes that were black in the middle with a fiery red rim, making him appear closer to a snake than a man. Although that wasn't what caught my attention, even past his lack of Aura, it was that he was hovering above the ground. Floating like an angel, or a spirit. His mind was a steel trap, unable for me to penetrate, as were his memories, although I knew exactly who he was. He had many names: Enhanced Being One, The Creator, CEO of Wakefield Laboratories, but I'd always thought of him as simply the terrorist asshole that killed my boyfriend.

"Hello, Eight Fifteen." Jonas smiled at me with white teeth that reminded me of a shark.

"Always wondered what a psychopath's Aura looked like, but it's as empty as your soul."

He made a sound that could be called a laugh, but it sent a chill up my spine. "One Eleven said that you were timid, I see time on your own has changed you."

I narrowed my eyes at Jonas. "You spoke to Reed?"

Jonas floated closer to me, hovering within arm's reach. "Who do you think instructed him to resurrect a platoon of my soldiers mere hours after he brought you back to life?" And maybe it was his lack of Aura that filtered through mine.

My limbs felt weighed down.

His words continued and were soft in tone like a secret. "I know he wasn't able to get all the scars to disappear before he died, so at least you have that memory of his sacrifice covering your skin."

I wanted to yell at Jonas, scream, but I couldn't find the words. My eyelids grew heavy, my knees bent, and I collapsed onto the roof. The only part of me that seemed to work at full capacity was my imagination, filtering through thousands of memories I had with Reed. "You killed him," was all I could get out. I felt so weak, I could have been carried away on the wind.

"Survival of the fittest." Jonas hovered above me, and even though the city was full of light pollution, everything turned black on the edges as his face neared mine. "Especially when it comes to you, Eight Fifteen." He reached out to me, cradling my face in his hand. And while I wanted to pull away, throw him off the top of the building, scream for help, I couldn't. His touch took what energy I had left, as if he were singing me a lullaby. "He always thought One Eleven was the answer, but I've always known it was you Eight Fifteen. After all, we're the only three telepaths that have ever existed."

I wanted to ask him to repeat himself, because it kinda sounded like Widmore was working with Jonas. After all, Widmore was the one who told me that I was the first telepath that had been created since Widmore had been given the serum. Instead, sleep took hold of me harder than any emotion, even fear, dimming a memory in me for the first time in my life. My momentary realization that Widmore had betrayed me was lost between Jonas' hypnotic powers and the drugs the Flashing Reds were about to inject into me. Widmore had only ever lied to me, which not only had brought me to this very moment, at Jonas' feet, but also brought about the Reed's death. The thought remained hidden in the depths of what would take place over the next few days, only to be remembered when it was far too late for me.

# CARL
## 10/17/2020 12:55 AM

She'd been gripping onto my hand ever since we stopped dancing to *The Night We Met*, and moments after we found seats she was gone.

"Talitha!" I yelled, standing up so I could look around the bus, but there were only four other passengers. "Where'd she go?" I shouted.

"Young man, you need to sit down," the bus driver called from the front of the bus.

"My girlfriend," and I almost said, *'totally just vanished'* but I couldn't get out the words out.

Phoenix stood up and met my eyes. "We're a block away from the Metro anyway."

The bus stopped and we all got off, but they turned toward Metro Center while I wanted to go back to the 9:30 Club. "Wait, where are you guys going?"

"Back home," Phoenix said, and the other three nodded.

All the sounds of the cars and people on the street went silent, in fact time might have stopped as I took in the nonchalance in Phoenix's stature. "What about Talitha?"

Frozenstar shrugged. "She's the one that made a copy of herself, so obviously she has a plan."

"She could already be at The Manor for all we know," Fidget added.

"Are you guys kidding me? You heard what those cops said, they *wanted her*, and you guys know what they'll do to her when they get her."

"That was her choice not to come with us, so she'll understand our choice not to go after her," Phoenix said.

"But you have superpowers…" I began.

"Yeah, and so does Jonas, even more than all of us combined. *She knows that* and that's why she made herself a distraction." Phoenix shook his head. "I'm in charge of the group now, so I say we go back home because Fidget's right, Talitha will probably beat us there."

I grabbed onto Phoenix's arm before he could go through the doors to the Metro. His skin was hotter than a stovetop, but it only made me hold onto him tighter. "I know you love her too. We have to do something."

"You're going on a suicide mission." Phoenix pushed my hand away. "And don't touch me again."

"Fine." I took a step back from Phoenix. "Then just tell me where they're keeping her and I'll go by myself."

"I burned that place down, probably have someplace new." He smirked at me. "And they'll just shoot you in the head *bendejo* ."

"I don't care, I promised her they'd never get her back." Every time I saw the scars The Lab had given her, I mentally made the promise again. That no one would tear her apart to see what she was made of again. I'd rather they took me, a hundred times over, peeled my skin off, and dipped me in salt, rather than taking her. "I'm not just going to let then use her as a science experiment." My teeth gritted together.

"Good luck with that, *ojete*." Phoenix turned from me and faced his friends, nodding toward the Metro. "C'mon guys I'll take care of you."

Frozenstar smiled, still staring at me, the sounds of the night dimming down as blood rushed in my ears at the look in her eyes. She took a step closer, her crimson smile taking over her face. It gave me a chill. "Can't believe you're asking Phoenix for help, after what he did to Talitha."

"What are you talking about?"

"My brother got a kiss." Frozenstar's beautiful face edged on evil villain as she continued. "Even knows how tight her ass is from firsthand experience."

"What?"

Phoenix shrugged. "A little misunderstanding, no big deal."

"Not like you could get her back anyway." Frozenstar dramatically sighed. "Phoenix will work it out to save her."

Lava filled up my veins as I recalled Talitha's face when she came back from the bathroom only a few hours ago. It was caved in, like she'd eaten something sour, and her bright blue eyes had tiny lightning bolts of red. I couldn't help myself, I grabbed onto Phoenix's tracksuit and pulled him toward me. "You kissed Talitha?"

He cocked an eyebrow at me. "You don't want to do this, Carl."

"I wanted to kick your ass for not wanting to help her, but now..." My voice darkened like the night sky, "I'm going to kill you for touching her."

He sneered at me. "Try it."

I raised my left fist in the air, but before it made contact, Phoenix brought up his palm which was filled with fire. My entire fist was engulfed in flames, the pain so excruciating that my brain wouldn't let me feel it at first. When I released Phoenix, the fire went out, leaving my clenched fist raw from the flesh bubbling.

"Holy shit," I muttered as I held my hand.

"You made him cry, *hermano*," Frozenstar giggled.

"Don't try to follow us," Phoenix hissed. "I know you can find The Manor, but I'll light you up if you do."

"Phoenix," Fidget's voice broke through my internal breakdown, "we can't just leave him here."

"Fine, you stay with him then." Phoenix didn't cast a glance back at me before he walked toward the Metro, Frozenstar and Siren following him.

Fidget took a few steps toward me. "I'm so sorry, Carl."

"Talitha," I moaned, connecting to her green eyes through my tears.

"They're right, she's probably back at home, and if she's not then Widmore will know what to do." The tips of her fingers gingerly examined my fist. "Wrap this up as soon as you can."

"You're seriously going with that asshole?" I spit out the words.

"I don't have another choice." She took her hand back and ran after Phoenix into the Metro.

# Talitha
## UNKNOWN DATE AND TIME

It was eerily quiet after they'd injected me with half a dozen vials of who knows what, stripped me, and redressed me in the teal scrubs they made all the prisoners wear. They didn't shave my head this time, nor had they stuck electrodes to my head and asked me a million questions like last time either. They finally tossed my limp body onto the cot in the cell Reed and I had shared all those years ago.

My only solace was that whenever they were done with me, I'd get to be with Reed again. I don't know how long they'd had me, much less how long since the Flashing Reds triple-locked and bolted the door. I was so high that I couldn't move anything but the tips of my fingers. They brushed against the scratch marks that seemed to move like ants on the wall. Reed made one each morning to count the days of our imprisonment. There were one thousand six hundred and forty-three marks. *Always knew I'd die in this room*, I thought as I tried to get my eyes to focus, and found control of even my most basic motor functions impossible. *Maybe I never left this room?*

But I had met Carl, and I was so glad that I had. That I had one more chance to be in love before I died some horrific death in the basement of The Lab.

The room glowed blue, and at first, I thought it was because I was high, but then I felt someone sit at the end of the cot. A hand reached out and touched my calf and Reed murmured, "Litha."

Reed.

Reed was here with me.

I turned from the wall to face him, as if his touch had broken the spell of barbiturates. However, as my eyes charted his dark skin that looked as smooth as silk, his hair faded close to the scalp, and his eyes clear and chocolate brown, I wondered if they gave me too much. I sat up and reached out for Reed's hand, our fingers interlocking. I brought his hand up to my face and his skin was warm against mine.

"Like the keys of a piano, right?" He smiled at me and his tone was rhythmic with the hint of his Dominican accent.

Every word I wanted to tell him was caught in my throat as my eyes filled up with tears. All that came out was, "Why didn't you come sooner?"

His smiled faded away and he cleared his throat. "I came to say good-bye, because it's my time."

"Time for what?"

"There's something after the never-ending darkness." His eyes fixed with mine. "That's where I'm going now, but I wanted to see you one last time." His hand stroked the side of my face. Nothing felt sweeter than his touch. "I never got to tell you goodbye."

I crumpled like a piece of paper in the hands of a toddler. "No," I managed and shook my head.

"It's time, Litha. You don't need me to watch after you anymore."

"They're going to kill me, Reed, at least stay until they do." I pulled on his arm because if I couldn't have Carl, then I'd take Reed.

"No, they're not. You still have so much else to do."

"Please," I sputtered trying to get my plea out.

But Reed stopped my words when he pressed his lips to mine.

It was the most perfect kiss to have with what was most likely a hallucination as I waited to die. The sparks traveled over every inch of my body, and every kiss we'd had spun like a Rolodex of pictures in my head. From a peck in between classes when we were teenagers, to the first time we made love, to the evening of November 10, 2014, when he set every cell in my body on fire. Our entire epic love story lasted no more than a minute as it cycled through the forefront of my mind.

"That's how I'll live on, in your memory, Litha."

I clutched onto him. "But I want you. I *need* you."

He smiled. "You *need* Carl now."

My breathing stopped. "How do you know about Carl?"

He chuckled, and it sounded sweeter than honey. "You think it was happenstance that you literally ran into the only person on Earth that's Blue?" He threw me a smirk. "And that he just happens to live in Baltimore? Or that your powers have become so much stronger since you met?"

"You're telling me he's like us?"

A smile covered Reed's face. "You think I'd let you fall in love with someone who couldn't save you?"

"Reed." Soundless tears began to fall like a waterfall down my cheeks. "I still love you, too. I love you both."

"I was just a part of your life." He tucked a lock of hair behind my ear. "But you. You were my everything. And I will love you even if I am on some other plane of existence." He took his hand off my leg. "You have to let me go." His eyes locked with mine. "You need to concentrate on the future, firstly getting out of here."

I shook my head. "I'm so fucking high I'm hallucinating, and you want me to get out of here?"

"You know why Widmore wouldn't let you read *Carrie*?"

I shook my head.

He brought his face next to mine. "Because he didn't want you to realize you're more powerful than him."

"I don't feel powerful."

"Do you trust me?"

"Yes."

"Then believe in yourself, as I do."

I rested my forehead on his. "Can you say it, one last time?"

His lips were next to my ear, and his words softly found a home in the center of my heart, as he recited *Un Amor* a final time. As the last stanza began, his breath didn't seem to reach my skin, and his hand loosened its grip on mine.

"Go into your memory and find Carl," he murmured as his lips danced on mine. "He'll give you strength so you can get out of here and find Lola."

"Who's Lola?"

Reed's dark eyes charted my face, memorizing me, and he smiled before he whispered, "Lola's going to kill Jonas. But she can't do it without your help. Not everyone thinks you can, but I have faith in you, Litha."

Before I could ask anything, like *'can you give me a hint on how to find and save this Lola chick?'* Reed's lips were on mine again, which made me forget how to form a question. His tongue in my mouth. His hands moving over me. Carl, Lola, Jonas, everyone and everything, vanished from existence because, for just a few minutes, I was Reed's once again.

Another moment to be added to our epic love story.

Or the conclusion that is.

Because when I opened my eyes, Reed was gone. Really gone. I brought my knees to my chest, wrapped my arms around my legs, and sobbed because it didn't matter who the fuck Lola was. There was no way I'd be able to help her because Jonas was going to kill me first.

# WIDMORE
## 10/19/2020 7:45 AM

I let the phone ring half a dozen times as I sat in my office in Johns Hopkins, surrounded by essays comparing *The Canterbury Tales* to *Piers Plowman,* but worried that the incessant sound would alert the faculty that I was essentially living in my office since Talitha's capture. I picked up and before I could speak Phoenix began.

"I'm going crazy." I could practically hear Phoenix's tears over the phone. "If we all go together then we can get her back."

"No." I shook my head although he couldn't see it over the phone. Because no matter how much emotional pain I might feel for the possible death, and her inevitable torture, it was overridden by my belief that she was the key. Jonas would test her to find how strong she truly was, and then we'd come up with a plan to get her to infiltrate the CDC for their research on immortality. "Even all together we're not more powerful than Jonas." The sober truth brought me out of the possible future to the present. It was the first time I hadn't lied to Phoenix since The Lab took Talitha, and was the main reason I'd stayed away from my charges. I couldn't stand the despair in their thoughts.

"We'll never know if we don't try," Phoenix's voice broke, "they're going to kill her."

"She's too important for them to kill." The words were quick, and I couldn't be sure if I said them for my benefit or his.

"Reed could bring people back from the dead. What's more important than that?"

I let the air hang in between us as I leaned back in my chair. "She took you inside her fog, correct?"

"Yeah, so?"

"Imagine you have an army; how useful would it be to have someone that can do what she can do?"

"*That's* what I'm fucking talking about. They're just going to use her, which is going to get her killed."

I knew Phoenix and I were about to hit an impasse, a troublesome issue since he was in love with Talitha. And I knew the power of love—for that was the reason I did everything, my unbridled desire for my lost love Cordelia was so powerful, it made the Talitha's sacrifice a non-issue in my mind. Therefore, I had to really drive the message home to him. "Are you willing to sacrifice Frozenstar's life for Talitha's?"

"What?" I could hear the gears in his mind stop turning.

"If you want to break her out of The Lab, we'll need everyone, including your sister. You can turn anyone to ash, but it's not as hard as you think to break out of ice. And what if Frozenstar dies and we save Talitha? All you'll have is memories of your sister, because it's not as if Talitha will ever love you back."

On the other end of the line, he gasped for breath as if he were taking a physical beating. "It won't be like that, I can protect both of them."

"No, you can't, one of them will die in The Lab, and the choice is up to you: Frozenstar or Talitha?"

"No," he growled, "you can't make me choose."

"Frozenstar or Talitha," I hissed.

There were sniffs, and a soft moan before the whisper of, "Frozenstar," from the other end, "my sister."

I smiled, because at least I'd saved his life. "Very good, now make sure no one else wants to go off on a suicide mission."

"I'll convince Fidget," Phoenix's voice reminded me of a deflating balloon.

I hung up without saying another word, hoping that Jonas pushed Talitha enough to access her powers, but not enough to kill her.

# Talitha
10/20/2020 7:55 AM

"Eight Fifteen, we're coming in."

The light was so bright when they opened the door to my cell, I brought up my hand to block it out.

"Put your hands down, Eight Fifteen!" one of them shouted at me.

My hand remained where it was, their Flashing Red Auras pounding into my grey matter. "You haven't fed me, and I'm still high, I can't do anything if I wanted to." At least that's what I tried to say, but instead I gurgled the sentiment. My pounding headache had proved so debilitating that I couldn't even read the minds of the two Flashing Reds in the doorway.

One of the Flashing Reds grabbed my arm. "Are you deaf, Eight Fifteen? Come with us!" he yelled as he tossed me out into the hallway.

I tripped and fell face-first onto the cement ground, one of them gripped onto my scrub top and righted me on my feet. That's when I realized just how much smaller I was than them. They towered above me, blocking out the light not only with their height, but also weight. They were in full riot gear, and the one who'd grabbed me had a revolver in his hand hovering near my face. The only reason I knew he hadn't been fully enchanted by Jonas to zombie level was that his Aura wavered Yellow in the center.

Zombies didn't fear anything.

"You're scared of me," I giggled, finding that my stomach was floating inside of me like I was on a roller coaster.

He pulled me closer to him, the Yellow in his center shrinking as his eyes focused on mine. "You're drugged, but I still hope you feel everything he does to you."

Even weakened, I caught the name that jumped to the forefront of his brain. "Who's Mary?"

I could see my reflection in the face shield of his helmet and he was right, I was very high. Drool was coming down the side of my mouth, sweat covered my skin, and flying saucers of black had taken over my eyes. His fear gave me the ability to see the footage in his head, of the Flashing Red that had turned into a melted puddle in the middle of a dark room. He'd been killed because I'd escaped him at Ottobar. Mary, she was the melted Flashing Red's daughter who'd been injected with the serum as further punishment for not capturing me. And now the Flashing Red that wished for my torture also prayed for his own daughter.

"Jonas will never stop." The words were in my voice, but my face was so numb I couldn't feel my lips move. It was like I'd just been pulled out of snowstorm without a jacket. "He'll hurt me and Mary."

"Better you than me." The Yellow in the center of his Aura engulfed the Flashing Red as he dragged me down the hall.

It looked like the corridor that had the door to my fog, a bright angelic white that seemed more ominous than if it were pitch dark. I reached up to the Yellow soldier's face, hoping I could touch his temple and enter his mainframe. While I didn't see it coming, the first physical sensation I could recall since I felt Reed's velvety lips on mine was a crunching pain in my jaw as the solider punched me. Without as much as a blink in retaliation, I landed on the floor, my head knocking into it. For a split second, my mind filled up with color and thoughts from who knows how far away. Then his boot made contact with my face and everything went silent.

"What the fuck are you doing?" A second soldier approached. His Orange Aura flickered above me to the left.

"She tried to touch me!" The Yellow in the center of the first soldier's chest began to spread, even though I hadn't moved from off the floor, and my mouth was filling with iron.

"Boss says we can't kill her."

"You saw what she did to Greene?" Yellow turned to Burnt Umber. "He just had a new baby with his wife and this bitch killed him. Made him slit his own throat. Same with Williams, Tanner, and Jefferson. I'm only alive from the last station because it was my day off."

Orange Aura's flicker picked up half a beat in speed. "Her freak boyfriend can't bring her back to life again."

"What if we tell boss she tried to escape?"

Something was pressed against the back of my head.

Cold metal.

"You want to lie to a man that can read minds?"

While they continued to bicker about the ramifications of killing me, I almost told them to do it. Because they were right—I'm a murderer. Massacred a building full of soldiers without a second thought and with the same ease as brushing my teeth. And if they did kill me, then it would all be over, all the pain. No more running or being scared. Wouldn't have to relive the torture because it was impossible to extinguish. Soon it would all be over.

*But Reed said Carl and I had to save someone…Lola.*

Yellow soldier's Aura turned full tilt Crimson, with a fountain of Black pouring from the center and expanding all over the floor. It was either that, or the blood in my mouth from having my jaw broken that was causing me to choke. Then everything lit up. I thought it was the light, the one you see before you die. I'd never seen it the two times I'd died before, but that didn't mean I'd lost hope that it existed, especially now as the corridor glowed brighter than a full moon.

Brighter than a comet.

Hotter than the sun.

Their Auras extinguished along with their words, but I still couldn't move, mouth full of blood.

"Wake up, Eight Fifteen."

# Carl
## 10/20/2020 8:55 AM

Instead of going back to The Manor with that flame throwing psycho, I went to Johns Hopkins where Widmore was easy enough to find even without superpowers.

The wind had a bite to it, so I shoved my hands deeper into my pockets, which was honestly a respite because I hadn't stopped staring at my left hand since I woke up. I had a trashcan full of bandages coated in blood and the outermost layer of skin. And I *know* Phoenix engulfed my fist in flame outside of the Metro a few nights before. I could only remember the agonizing pain, and the smell of burning flesh. However, when I went to change the bandage this morning, the skin looked just as healthy as any other on my body. Not a mark, mar, or even discoloration. I had normal sensation in the hand, full range of motion, and not the faintest hint that a superpower pyromaniac had set me on fire.

*Okay, yeah that's super weird that my third-degree burns healed so quickly but right now I need to find Talitha,* I reminded myself as I moved through the students that were exiting Widmore's Shakespeare lecture. Under normal circumstances, I might have talked to him about Shakespeare, *maybe he even knew him*. My mom had been obsessed, so I was familiar with Othello and Desdemona long before everyone else read about Romeo and Juliet. Although Hamlet had always been my favorite and now I wondered if I wanted 'to be' without Talitha.

"Can I help you?" Widmore gathered his things from the podium of the lecture hall and packed them in his briefcase.

"Are you seriously at work when Talitha is missing?"

He shut the briefcase. "I'm not sure I understand you, seeing as I don't know a Talitha."

I grabbed Widmore by the forearm with my left hand, just as I'd done with Phoenix the night before. Widmore's eyes scanned the pristine skin, and my head started to hurt when our eyes met.

"Stop that." I released him. "She told me you can't read my mind anyway."

"It's best you go back home, or maybe go visit a family member. I'd remove your time with us if it were possible, but we both know it's not." He shifted away from me.

"I'm not just going to leave her there with them. I promised her."

Widmore pushed the glasses up the bridge of his nose. "She wouldn't want you to come after her."

"She's just saying that." The words rushed out of my mouth. "I don't know if I *can* save her, but I need to try."

He scanned my face. "It's not possible. You are literally and figuratively useless. She did a disservice not erasing your memory."

"You're the one that told us to go out, and that just happens to be when she gets caught?" While I tried to come up with a plan on how to save Talitha, I had begun to wonder if she'd been double-crossed.

"You must be insane if you think I'd hurt Talitha, Mr. Anderson." His nostrils flared.

"Well I'm not insane, and unless we do something she will get hurt." I slammed my hand down on his desk.

"Please don't make me call security. Wouldn't want to be arrested seeing as you're not a student of this fine institution." He snapped shut his briefcase as he mumbled, "Don't understand why she didn't erase your memory."

"She didn't because she loves me."

"When she does get out, and that is a *when* Carl," his voice lowered to just above a whisper, "she will take your memories of her, because she might be powerful enough to evade The Lab on her own, but as long as she has a weakness, they will always be able to control her."

"Doesn't matter," my voice wavered, "I'll never be able to forget her."

"I thought that once as well." Half a smile took over Widmore's wrinkled face. "But I was wrong, and in order to save the woman I loved, I blocked her mind from mine. Can't read her thoughts just as I can't see yours. Couldn't find her no matter how much I wished to know if she still dreams of me as I do of her."

"But you could have something now. And that's all I want, a chance, so just tell me where they have her."

"Be glad for what memories you have." Widmore pushed past me. "Don't come back here, Mr. Anderson."

"Why am I even talking to you?" I groaned looking for something to punch but instead I just gritted my teeth and muttered, "Like someone who's immortal can even relate to sacrificing for someone."

Widmore stopped in the empty hallway. "I've sacrificed more than you'll ever know," and he continued to his office, leaving me unsure of what to do next.

I went back to my house on instinct, barely had time to shut the door before I passed out and collapsed on the floor.

# Talitha
## 10/20/2020 8:35 AM

When I opened my eyes, I was sitting upright. My jaw was reset, which was a blessing when I saw what was before me: a table full of deliciousness that would have been truly appreciated by a frat house full of stoners. A bucket full of crab legs, seasoned generously with Old Bay, potato chips in both the rippled and plain variety, a mound of peanut butter cups, buffalo wings, six liters of soda, a gallon of Neapolitan ice cream, nachos, and across from me a bowl of mac and cheese. Not just any kind, like from the box, but oozing with bubbling made-from-scratch goodness, browned on the edges of the casserole dish, bread crumbled on top, three types of cheese poking through. Each was easily identified by my taste buds as cheddar, Monterey jack, and a touch of cream cheese to bind it all together, as the center of the most scrumptious meal that a lab rat could ever encounter.

It was more than likely my last meal, so I didn't bother with a napkin, or any form of etiquette. After all, there was no one to hear me chomping, slurping, and burping in the circular room made of brushed steel in which I was positioned in the center of. If there was any hope of getting the fuck out of here, then I'd need all the energy I could get, which meant I had to eat until there was nothing left. As I ate, I kept trying to push Carl out of my mind. I wanted more than anything to be able to forget him. Forget his jawline, his gray-green eyes, or the way it felt to have him move inside of me. To have parts of me spark and flicker when he'd look at me, or say my name, or that his hand always seemed to find mine.

"I have to say, I understand the attraction," a voice came from behind me. I didn't turn toward it, but I did set down my crab claw, realizing that I'd never get a chance to eat the last two as the voice continued. "Carl is quite handsome."

I turned toward the being with no Aura. "Leave him alone."

"As long as he doesn't try to perform a gallant rescue attempt on your behalf." Jonas' teeth were as bright white as the light that blinded me before I woke up in this room.

"He won't." I wiped my hands on my scrubs, only then seeing the stains of sticky crimson that were splattered next to wing sauce.

"Well, at least he's talking about it. Or, at least I'm tracking him right now as he's driving to the University, although I can't read his thoughts, so I'm not sure of his true motivation." Jonas stepped closer to me, and all the energy I'd incurred by eating a month's worth of calories began to slip away as I tucked away the knowledge *even Jonas can't read Carl's mind*. "That's more than what I can say about your friends."

I couldn't be sure how deep he was into my head, because his presence wasn't simply stronger than Widmore, but on an entirely different level. He slipped into the memory of October 13, 2020, as if Jonas were there in the room as Carl made love to me, murmuring in French as I rattled the windows in his house.

Jonas' lips turned up. "He did make you more powerful, *and* he's Blue like One Eleven."

I shoved Jonas out of my head and the lights flickered above us, making Jonas' grin expand, hoping my words were the definition of nonchalance. "Just a coincidence."

He continued to move toward me, gliding like a ghost, until he was close enough that my Aura began to wrap around me. "You're willing to sacrifice yourself for him? This *coincidence?*"

Jonas tried to slither into my brain again, this time drawing on the shape of a fillet knife, but I managed to pour concrete over my grey matter. "Yes."

"Why, because you think you're in love?"

With the word 'love', an image popped out of Jonas' head and into mine. She had dark almond-shaped eyes, caramel skin, and a mess of coco curls that framed her heart-shaped face. I didn't know her name; somehow, he kept that from me. But she had a tattoo like mine and was called One Hundred and Eight, and once I read her Sea Glass Aura, I found out so much more. She was Indian, raised in London, an orphan, and that Jonas had raped her on her eighteenth birthday, which fell on October 10, 2020. My irises shot to the scratch on Jonas' neck, four nails digging so deep into his flesh her mark was still visible.

"One Hundred and Eight must be really strong." I nodded at Jonas' throat as the red in his irises shone like a Las Vegas sign. "If she could leave a mark like that on someone so powerful he doesn't even emit an Aura."

I expected to be beaten, thrown against a wall with the flick of his wrist. Instead, Jonas laughed, and cradled my head in his hands as the image of the young Sea Glass girl he was obsessed with faded into the background. "We are going to do so many astonishing things together."

"I'm not a traitor like you."

"It would be so sad if Carl were to get into a car accident like his parents." The red in Jonas' irises swirled.

He had me, but he already knew that, so I didn't bother begging for Carl's life again.

"If you can break out of this room," Jonas' mouth made its way to my ear as if we were lovers, "then you can go back to Widmore, and I'll let Carl live as long as he returns to Baltimore."

In the time it took me to blink, Jonas, the table, and food were gone. Jonas put me in a tin can and wanted me to get out, which was scary enough, until I heard a chuckle behind me and realized I wasn't alone.

"That you, Annie?"

# Talitha
## 10/20/2025 9:30 AM

Joe, the serial rapist that I exposed at the party Carl took me to, stood before me. "That's just one of your names though, right, Annie? Because I've heard them call you Talitha and Eight Fifteen. They told me you can read minds and that's how you did it." He gritted his teeth at his last few words as he walked toward me. "You put the memory of what I did to my ex-fiancé in everyone's heads at that party."

"It was an accident," I murmured as his Ink Black Aura rippled out around him like a riptide in the ocean, holding me down. Even after eating enough calories to feed a boy scout troop, I found myself completely weakened and unable to do anything but continue to step back. Jonas had put me in my worst nightmare to see how far my abilities had progressed.

"An accident." His bottom lip quivered. His aroma and the dark stains on his teal scrubs that matched mine told me that he hadn't showered since the party ten days ago. However, his blond hair still sparkled under the bright lights in the center of the circular metal room Jonas had locked us in. "You ruined my fucking life with that *accident*."

My back pressed against the wall. "I'd never done it before, ever since I met Carl my powers have…"

He growled over the rest of my sentence. "Don't even mention that asshole's name. If he hadn't brought you to that party, I wouldn't even be here. I'd still be in Baltimore, instead of this hellhole for mutants." Joe leaned in, his blue eyes flashing as he rested his palms against the wall on either side of my head and hissed, "I've been thinking about you a lot."

"Please." I found my powers frozen deep inside of me out of fear.

He grinned, which brought a chill up my spine. "I was hoping you'd beg." Joe pressed his chest against me, suffocating me, leaving me with only one option, to knee him in his chest. He faltered a step or two, and laughed. "Hoped you'd fight, too."

He grabbed for me, but I wriggled away. His fist clenched onto my scrub top, tearing it as I pulled away. It was like that for a while, a cat and mouse game. Then his face changed, the smile slipped away, and somehow his Aura became Darker as it wrapped around me. All of that slowed me down so that I was close enough for his left fist to make contact with the right side of my face.

I saw stars.

With another punch and kick to my chest I collapsed on the floor with broken teeth filling up my mouth.

There was a throbbing pain in my face as my lungs tried to fill back up with air. Joe's hand made its way up to my sports bra. "Not even worth taking off," he mumbled as he hovered above me. I tried to crawl away, but his knee pinned down my leg. His hands were everywhere, exploring me, and suddenly I was Annie, a helpless girl that was trapped by a man, not Talitha, a powerful telepath.

But either way I didn't want to die, not like this.

I wouldn't let this sociopath rape and murder me in the trap Jonas had constructed.

With all this skin-on-skin contact, it was easy to get my hand on his temple as he started to pull down his scrub bottoms. Once my fingertips touched Joe, we traveled in a flash though the bright white corridor in my brain, through Joe's door made of plywood like an abandoned building, and up to his screening room. I scrolled back to October 10 to the party where Joe and I met.

Once I hit play it was as if the floor beneath me disappeared as Joe and I fell onto the Persian rug next to the coffee table made out of an old door. All the lights in the room, including the Christmas lights strung along the staircase, flickered and the volume on speakers blared *Two Weeks* by Grizzly Bear. Everything was as it was the night of the party, and even though Joe and I basically fell from the sky into the middle of the party, no one seemed to notice us.

Yet.

Joe was still on top of me but distracted as he looked around. "What the fuck did you do?" He murmured as his grip loosened and Joe's eyes fell on Tonya. His ex and rape victim cheered on her brother, Clint, who was playing on the Jaws-themed pinball machine.

I used this opportunity to crab crawl away as Joe grabbed onto my leg and yanked me back under him. "What the fuck did you do!" He bellowed at me.

"Joe?" The music stopped, the lights flashed again, and every set of eyes zeroed in on Joe and me. Tonya rushed toward us. She knocked Joe off of me, which gave me time to get to an empty corner in the living room, bringing my knees to my chest as I watched karma unfold before me.

Tonya hollered at the 'asshole bastard' also known as Joe, and with each curse she kicked or punched Joe. The other girls at the party began to join in, forcing Joe into fetal position to protect himself. Which worked for a while, until Clint joined in and pressed his foot into Joe's neck as the girls continued to thrash and curse.

I didn't realize I'd been holding my breath until someone came up and touched my knee.

"Talitha?"

I knew Carl would be here in Joe's memory, since he was at the original party, but the fact that he could interact with me and remain invisible to everyone else was beyond shocking. I was relieved to see Carl. I was about to wrap my arms around him, but I stopped short when his palm glowed and the pain in my knee began to subside. Carl looked just as shocked as me, but it didn't stop him from raising his hand to my face. I could hear the bones in my face set themselves, and all the iron dissipated from my mouth.

"You're a healer," I said before I could even take a moment to realize the implications of the fact. My hallucination of Reed told me that Carl was special, that his Aura wasn't a coincidence, nor my increase of abilities. Which I began to understand as the glow from Carl's palm energized me as if I were made of solar panels and the light he emitted from his palm was the sun.

"I kinda already guessed that." Carl showed me the memory of Phoenix burning his hand, leaving third degree burns, and it miraculously healing the next morning. "But I didn't get a chance to think about what it means, just wanted to save you."

As his glowing palm continued to travel over my body, taking away even a hint of pain, it made the energy in me rise to a level higher than I'd experienced even after the largest feast. I smiled from the inside out. "You did."

"How?" His gray-green eyes held onto me. "You're still in the lab, right? You just went into a memory, which means you're still with a fucking rapist." Carl's voice cracked at the end.

"Yeah, but I'm going to trap him here in his memory." I threw a glance at Joe, who was still getting his ass kicked by everyone at the party, save Carl and me. "He'll spend an eternity paying for what he's done. You've healed me." I turned back to my savior.

"Can you do that?"

I smiled at Carl. "Yes, I can feel my power increasing. I'm going to get myself out." I kissed him as the bubbling energy flowed through me. "And after I do, I'm going to call you so you can bring me back to Baltimore."

"But you don't have my number."

I telepathically told Carl, *I can get a hold of you without a phone.*

*See you soon then?* he mentally responded.

I gave Carl a quick peck as I ejected myself from Joe's memory. I stuck a screwdriver in the reel that played Joe's biopic, that way he'd be stuck at that party forever, until the end of time he'd have his ass kicked. I shut the door to Joe's theater, bolted it, and returned to the bright white corridor in my mind. But instead of retreating to my fog, or going into one of the other thousands of doors on either side of the hallway, I returned to The Lab.

It was the first time in as long as I could remember that I felt no fear.

Once I found myself in the brushed steel circular room, I cut myself out with my mind like a chainsaw. The jagged edges of metal cut into the bodies of the soldiers guarding the room. The Aura of the soldiers that were closest to me turned Neon Yellow as I stepped out of the tin can and into the hallway that I'd been beaten in. Blood dripped from the beating Joe had given me as I hadn't let Carl heal me completely. It seeped into the concrete and melded with that of the soldiers who I'd already killed.

I turned left, knowing it was the correct way out, but not sure *how* I knew it.

A rush of footsteps came upon me. "Holy shit, she got out." Were the last words the Flashing Red in front of his team said before he aimed his rifle at me.

With the snap of my fingers, his head exploded inside of his riot gear helmet. Through the clear helmet I watched as the blood rose up inside the sphere; if his brain had been intact, he would have drowned in his own blood. His knees buckled and he dropped to the floor. The helmet cracked and crimson seeped out. There were a dozen others, who each befell the same fate of a blown-up skull. Their brains and blood seeped out of their helmets and coated the floor as I walked toward the elevator, only then realizing I wasn't wearing shoes anymore. With each step, my feet made a *squishing* sound, but that was easily muffled with the screams of the Flashing Reds as they begged for their lives.

I couldn't sense Jonas, and didn't expect to. He'd threatened to hurt Carl, and wished I'd push myself further than I'd ever gone before. Although I didn't want to grant his wish, at least it meant that I'd soon be free. Once in the elevator, I didn't even need to snap my fingers anymore. The glow from Carl had given me the same amount of energy as if I'd been powered by four ships full of dynamite, and sharpened my mind so I could focus on each Aura that existed inside The Lab. And once I focused on them their life was over.

Most of them died instantly as I telepathically crushed their heads, a bunch pointed their weapons at their heads and pulled the trigger, some were thrown against a wall until their hearts stopped, a few that tried to cut the lines to the elevator and stop my escape were easy to electrocute. However, I left the two that had pulled me out of my cell that morning for last as I locked them in the room in which they'd hidden once I broke out of the round metal room.

I made it to the ground level, I found the employee locker room and, with a thought, all the doors unlocked and popped open, exposing their contents. After a short search, I stripped off the scrub pants, tugged on the jeans from inside, laced up the sneakers, pulled on the long sleeve t-shirt, and put the gray hood up on the jacket. I didn't bother wiping my fingerprints, or locking anything back up, considering the owner of the contents had been eviscerated.

Save the two Yellows that I'd trapped inside.

I continued working on instinct until I pushed open the double doors with my mind and felt the sun on my skin. The air was clear and was just cold enough to feel harsh as I filled up my lungs. Around me were trees for about ten miles. The Lab was positioned at the top of a hill, a muddy trail leading down about five miles to a paved street. I could hear cars honking, birds chirping, and thoughts of the inhabitants that lived in the nearest town that were in the next zip code. My feet started the trek back toward civilization as my mind focused on the basement of The Lab, the gas main more specifically.

There was a spark that began when Jonas captured me all those years ago, finally ignited. But the soldiers that I'd saved for last would have lungs full of smoke before they turned to ash. Their fingernails would be bloodied from trying to scratch their way out of the room I'd trapped them in. They would lose their voices, screaming for help from God or a fellow solider at least. I made sure that they felt the flames before they died.

While I turned The Lab, and every living soul inside back to their natural state of carbon, I couldn't help but wonder what it meant that I felt no guilt or anguish for my actions. It was the second time in my life that I'd killed a building full of people. True, they all didn't care for my safety, a fact I knew to be true because I could read their minds. And because I could read their minds, I knew that they thought, *better to kill than to be killed*.

Which is in essence how I felt as a fire raged that only stopped short of taking down the forest because of me. For hours, all I could wonder was, *is this what my life has become?*

It was dusk when I'd made it to a bodega. The streetlights flickered, the power inside of me still trying to find its way out. But my power held steadfast as I put a stopper to block its escape like a cork in a wine bottle. I didn't let myself contemplate that there had to have been some people inside that were innocent. Custodians, cooks, maybe even someone who answered a phone were all dust because of me. However, now wasn't the time for any emotion, much less guilt, now that I'd fully accepted that from now on, my life would be kill or be killed.

A chime twittered above me as I opened the door and maneuvered through the empty store back toward the cooler. I took a gallon of orange juice from the shelf, returned to the front, and set it on the counter. I paid using the money in the wallet of the woman whose clothing I'd stolen. *Tiffany Walker*, my eyes scanned her New Jersey driver's license, *that's one of the people I killed today.*

"You alright, miss?" The fifty-something attendant rose an eyebrow at me as he slid the change toward me.

"Yeah." I put it back in Tiffany's wallet and shoved it into my back pocket. "Where am I?"

"How come you don't know where you are?" The wrinkles in the old man's tan skin deepened as his eyes narrowed in on me.

I opened up the orange juice, took a long drink, wiped my mouth, and said, "I'm telepathic, and was kidnapped, now I need to mentally tell my boyfriend where I am."

The old man crossed his chest with his arms and smirked. "If you're telepathic, then why can't you just read my mind and find out where you are?"

I took a long pull from the jug. "You wouldn't want to be in everyone's head if you didn't have to, either." For a moment, I became acutely aware just how all-encompassing my powers had become, that if I wanted to, I could read the minds of people that spoke other languages. French, German, and what I assumed was Italian because I knew it wasn't Spanish.

"Probably need to tell your boyfriend that you need a visit to rehab too, miss. You're in Red Hook, New Jersey, and there's a bus stop on the corner where you can wait for him."

The wind nipped at me as I left the bodega and turned toward the bus stop. *Carl, you there?*

*Yeah,* he thought back, *where are you?*

*Red Hook, New Jersey.*

*Whoa, that's practically New York.*

I made a map appear in Carl's head, with a red blinking dot where I sat on the bench. I closed my eyes and waited. I kept the radar up, tracking the Auras of everyone in a ten-mile radius, and knew I was safe. I also knew that if anyone did come for me, then I'd still be okay, because the closer Carl got to me, the stronger I felt. Not only was my battery power at full capacity, but my backup cells filled up on top of that. It was like I'd figured out the code for infinite lives, but mentally I was nearing a system crash.

As all this new data overwhelmed me.

Carl being Enhanced as well.

Jonas setting up the ultimate test only proving that I'm far more powerful that I even imaged.

And that my dead boyfriend came to me in a hallucination, that together Carl and I were to save a girl named Lola so she could kill Jonas.

It was times like these that I was thankful I could recall any song from Justin Beiber's catalog, choosing *Lonely* and finding myself soothed. Although, something else lingered in the background. It wasn't as strong as a normal memory, as if it was a xerox copy that had been left out in the sun, leaving behind only one word.

Widmore.

Widmore didn't respond to any of my telepathic messages as I was being chased by the Flashing Reds, which was reason enough not to trust him. Yet there was a nagging suspicion that I had no idea what was really going on. But it almost didn't matter that I couldn't trust him, because now I was powerful enough to shield my thoughts from him. In fact, if I concentrated hard enough, I could find his Aura at Johns Hopkins.

Carl needed to be kept away from him at all costs, otherwise he'd be found out and tested on. Right now, only Carl and I knew he was a healer, and in order to maintain that reality, I had to pick one life or the other. On the run, protecting Carl, or trapped at The Manor where I could protect my friends and kill Widmore if need be.

I didn't have time to ponder that question or any other for that matter before a car pulled up and Carl rushed up to me. "Talitha." He wrapped as his arms around me.

"Annie," I said as I pulled away just enough so I could see his whole face, which was blotchy and red. "Call me Annie now, okay?"

"Why?"

"Because I don't want to be Talitha anymore. I want to be normal and live far away from here."

"But I'm Enhanced like you." A smile took over his handsome face. "We can be not-normal together."

I took his face in my hands, his skin so warm against mine. "But we don't have to be. I want to be Annie. And I want you to stay Carl. And for us to be free. Maybe we can live on your family farm with the flowers?"

"Okay, Annie." He put his hands over mine. "I'll take you to live with the flowers."

Carl picked me up, held me in his arms, slid me into the passenger seat, and buckled me up as he leaned down and gave me a quick kiss. He turned the key in the ignition and *Thrill* by Future Islands came on as we drove as far away from here as possible, with a stop in Baltimore on the way.

# CARL
## 10/21/2020 7:45 AM

"You sure you're okay?" I asked as the violence that I'd seen perpetrated against my girlfriend hammered in my head.

She nodded from across the tiny, round table in the kitchen of my rowhouse in Baltimore. She wiped her mouth with the back of her hand although a streak of buffalo wing sauce was left on her chin. "I've already told you a million times, he didn't rape me."

"Still looked horrible," I muttered, gazing down at the table, unable to find the food on the table appetizing, mainly because I couldn't get the image of Joe on top of Talitha out of my mind. *Wait she wants me to call her Annie,* I reminded myself.

"You can call me whatever you want, Carl." She picked up the liter of soda and finished it off.

*Have I told you how weird it is that you answer me after reading my mind?* I thought knowing what she'd probably say.

"Do you want me to answer that?" She smirked as she tossed the plastic bottle atop the half dozen in the trashcan behind her.

I couldn't help but smile back and that simple change in the muscles in my face altered my whole outlook on the situation I found myself in. The feeling of hope started from the outside but made its way into the very center of myself. Like my heart was given a cup of cocoa, a warm blanket, and a bedtime story. "I like Annie, it suits you."

Her grin seemed to take over her face, her blue eyes sparkled even in the dim lighting, competing with the ruby studs in her right ear. "And why is that?"

"It's short and cute. Like you."

She laughed. "Did you just say cute?"

"Yeah, I'm confident enough in my masculinity to call my girlfriend cute."

"Your girlfriend, huh?"

"Yeah, after all we've been through, you're at least my girlfriend, Annie."

"I like it," she mused before she started in on another hot wing. "Very normal."

I let the silence wash over me. Well, there were the sounds of Annie eating and My Morning Jacket playing on my speakers, but I was left to my thoughts, which threatened to pull me back into the darkness. I realized that Annie so desperately wanted to be normal, but that it would be impossible for either of us. I thought for a beat about the fact that my palms lit up like a glowstick and made all the wounds and bruises on Annie fade away instantly, which meant I could probably heal other people too. That I had superpowers hidden within me only to come to the surface when a girl ran into the bathroom at Ottobar and called me Blue.

"Maybe normal isn't the right word." She handed me a wing, which I took more out of habit than hunger. "I just want to have a house, a job, and have a dog that we can walk every morning."

Imagining Annie as a waitress in a small French bakery in the Provence village proved enough to quell my fears once again. Together, we'd go to the weekly market to sell the flowers, mostly so I could sketch the patrons, because after the inheritance my parents left me we didn't need money. We'd go on picnics in the Maldives, take a tour of the churches in Spain, sail in the French Rivera, and see the Opera House in Sydney that my mother always dreamed of seeing. I'd do all the things she didn't get a chance to do. Do all the things I *should* have been doing in my twenties rather than living in an empty house with a bartending job just so I wasn't alone every day.

We could be normal together.

Which was something I never knew I wanted so much.

"As long as you don't want one of those purse dogs." I sunk my teeth into the wing.

She rose an eyebrow at me. "Purse dog?"

"Yeah." I swallowed. "They're little dogs. Some girls carry them in their purse, you know? But I'd want a big dog like a collie or something."

"Like Lassie?"

I nodded, the picture crystalizing in my mind. "We'll live on the farm with Lassie."

We kept looking at each other like a couple of idiots in love until her gaze flashed to the time on my phone. "Widmore's been at Johns Hopkins for hours, and we need to get back before he figures out that I'm not a hostage anymore."

I clenched my fist. "I still don't know why you have to go back."

"I know it's dangerous, but Jonas has taken everything from me, and I want to get back what little I have left."

"I will buy you a hundred copies of *The Hunger Games* if we can leave Baltimore tonight."

"Your sketchbook is still there too, under my mattress."

I shrugged, even though losing a gift from my mother felt like a shot in the gut. "I can buy a new sketchbook then too."

"It's not just the book, there's a picture that I used as a bookmark. It's a picture of me and my mom." Her eyes held onto me. "It's all I have left of my mother, Carl."

The weight of her words sunk me, because even if my house was nearly empty, it was *my* house. And I had pictures of my mom, including one I kept in my wallet of us as I tried to teach her how to do an ollie on my skateboard. Also, no matter where we were going, I was taking my records when we left Baltimore. So even though it might be dangerous, the least I could expect her to take would be a picture of her mother. "Okay, I get it, it's just that if Widmore can't be trusted…"

"He can't. I know that now."

"There's no way I'm letting you go into that house alone."

Annie leaned closer. "If Phoenix sees your hand is healed, he's going to say something about it, because that's never happened before. And he was best friends with Reed, so once he realizes that you're a healer, he'll automatically go to Widmore. The only way to protect you is to keep everyone in the dark. It's crazy how powerful you are already."

"Why do you think it happened so fast?"

Annie shrugged. "I've become so much more powerful too, maybe we're making each other stronger?"

"No matter how strong you are, I think you should be afraid, especially of Widmore. It can't be a coincidence that he tells us to go out to party and then you get caught. I think we should just run away, Annie."

"You're acting like a scared little girl, Carl."

"I'm not afraid for me, I'm afraid for you. I need some answers too, and I'm not going to let you go back there alone." I still hadn't had time to really figure out what it meant to be Enhanced. I mean, did that mean that my parents weren't my parents? Although, I didn't see how that was possible since everyone always told me how much I favored my mother, but I was nothing like my father. Never had been. That's why we fought so much, even that last night when he was late to his performance, and they sped off only to get murdered by a drunk driver. All this time I'd felt so guilty for being the reason they were even at that stop light at that exact moment, but what if this whole time I hadn't killed my father. Not my real father at least.

Thoughts collided in my head: *So, does that mean she cheated on my dad? Who really wasn't my dad? Then who the fuck is my dad?*

"We'll figure that out." Annie squeezed my hand. "There's got to be a file on your mother somewhere if she was tested on like my mom."

My heart fluttered as my worries spiraled out of control. Thinking of my mother trapped in a steel room like they'd done with Annie... What if Jonas locked my mom in a room with a rapist too, and what if that's how she got pregnant with me?

All of those thoughts whirled with Annie's dead boyfriend telling her that together Annie and I would have to save a girl named Lola. A girl Annie had never met, had no idea where she was, much less what she looked like, but yet somehow, we were destined to find her? Nothing that had happened in the past week made any sense. Well other than the fact that I loved Annie.

*And if Reed was right about me being Enhanced, then he must be right about Lola killing Jonas, all we need to do is find her, and I can forget everything about my mom, and—*

"Carl," Annie tugged on my arm, and that along with her voice was enough to cut through all my uncertainty. "I know it's a lot, but we'll get through it together."

I couldn't say anything, as if my mouth was frozen.

"Just try to remember that I love you, and your mom and dad loved you, too. Even if you and your dad fought. Charles Anderson is your dad no matter what, because at least he was there for you to fight with." She laced her fingers with mine; now both of us were coated in wing sauce. "You took me into enough memories that I know they loved you, and they wouldn't want you to be hurt. Which is why neither of them told you, they wanted you to live a normal life. That's how we honor your parents."

I didn't realize I was holding my breath or biting the inside of my cheek until I finally exhaled. "You're right, my mom never told me anything, and it's not a secret that Wakefield tested on pregnant women. She would have told me if she wanted to. So, yeah, you're right, let's leave Baltimore and start over."

Annie leaned forward and kissed me. She tasted like hot wings, garlic, and pepperoni pizza, and I loved every second of it. "I think we have time to take a shower before we go," she murmured.

Annie stood up, took my hand, and directed me toward my bedroom.

# Fidget
## 10/21/2020 9:55 AM

When you could walk through solid objects as if they were air, privacy isn't something that you think about. Or, at least I don't. Especially when my best friend reappeared at The Manor and didn't bother even saying 'Good Morning' before she rushed to her room. The door Talitha slammed and locked was easier for me to break through than a spiderweb. Talitha grabbed a bag and threw all shades of gray clothing into it, along with Carl's sketchbook, and was about to add *The Hunger Games* when she stopped, turned the pages and stared at a picture.

I had suspected that she'd become more powerful if she were able to hide for so long. Hell, she'd even told me that her abilities increased since she'd escaped. However, it was still a shock to see her snap her fingers like Widmore, making the mattress flip, sending pillows, sheets, and a comforter throughout the room.

When I attended school at The Manor, I'd met nearly three hundred other Enhanced Beings like me. None had been a telepath. In all the hundreds of years Widmore had been alive, he'd told us the only others to have telekinetic powers was Jonas and himself. It was only a matter of time before she became as powerful as Widmore, and maybe I should have been afraid of her. After all, Talitha had killed two fortified buildings full of highly trained soldiers and, from what I could see, she didn't have a mark on her. Although she was wearing jeans and that leather jacket that covered up nearly all of her skin.

Thing is, I remembered her as the scared girl that had been shuffled from the burbs of wealthy Maryland, who spent months crying herself to sleep.

"Were you even going to say 'I'm alive'?" I stood five feet from her, my arms crossed my chest.

Talitha's eyes met with mine. "Well you obviously know that I'm alive."

"We've been friends our whole lives and you're seriously going to pick a guy over me?"

"I'm not picking a guy over you." She shut the book with the picture inside and shoved it into the duffel bag. "I'm picking freedom, and you can come with us."

My body stilled, my anger stifled as I contemplated leaving with Talitha. I'd been born in Berlin, and hadn't even been outside of Maryland since I was three and walked through my first wall. Widmore had been the only parent I could remember. If I left The Manor, under Talitha's safety, then I could travel, meet new people, maybe fall in love like her. But then I realized in all these dreams there were only three of us, and there was someone else who had been here almost as long as me.

"Siren can come too, right?" I asked. "And Phoenix and Frozenstar?"

Talitha pursed her lips. "Siren can come, but not the drama twins."

My anger spiked once again. "You can't just leave them here, and Phoenix can set our enemies on fire."

"Our enemies?" Talitha scoffed. "You saw him set *Carl* on fire and he is definitely not an enemy."

The memory of Carl's hand engulfed in Phoenix's flame returned to the forefront of my mind. I could still smell his burnt and bubbling skin. "Is Carl okay?"

Her cheek twitched. "He's going to be fine, just in a lot of pain." She slung the bag over her shoulder and started toward the door.

I grabbed onto her arm. "Are you seriously abandoning us again?"

"Again?"

"When you and Reed left, after Micha died. You left me alone, Talitha!" I cried. "I've been all alone here for so long."

"You can come with us." Her voice was soft. "You and Siren."

I shook my head so hard my hair hit me in my face. "You have to take all of us."

"I can't." Talitha shook me off and made her way to the door.

"You're killing us too then, you know?" I called out to her.

"You'll be fine here with Widmore," she started.

*I know you're not that stupid and still trust Widmore,* I telepathically hissed. *He's the one that sent us out and you got caught.*

Talitha froze. "Who else knows?"

"Phoenix loves him like a father and reveres him like a god," I insisted. "But Siren and I have no chance on our own." I shook my head.

"Look after each other then." She turned the knob on the door.

"You're a selfish bitch!" I called out.

She turned back to me and glared. "What?"

"You're given all this power to protect us and you're going to waste it on a fuck-a-thon with your boyfriend." I pushed past Talitha and drifted through the closed door.

"Nice last words from a best friend!" Talitha yelled into the hallway.

I didn't turn to look at her one last time, and I didn't need to read minds to know she was conflicted. But she proved me right, and left The Manor without a word to anyone else. Whether she was Talitha, or the crying little girl Annie, she was a selfish bitch.

With no idea what to do next, I went to my own room and turned on the stereo, hoping that Tegan and Sara would solve my problems. Or at least let me forget them.

# CARL
## 10/21/2020 10:25 AM

Annie climbed back into my car, handed me my sketchbook with a smile, and asked, "So, how do you want to spend your last day in Baltimore?"

I shrugged, turned on the ignition. "I've seen it all, a hundred times. What about you?"

Her smile turned into a smirk. "I've never been to the Aquarium."

I turned the car around as confusion washed over me. "It's not that long of a drive from the suburbs for at least a field trip, we went when I was twelve."

"I was nine when Widmore took me to The Manor." The seat squeaked as Annie slumped into it. "And when you're a telepath, going to places with a bunch of people isn't exactly fun."

"But that won't be a problem now?"

"No." She shook her head. "Just sitting next to you is charging me up."

I chuckled. "It's so weird how I completely understand what you're talking about."

She raised an eyebrow at me. "What does it feel like to you?"

"It's like…" As I searched for the words to explain, I could sense her blood pumping. I knew her current heartbeat was fifty-seven, the same as you'd expect from an Olympic athlete, and I felt it rise when I'd call her name, touch her hand, or kiss her. I was able to go so far as the division of the cells in her body, leaving only the deepest scars from her torture intact as her skin rejuvenated at a record rate.

"I can just feel you," I finally said as we turned onto the highway. "I can hear other people too, but you come through the strongest."

It was quiet for a while until Annie turned on the radio and *Walking on a Dream* started up when I realized something. "Wait, does that mean you've never been to the Baltimore Museum of Art then?"

Annie shook her head.

"Holy shit." I smacked the steering wheel with excitement. "It's, like, famous for having the most works from Matisse in the world."

"Is he the guy that painted those waterlilies?"

"That's Monet. Didn't Widmore teach you all that when you were at school?"

"Taught me how to survive on my own for over two years." She shrugged. "And we read The Canterbury Tales in Latin."

"Trust me, a morning with sharks and an afternoon with Matisse is a hundred times better than Canterbury's Tales."

She giggled. "Canterbury is a place, not a person, and that sounds like fun. Did you have any plans for our last evening in Baltimore?"

My foot pressed into the accelerator. "Maybe a tour of the neighborhoods of Baltimore."

Many hours later, after the Aquarium, Museum, and cooking some mac and cheese with the crab cakes we'd picked up on our way back to my rowhouse, we were naked in bed. The tip of her index finger traced the tattooed gears on my chest, which were still sweaty from our last session, which matched our record of four times in a day.

Annie's limbs were tangled in my mismatched flannel sheets. The light from the street filtered in through the window, bathing her fair skin. Her crystal-clear blue eyes still sparkled in the dark, and her lips were red and slightly swollen from all the friction of skin on skin. She sighed and rested her head on my chest, kissing the tattooed heart in a cage.

"Did I ever tell you how hot your tattoos are?"

"Enough times to make me question if I should get some more."

"You should get 'Annie' right here." She pointed at the center of the heart on my chest.

"Only if you get 'Carl' here." My fingers gingerly moved over her chest.

"Okay," she mused as my hands continued to chart her body.

My glowing palm had nearly erased all of her scars at this point, especially after she pushed her power into me each time we had sex. It was better than breaking anything in my house and gave me the energy to run a marathon, climb a mountain, and run from each corner of the city and back. Beach House played from the record player atop a side table as the rest of my prized albums were scattered on the floor, easy to step on if we weren't anchored to the bed.

"Thanks for being a tourist with me today."

"Of course." I stroked the side of her face. "And might as well, if it's going to be my last night in Baltimore anyway."

Her blue eyes darted to the left before they connected back with mine.

"You having second thoughts, Annie?"

Her heart rate rose when I said her name, but I could feel a bubbling underneath the façade of bliss that shrouded her. She met her eyes with mine. "I have no second thoughts when it comes to you, Carl."

I sensed her body heat up. "Why does that feel like a lie then?"

She bent her elbow, propped herself up, and gazed down at me. "You can read minds now too?"

"No, but I can read you." I sat up. "And even if it doesn't make sense, I know I'm powerful enough to know when you're lying."

"You're powerful because I'm powerful."

"How's that work?"

"Because we're connected. Your abilities coming up so fast are proof of it."

"Then I am right, and you're lying."

She looked down and the room darkened a bit. "I'm just worried about my friends."

"I told you we should take Fidget and Siren."

Annie's voice was still. "They won't come without the fire and ice twins, and maybe they'll be better off far away from us."

"You sure you can trust Widmore with them?"

"He hasn't hurt them yet, protected them in fact, and if they don't know where we are it's not like he could get any information from them anyway."

"You sure that's it?"

She smiled and all my fears dissipated, for a flash it made me wonder if she were using her powers on me, but I decided I didn't mind. "Yes, I'm sure."

"Good." I grinned back at her. "Because I want to see how much stronger you make me."

She cocked an eyebrow at me. "So that's all I am to you, a battery?"

My palm glowed as it hovered over the scarred skin on her left hip; the light dimmed when her scars were gone. "I heal you, and you power me up. We're like that figure eight symbol."

"You mean infinity?" She drew it on my chest.

"Yeah, like we were fated to meet."

"I like the sound of that," she murmured as I thought about our future. She'd finally get to be 'normal,' and neither of us would be traveling alone on the big blue marble called Earth anymore. We'd get married, and even though it wouldn't be some traditional event in a church, we would promise to be the others until death, and maybe even after that. I hadn't ever planned on being a father, considering I'd never loved a woman enough to want to have a child with her, but with Annie, that was different.

As my hand moved over her frame, taking in the health of her kidneys, how much oxygen was in her blood, and even tracked the density of the veins that ran through her body, it stopped where I found no data. The glow brightened above her lower abdomen, where there was no blood flow or cell division. While I hadn't excelled at biology, I knew she didn't have a uterus which made pregnancy impossible. Yet even as I thought about a future Annie with long blonde hair in a field of lavender, rubbing her round belly with my baby inside, my palm started to glow to near blinding levels.

Suddenly blood flow began, and the beginnings of a universe of cells started to spark inside of her.

She giggled. "That tickles."

"Yeah?" My glowing palm dimmed as I pulled it away and decided to ask a question I'd never asked a woman before. "Would you want to have kids with me someday?"

Her body stiffened. "I told you before we got together that they sterilized me when I was a kid."

"What if I healed you?"

She sat up. "That's not possible."

I sat up, too. "I just started to."

Her eyes doubled in size. "Started?"

"Yeah, it's like I said, I can feel your body working, but here," I nodded to her stomach, "there's nothing until...well, when I think about you pregnant with my kid." My palms glowed even if they weren't touching her. "I know I can do it," I murmured as the light dimmed.

"I've never thought about it before."

"So, Reed never tried?"

"He wasn't like you." Her voice was so quiet I could barely hear it over the music. "He couldn't control who he healed, and he couldn't feel my blood pump like you, so no, we never talked about having kids."

"I want to talk about it."

"You'd really want to have kids with me?"

"Yeah, I do."

She took my hand in hers. "Maybe."

"Maybe?"

"Maybe we'll talk about it." Her eyes were wide, and I wasn't sure if it was the light, but Annie looked as if she was about to cry. "But not today." She fell back on the bed and pulled me on top of her. "Although I do want you to break your record."

"Yeah?" I smiled as she lay back and pulled me on top of her.

Her hands explored me, and mine traveled over and inside of her until I could sink into her. We murmured 'I love you' in our respective native languages, and by now, I was used to calling her Annie as I thrust deeper and deeper. Afterward, I clung to her like she were the only lighthouse for miles, and I'd been lost at sea for years.

October 21 was the best day of my life, and I couldn't wait for a lifetime of more days like this.

# Talitha
## 10/22/2025 2:47 AM

October 22, 2020, would be the worst day of my life, but I deserve worse.

By now, I'm sure you think I'm the hero of this story, but that's not true. I'm a murderer, liar, and am about to hurt the only person that really knows me and loves me anyway.

But I had to do it. I had to do it now while Carl was asleep, because the last time I brought my hand to his temple, he kissed my palm, and somehow I ended up on his kitchen cabinet begging him to go harder. As I stood fully dressed over Carl, who was sleeping with a smile on his face, I knew there was no more time left.

A secret was more important than my feelings, and I had to keep it from every other soul on Earth.

Carl's a healer.

I would rather he be alive without me than be dead by my side.

Besides, the anger that was starting to take over would send him away anyway.

I have no fucking clue how he was Enhanced, but he was. Fidget's words were the tipping point. She's right; I had been selfish because I wanted him. I wanted him so bad that I was willing to put the life of my friends at stake by leaving them unprotected with Widmore. But I couldn't be selfish anymore. I couldn't be Annie, living in France without a worry in the world. I would have to be Talitha, the telepath who was so strong now, I could see not just Carl's dreams but the nighttime visions of everyone in Baltimore.

I leaned down and brushed the loose curls off of Carl's forehead as I wondered how evil I was, considering all day I was fully aware that I'd erase Carl's memory of this day.

Every day we'd had, for that matter, because it was better off for Carl if we never met. But I'd remember his smile with a lone dimple, his left-hand racing across the pages of his sketchbook, pencil in hand, the soft melody of his French accent when he murmured sweet nothings. Carl was too good for this world, much less me, and I was willing to do anything to keep him in the human world, no matter the sacrifice.

I took a deep breath, put my hand on his forehead, walked into the endless white corridor in my head, and opened Carl's door. It was covered in artwork, and when I turned the handle in the shape of Lloyd Dobler's boom box, *Sparks* from Beach House played throughout the theater. I turned away from the screen, which played images of me laughing, smiling, and moaning on a loop. His dreams were filled with me, just as mine were with him. I walked up the narrow spiral metal staircase up to the projection booth When I pulled open the door, I knew that there was no going back once I took a step inside.

I didn't bother shutting the door behind me as I went for the filmstrip. Spools and spools of the both of us, not nearly as many as my mother, but with the equal amount of weight as I lifted them into Carl's projector. Somehow, a relationship of ten days had more frames than 'Gone With The Wind', and just like with my mother, I would carry the weight of them around with me forever.

"This fucking sucks," I muttered as I found the cell of when I walked into the bathroom at Ottobar and started watching our love story unfold.

"Fuck Baltimore," I added as our walk to the party popped up in Carl's memory, "and fuck indie music," as a frame with the two of us walking along the Seine while *Moonlight* from Future Islands played as the soundtrack. Tears streamed down my face as I continued cursing everything that made up Carl Anderson as I watched us, realizing I had to remove it all and finding that I couldn't bring myself to do it.

So instead, I stretched the tape of Carl's memory out, and re-recorded something new. For the first time, I was able to implant a memory into someone else. With just the right amount of imagination, I changed the ending of our time together to have me die in his arms. The Flashing Reds put a bullet in my head and with all their resources were able to cover up my murder in the middle of the busy club. Carl wouldn't remember our race through the allies. Nor when I was caught, or came back to his house, or what I happened between us on October 21, 2020, which I knew he thought was the best day of his life.

We would still dance at the 9:30 Club.

Although it would be the last thing we'd do together as far as Carl knew.

I saved enough of his fight with Phoenix but altered it, so it seemed like he didn't want to join Carl on his quest for vengeance because of my murder. I wiped his burnt hand, which in turn took out his suspicions that he might be more like me than anyone believed.

In a few hours, Carl would awake, believing that he'd spent the past few days reviewing his life choices and decided to move to France. He'd tell Baltimore to fuck off, too, since everyone he loved died there, and he'd start over.

With my last few moments, I implanted the fantasy of a leggy brunette that lived in the village, that could give him a life with a family and a dog. Not being chased by Flashing Red freaks for an eternity.

Carl would be the hero of the story, and I would go where villains belong, in the shadows alone.

Once everything was in place, I turned his movie back on, and I didn't pick the song, so maybe it was his subconscious, but *Civilian* by Wye Oak became Carl's soundtrack. A tune I'd once joked to him sounded like a song to hang yourself to clicked on as I walked back out into the endless bright white corridor. Once back in the real world, I could still hear the song echo in his head. I set a glass of water next to the bed, because he'd be thirsty when he woke up, just as his ex Jenny had been when I erased her memory in this same spot ten days ago.

"I would say don't forget me," I murmured in his Carl's ear, "but I really hope you do."

As I stepped out into the cold, I pulled the hood up on my jacket and with each step I could feel the world vibrate around me.

Or that might have been the rage mixed with equal parts sorrow that sent a bolt of energy out of me. I didn't just make the streetlights flicker, but shatter. As I neared the end of the block, the traffic post bent as if a tornado had come down the street. With each step further away from Carl, the city began to crumble around me. Windows didn't just shake, but fractured, covering the cracking asphalt in glass. That's when the thoughts of the Baltimoreans began to fill up with cries for help from their various gods. Car alarms went off, a fire hydrant busted, water pouring out at a steady rate, and before I was out of the neighborhood the Baltimore Police showed up.

I guess it was worth calling them when people looked out their windows and saw the destruction in my wake. None of them could grapple with the fact that Charm City appeared to have been ravaged by several natural disasters that didn't affect the young woman that strolled in the apex. Their thoughts were filled with terror, their Neon Yellow Auras visible even from behind their doors.

The two BPD patrols stopped their cars, and called out over the speaker, "put your hands up!"

And for a second, I thought of snapping my fingers and watching their heads explode. I could blow up their cars, flood the streets, and make the foundation of these blocks quake. The power that I had, and my ability to dispense it as I deemed worthy proved mouthwatering.

I could really fuck up Baltimore.

I envisioned burning it to ash, leaving nothing in my wake but destruction, death, and pain. But the thought of one person stopped me from laying waste to the city. The only reason I saved Baltimore was for Carl.

I didn't raise my hands, but snapped my fingers, and Baltimore was as it was once again.

All the shattered pieces of glass reformed, stronger in fact, and sparkly clean in their original locations. No alarms chirped, the dogs stopped barking, the crevasse in the middle of the road reconnected and had a smoother surface. Water that threatened to flood the neighborhood evaporated while hydrating the trees that stood at the corner of the block, making the leaves a more vivid autumnal coloring. The air would be cleaner, all the cars gas tanks were now filled, and the BPD got a call to get a kitten down from one of those trees. They turned off their lights and drove away, completely forgetting why they'd come out in the first place. With a quick scan, I erased the momentary destruction of the city from the minds of every inhabitant.

Everyone's minds returned to pleasant dreams, except Carl, who couldn't help replaying my death. But better to have nightmares of me dying than his own torture at the hands of Jonas.

It was daylight by the time I made it to The Manor. My thoughts opened up the door and while I made my way to the dining room, I snapped my fingers and Widmore's finest bottle of Vodka appeared before me. I didn't need to use my hands to pull out my chair, pour a splash of orange juice into my glass, then fill it up to the brim with the vodka. Although I did decide to use them when I brought the glass to my lips and let the alcohol sting for a second as it went down.

Then I let the chorus of words take over.

"Talitha, thank God you're okay," Phoenix sputtered across from me.

"I told you she wasn't dead," Frozenstar added.

Siren's hands moved so quickly I couldn't catch a word, so I read his mind: *I hoped you'd come back to protect us.*

"Guess I was wrong," Fidget murmured.

"You weren't." I finally made eye contact with Fidget and wondered if she could see a difference in me now that I had nearly wiped Baltimore, Maryland, off the map.

Fidget nodded back, her gaze softened in apology as if she understood what I gave up. I took another deep swig of the liquor so I could push Carl out of my mind. Widmore was knocking on the door to my grey matter, and I could feel him trying to find a crack, knowing he wouldn't. His Aura flickered Orange in the center, which made me smile.

"Can't read my mind anymore, can you?" My tone was loud enough to override any other voice at the table.

Widmore was silent at the head of the table.

I turned and met eyes with him. "I'm powerful enough to repel you, powerful enough to destroy Baltimore and put it back together with a snap of my fingers. So don't bother trying to control me anymore."

"Talitha, I never wanted to control you," he began.

"I don't give a shit what you wanted, I'm not here for you anymore."

"Then why are you here?"

"Because I know that we're not the last five Enhanced beings like you told us. I know we're not alone and I'm going to find them, and together all of us are going to kill Jonas." I hadn't known that was my plan until I said it.

"And how do you expect to do that without going to Jonas for the information?" Widmore set his fork down on his pate of Eggs Benedict and his eyes held me.

Right now, all I had was a name, Lola, and I knew that Jonas was in love with a physically strong Enhanced being in London. If life had taught me anything, I bet they were the same girl, because who better to kill Jonas than his own victim and obsession. I'd find Lola, somehow, and then there'd be at least one ally on our side. "I'm not sure yet." I finished my glass. "But I do know that I'm going to get drunk."

"What about Carl?" Fidget asked.

"We don't have to worry about him anymore, he thinks I'm dead."

Widmore scoffed from the head of the table. "You should have used your all-encompassing new abilities to erase yourself from him entirely."

"Maybe I didn't want to," I hissed back.

"And why not?"

"Because then it would be like he never loved me." I didn't give the words a chance to linger as I stood up, took the bottle with me to finish off in my bedroom.

# 2 HOURS/ 3 MINUTES/ 15 SECONDS

F*eels Like We Only Go Backwards* played as I once again reviewed in my mind what happened the ten days, but it still brought me to the same conclusion. If I were a real man, I suppose I'd find Jonas and kill him for sending those cops to kill Talitha instead of sitting in my empty house for the past two hours lamenting her death.

Only I wasn't sure she was even dead.

Although, I also wasn't sure if I was completely crazy because I could hear people's heartbeats. *That's not possible*, I told myself the last time I went outside to search for her, *just got to get my hearing checked*. However, I haven't left the house since then because it's also not possible to fall in love with a telepathic girl who died in my arms.

I wouldn't necessarily call myself an intelligent guy, but Talitha was smart and resourceful. She'd been on her own for over two years with the power to control memory and the added asshole detector She might not be able to blow things up, freeze them over, or glide through walls as if they're made of air. But she could alter what you think happened in the past, and if she altered my memory, then I lost who knows how much time. Talitha was more powerful than any of her friends. She told me altering a memory was like changing the spool in a movie theater—

like they used to do when we were kids, and they had things like movie theaters. I tried to replay October 11, 2020, the first night we slept together, over in my mind. It seemed faded, like an old VHS from a millennia ago.

My eyes flicked to my nightstand, which had a glass of water on top of it. It had been there when I woke up, although I don't remember putting it there. I rushed out of my house, searching for Talitha. As if I'd find her on the street when I had a memory of her dying in my arms at the 9:30 Club. But instead, I was bombarded with the beating hearts of everyone around me. I didn't know how or why I could do it, but I knew I could.

I focused on the glass of water that reminded me of the day Talitha erased Jenny's memory. *'Give her a glass of water. She'll be thirsty when she wakes up.'*

When I picked up the glass, the hair on the back of my neck pricked up as if it were proof. However, I wasn't just basing this on a glass of water. My vintage record player was still on. It had been since I woke up a little over two hours ago. The indie record store edition of 'Lonerism' by Tame Impala had been spinning for who knows how long. I stood up, leaned down, and set the needle back on the vinyl to start *Feels Like We Only Go Backwards* once again. I had a teal case full of music next to me, the only thing I kept sacred. My index finger ran along the edge of the spine of the record's artwork, and I realized that I might not be crazy.

Tame Impala was squeezed between Chromatics 'Kill For Love' and The Flaming Lips' 'American Head', which would never happen. I'd kept my music in alphabetical order since I learned the English alphabet. All my records were out of place, some were flipped upside down so I couldn't read the album's title, and one record was not even with the rest. 'Singles' by Future Islands is arguably the best album pressed this century and one of my most cherished possessions.

There was no way I'd leave it on the floor of my bedroom amongst my discarded clothes.

The last time I remembered seeing Talitha was five days ago, when she died in my arms. But the water and the record on the floor told me that maybe she'd been here only a few hours before I woke up. I looked around the rowhouse and found more things out of place. Dishes in the sink still stuck with mac and cheese, which I didn't remember cooking. I had no memory of putting half a crab cake in the fridge, much less bringing it home. And there was a faint smell of lemon that echoed on each surface that was now devoid of dust and debris, but I couldn't remember the last time I'd cleaned.

There were a handful of texts from friends and just as many from Jenny, but not a single one from Danny, which was also super weird because we'd never gone a day without talking since we were ten. The last text I sent him was dated October 20 and said, '*call me now*', but there were no incoming calls, just me calling him three times the past two days. I hit his number again, only to be told that his mailbox was full. And if my girlfriend had been shot right in front of me, I would have called him first.

*Where Fuck r u?* I texted quickly before I dropped my phone back onto my bed, trying not to worry too bad about Danny because everything else was weird.

I took a shower because now I didn't know the last time I took one, didn't bother to shave, which it looked like it had been a few weeks since I had. Finally, I picked up some clothes from the floor and smelled them before putting them on. I laced up my boots, slid my arms into my jacket, put my hands in the pockets, and pulled out a ticket stub for the National Aquarium.

*There's no fucking way I went there by myself*, I thought as I crumpled the ticket and shoved it back into my pocket. I had no reason to go there other than to impress a girl.

I must have taken her there, then to the seafood market. I could still see her smirk when I made fun of her for her obsession with mac and cheese; *how can live in Baltimore and never had it with a crab cake?*

My breathing quickened as I made my way to the front door. I wasn't going to yell at her for literally stealing time from me, or get on my knees and beg for her back. All I wanted was an answer to the question: Why?

The door to my childhood home slammed behind me, but I didn't bother to lock it. I was not worried if someone broke in since I had nothing worth stealing. I went East toward Johns Hopkins, remembering where I'd last found Widmore, who would be the only person that could give me an answer.

*Why did you leave me?* I kept thinking on repeat if she was reading my mind from wherever she was.

Carl's story continues in **The Boy With The Glow**

# About the Author

Melissa Algood is a true-crime-obsessed dyslexic who read Helter Skelter and Harry Potter and the Deathly Hallows in one sitting.

Although not at the same time.

Her hometown, Annapolis, inspired the setting of *Everything That Counts*, a coming-of-age story of a geek who yearns to be cool. *The Greater Good* series follows a blood-thirsty assassin and her ex-Navy S.E.A.L. handler; the three-book series has a body count which matches the make-out count. Her award-winning short fiction can be found in *Everyone Dies: Tales from a Morbid Author*. She revisits Maryland, and rewrites 2020 with a sci-fi twist which begins when readers meet *The Girl In The Fog* and follow the journey of a telepathic twenty-something on the run from a lab that created and continues to test on her with the help of a guy she met in a bar.

Melissa's moved over twenty times in her life, including California, Puerto Rico, and D.C., before making Houston her home. She's a hairstylist in the real world and lives with her longtime love, Izzy, and Madame Bijou, their tuxedo cat.

# Music To Memorize

### 2 years/ 3 months/15 days
- Running from the Cops - Phantogram
- First – Cold War Kids
- You Already Know – Cold War Kids
- Yummy – Justin Bieber
- Star Guitar – The Chemical Brothers
- So Tied Up (feat. Bishop Briggs) – Cold War Kids

### Jonas 10/9/2020 9:42 PM (aka enough humans today)
- Celestica – Crystal Castles
- Psycho Killer – Talking Heads

### Talitha 10/9/2020 9:55 PM (aka un amor)
- Your Cloud – Tori Amos
- Hang Me up to Dry – Cold War Kids
- lovely – Billie Eilish & Khalid
- Still Have Me – Demi Lovato

### Talitha 10/10/2020 8:38 PM (aka the beginning)
- Trouble – Father John Misty

**Talitha 10/10/2020 9:55 PM** (aka Joe & Tanya)
- Take Care – Beach House
- I Dare You – The XX
- Popstar – DJ Khaled
- Two Weeks – Grizzly Bear
- Brb - Leet

**Carl 10/10/2020 11:45pm** (aka radioactive spiders)
- Confines (Live in Studio) – Black Pumas
- Heavy Balloon – Fiona Apple

**Talitha 10/10/2020 11:45pm** (aka thought you were a telepath)
- Take It All Back – Judah and the Lion
- Kim & Jessie – M83
- We Own The Sky – M83

**Widmore 10/11/2020 12:27 AM** (aka the mentor)
- Immortal - Marina and the Diamonds

**Carl 10/11/2020 11:27 PM** (aka monsters having monsters)
- Will Do – TV on the Radio
- Hit My Line – Logic

**Phoenix 10/12/2020 10:28 AM** (aka always a prisoner)
- 7 Years – Lukas Graham
- Me Gusta – Shakira & Anuel AA

**Talitha 10/12/2020 3:45 PM** (aka no bra)
- Available – Justin Bieber
- Maps – Yeah Yeah Yeahs
- Blood in the Cut – K. Flay

**Talitha 10/12/2020 5:55 PM** (aka forgotten by Rick)
- Falling Asleep at the Wheel – Holly Humberstone

**Widmore 10/13/2020 12:27 PM** (aka what amounts to a roach)

• Space Oddity – David Bowie

**Talitha 10/14/2020 12:07 AM** (aka the date)
• For Sure – Future Islands
• Heart in Slo Mo – Young Summer
• Boyfriend – Justin Bieber
• You and I – Washed Out
• In Your Eyes – Peter Gabriel

**Widmore 10/14/2020 1:37 AM** (aka hear you say it)
• The Magic – Joan As Police Woman

**Talitha 10/14/2020 11:57 PM** (aka only said it during sex)
• Silver Soul – Beach House

**Talitha 10/15/2020 1:56 AM** (aka they're waiting)
• 1-800-273-8255 (feat. Alessia Cara & Kahlid) – Logic
• Renee – SALES
• Aristocrats – Raleigh Ritchie

**Carl 10/15/2025 9:29 AM** (aka I'm Blue)
• Black Mambo – Glass Animals
• Kill for Love – Chromatics

**Talitha 10/15/2025 11:55 AM** (aka the polka dot dress)
• 3 Hour Drive (feat. Sampha) – Alicia Keys
• Sorry – Justin Bieber

**Fidget 10/15/2020 *1:55 PM*** (aka addicted to Estrella Ramos)
• No One Like You – Best Coast
• Nineteen– Tegan and Sara
• Wasted Time – Best Coast

**Widmore 10/15/2020 2:00 PM** (aka the test)
• Amoreena – Elton John
• The Chain – Fleetwood Mac

# Music To Memorize

**Fidget 10/15/2025 3:47 PM** (aka you can never leave)
- Better Than Feeling Lonely – Olivia O'Brien

**Phoenix 10/15/2020 4:00 PM** (aka you belong with us)
- Pineapple – KAROL G

**Talitha 10/15/2020 4:14 PM** (aka Annie & Nina)
- So Like A Rose – Garbage
- bon iver - mxmtoon

**Phoenix 10/15/2020 5:17 PM** (aka pick me)
- Love Goes - Sam Smith & Labrinth

**Carl 10/15/2020 10:38 PM** (aka the famous Napoleon)
- Paralyzed – Washed Out
- Red Eyes – The War On Drugs
- Midnight City – M83

**Talitha 10/15/2020 10:38 PM** (aka *je serai toujours à toi*)
- All Around Me – Justin Bieber
- 10,000 Emerald Pools - BØRNS

**Widmore 10/16/2020 7:45 AM** (aka the betrayal)
- The Happening - Pixies

**Talitha 10/16/2020 9:15 AM** (aka first battle of the telepaths)
- Name (feat. Tori Kelly) – Justin Bieber
- ooh la la (feat. Greg Nice & DJ Premier) – Run The Jewels
- Edge of Seventeen – Stevie Nicks
- Immortal – Marina and The Diamonds
- 24 - IDK

**Phoenix 10/16/2020 9:55 PM** (aka forever and ever and whatever)
- LA NOCHE DE ANOCHE – Bad Bunny & ROSALÍA
- No Brainer (feat. Justin Bieber, Chance the Rapper & Quavo) – DJ Khaled

**Talitha 10/16/2020 9:55 PM** (aka the night we met)
• Without Me - Halsey
• Stuck with U – Ariana Grande & Justin Bieber
• No Brainer (feat. Justin Bieber, Chance the Rapper & Quavo) – DJ Khaled
• The Mother We Share – CHVRCHES
• EVERY CHANCE I GET (feat. Lil Baby & Lil Durk) - DJ Khaled
• The Night We Met (feat. Phoebe Bridgers) – Lord Huron

**Talitha 10/16/2020 11:57 PM** (aka whatever you do)
• Setting Sun – The Chemical Brothers
• The Keeper – Kai Wachi & Macntaj
• Seal – The Chemical Brothers

**Carl 10/17/2020 12:55 AM** (aka you love her too)
• Temple of Sorrow – M83

**Talitha Unknown Date and Time** (aka gone really gone)
• The Funeral – Band of Horses

**Widmore 10/19/2020 7:45 AM** (aka Frozenstar or Talitha?)
• You Don't Know How It Feels – Tom Petty

**Talitha 10/20/2020 7:45 AM** (aka Greene, Williams, Tanner, and Jefferson)
• Queen – Perfume Genius

**Carl 10/20/2020 8:55 AM M (**aka the bandage)
• The Less I Know the Better – Tame Impala

**Talitha 10/20/2020 8:35 AM** (aka last meal)
• Fetch The Bolt Cutters – Fiona Apple

**Talitha 10/20/2020 8:35 AM** (aka hope this works)
• Close Your Eyes (And Count to F**k) [feat. Zack De La Rocha] – Run The Jewels

- Two Weeks – Grizzly Bear
- Tear You Apart – She Wants Revenge
- Nitrous Mafia – Subtronics
- Lonely - Justin Bieber & benny blanco
- Thrill – Future Islands

**Carl 10/21/2020 7:45 AM** (aka live with the flowers)
- Tropics (Erase Traces) – My Morning Jacket

**Fidget 10/21/2020 9:55 AM** (aka selfish bitch)
- I'll Be Back Someday – Tegan and Sara

**Carl 10/21/2020 10:25 AM** (aka the day that won't be)
- Walking On a Dream – Empire of the Sun
- Holy (feat Chance the Rapper) – Justin Bieber
- Myth– Beach House

**Talitha 10/22/2025 2:47 AM** (aka fuck Baltimore)
- Forever (feat. Post Malone & Clever) – Justin Bieber
- Sparks – Beach House
- Moonlight – Future Islands
- Civilian – Wye Oak
- Coming Back (feat. SZA) – James Blake

**2 hours/ 3 minutes/ 15 seconds**
- Feels Like We Only Go Backwards – Tame Impala

# Acknowledgments

When I finished the Greater Good Series, I was worried that I didn't have any more stories to tell because the voices in my head had gone quiet. For about 24 hours, that brought about a great depression, so I went home and picked a random movie on Netflix, unaware that it would change my life. *The Old Guard* starring Charlize Theron was that movie, and I'm forever thankful that I chose to watch it because Talitha became the new voice in my head.

The Baltimore music scene, with the addition of the Chemical Brothers and Justin Bieber, proved a strong influence as well. I wanted to make this book, and indeed the series, a love song of sorts for my home state of Maryland and Baltimore. As you might have noticed, the book was set in 2020. I did write this one, started a rough draft on the following three books, and did an outline for the entire series during the lockdown when I was out of work, home alone, and terrified that I could contract a deadly disease from just about everything. I decided to reinterpret 2020 and create a new world in which there wasn't a global pandemic, but a covert agency that tests on pregnant women and children, which I found much less terrifying than a virus.

I also wrote this book to bring new characters to the sci-fi/fantasy genre where they would seem familiar but with a twist. Sure, there are characters written that can conjure fire, but they weren't Mexican immigrants with a twin sister who can freeze you to the core. I wrote several full-length novels, poems, and flash fiction during the shutdown, but only one series proved strong enough to share with the world, which began with my critique circle of David Welling, William Mays, and Carla Conrad. A few other authors read a bit of it, and I'm thankful for Jessica Raney and Chantell Renee's input as well. My beta readers let me know what made sense and what I had to cut, so I'm thankful to Omar and Jennifer for taking the time to read it as well. But I couldn't have written a word without my husband Izzy understanding that, to keep my sanity when the world was crashing in on us, I had to create and not deep clean, learn to make sourdough, or go back to school.

I'm also indebted to all the writers who've penned their sci-fi tale, from comic books to screenplays, and the musicians who keep me going when I've been writing for hours. I hope you love this story as much as I do, and you give me patience as I work on the following five books in the Enhanced Being Series.

# Also by Melissa Algood

*Enhanced Being Series*
The Girl In The Fog

---

*The Greater Good Series*
Unseen
Gone
Home

---

*Novels*

Everything That Counts

---

*Short Fiction*
Everyone Dies: Tales from a Morbid Author

---

*with Chantell Renee*
Hair Raising Tales of Horror
Hair Raising Tales of Villainous Confessions

---

*Short Pieces Included in*

100 Word Zombie Bites: An Undead Drabbles Anthology

Approaching Footsteps

IN THE QUESTIONS

That Moment When

Eclectically Carnal

Eclectically Criminal

Eclectically Vegas, Baby

CPSIA information can be obtained
at www.ICGtesting.com
Printed in the USA
JSHW041809060722
27597JS00001B/45